Praise for *An Invitation to the Party*

"MJ Werthman White's *An Invitation to the Party* is a novel full of depth and heart that explores the complications of a complicated family with plenty of wit and empathy to go around. The success of this wise, endearing tale lies in a most memorable main character, Garnet, who is not going gently into any good night. White's background as a poet helps her create a compressed, nuanced style that draws readers into every single scene—every moment, every brief exchange. A masterful book by a writer who never misses a beat."

- Jim Ray Daniels, author of *The Perp Walk* and *Gun/Shy*

"Garnet Delaney is turning seventy. She misses the rotary telephone and the satisfaction of slamming down the receiver. And sometimes she thinks her entire family could use a refresher course in adult behavior. In this humorous, tongue-in-cheek novel, MJ Werthman White celebrates the uncertainties of aging, with characters so deftly drawn they already feel like family. *An Invitation to the Party* is the novel you will invite your friends to read, again and again."

- Cathryn Essinger, author of *The Apricot and the Moon*

"At a time when the world feels so disconnected and mean, I adored this warm, funny, moving book about real community and connection. Trust me, this is an invitation you want to accept."

- Katrina Kittle, author of *The Kindness of Strangers*

"It's impossible not to be completely captivated by this wonderful novel and its memorable cast of characters. With a potent mix of wit and empathy, MJ Werthman White shines a bright light on the American heartland, illuminating all the extraordinary facets of ordinary life."

- Joanna Scott, author of *Excuse Me While I Disappear* and *Careers for Women*

"In *An Invitation to the Party* Garnet tempers her keenly observed Truths with a capital T with crackling sarcasm, not only transcending grief, rage, fear, and consideration of imminent mortality, but also leading the reader to a resonant, sustaining gratitude long after the final page has been turned."

- Kimberly Willardson, editor of *The Vincent Brothers Review*

An Invitation to the Party

MJ Werthman White

Regal House Publishing

Published by
Regal House Publishing, LLC
Raleigh, NC 27605

ISBN -13 (paperback): 9781646033409
ISBN -13 (epub): 9781646033416
Library of Congress Control Number: 2022942657

Cover images and design by © C. B. Royal
Author photograph by © Connie Gifford

Regal House Publishing, LLC
https://regalhousepublishing.com

Printed in the United States of America

For my teachers, especially Charles Mills,
who declared me a writer in 1962.
I never forgot, although it took me a while to prove him right.

The universe's favorite word is yes.
The word she uses most often is no.
It's a mystery. She doesn't understand it herself.

from *How the Universe Says Yes to Me*

March

2017

Personal Ad

Cranky, nearsighted, elderly female with wrinkles,
scars, and age-related blemishes, has hearing loss,
hip replacement, and short-term memory gone south,

looking for someone who will never grow old,
a dog that will not die, looking for solace,
for someone to tell her lies. No calls after 7 p.m.

Earlier this morning Garnet was awakened by the pre-dawn clanking of the Village of Haven's garbage truck outside her bedroom window, air brakes squealing like a stuck pig. Getting out of bed, she'd thought, *Awful simile that*, her resident critic already wide awake and on the job despite the hour. She'd been in the midst of a beautiful dream, one where all her dead were returned, best friend back, her parents, even two beloved mutts preceding her current and much-loved Vera, presently asleep on the kitchen floor, muzzle resting on her foot. It had been, all of it, simply a misunderstanding, a terrible mistake.

Having recently given herself a pass—permission to feel what she's feeling, to want what she wants, Garnet wishes that her dream could come true. Unfortunately, actually getting what she wants does not seem to be part of the deal. Even Vera, willful Great Pyrenees, seems determined to go her own way, ignoring Garnet's pleas to *sit*, *stay*, or (laughably) *come here!* So Garnet is left to consider what might be possible. How about growing old with all? most? okay, she'd settle for some of her marbles intact. Garnet desires agency, to be the one who decides what will make her happy—or maybe just not completely miserable. She refuses to allow age to render her invisible; she wants others to see her, to hear what she has to say. Not such a large order really. Nothing that could not be termed reasonable, though she knows what she's just described to herself is not something the world actually finds reasonable. It's something the world finds amusing; something that makes it smile a mean little smile while muttering, *Dream on, Garnet.* And as so often happens when she is confronted with some unpalatable truth, she's chosen to ignore it.

So. Moving on. A cup of coffee would be lovely and easier to accomplish than any of the above. See? Garnet is nothing if not flexible, ever willing to adjust her expectations. And Mr. Coffee awaits on the counter next to the sink, ancient but perfectly serviceable, much like the majority of males in her peer group. Vera, pottied and fed as soon as they came downstairs, snores softly, first nap of the day always a long one for the old dog.

Garnet measures Maxwell House into Mr. Coffee's basket. As she turns the little machine on, she wonders what the odds are anybody else at this very moment is also thinking of joltin' Joe DiMaggio, the Yankee Clipper, and his coffeemaker commercials. For sure, no one born after 1970. She adds a spoonful of sugar to her cup and, leaving the coffee to cool, takes her puffy coat off its peg by the back door and goes out into the March darkness to retrieve her soggy *New York Times* from a frosted front lawn—no thanks due the geriatric newsboy who daily maunders down the street in his muffler-impaired car, aiming for driveways and missing. Every. Single. Time.

Trees do elicit her sympathy but Garnet finds herself unable to bear reading the reliably awful news on anything but actual paper (there is an idiot installed in the White House like some regrettable online appliance purchase, the country apparently having neglected to check out the myriad negative reviews before its ill-starred purchase). Like Madonna, she is an analog girl.

Setting the newspaper on the porch step, Garnet refills the feeder, grateful she has the twenty dollars a week to spend on premium seed, even though the birds do not care. The birds do not know what care is. The birds are. A lesson here? Not today. Inside again, she drapes the newspaper over the back of a kitchen chair to dry, nukes her cooling coffee and, retrieving her journal from the antique desk in the front hall, begins to write at the kitchen table.

When Garnet retired she'd begun this daily exercise, writing by hand, at first keeping a diary. It didn't take long for her to realize her entries were incredibly boring, the blank page at her approach each morning seeming almost to emit a low complaining whine as if in actual pain. No longer recording the quotidian events of an uneventful life, she now begins her days composing poetry, something she's done sporadically her whole life. She writes poems about what interests her, which more and more is aging, gracefully or otherwise, mostly otherwise. The only rhyme involved is the occasional involuntary one she catches as she revises, often allowing it to stay.

The front of her journal is saved for these efforts, the writing annotated with substitutions and alternative word choices, filled with crossings out. Only after three, four, five messy pages of small, Palmer-method cursive, can a final draft be found neatly recopied and honored with a whole page, front and back, of its very own—though even that is sometimes revisited and marked again with more additions and deletions.

Garnet loves poetry, her own and others, mostly others if you want to know the truth. In fact, this very day she's expecting a chapbook ordered from a small press she favors. And when there is no poem of her own to work on or no subject appeals, she uses the back of this same notebook to copy out some favorites. There are so many, perhaps one from Sexton's *Transformations*, or a Stephen Dunn—because he loves the dogs as much as she does and is apparently not afraid of someone lobbing "sentimental" at him for occasionally writing about them. Her hand forming others' words on the page, others more proficient than she, allows each poem to become its own small instruction manual for a student willing to attend and learn.

She does not send out her work, has no desire to see her name on the cover of one of the volumes in the large bookcase next to the refrigerator, its shelves filled with poetry (and with cookbooks—Garnet's furniture arrangement and cataloging idiosyncratic), the poetry collection here begun when she started working in her late twenties at the bookstore in the village, and added to over the years. She misses that small bookstore she managed for so long and wishes it, like so much else—rotary phones, typewriters, manual transmissions with stick shifts, drive-in theaters, she's embarrassed at how long the list could become—was still around. She would not mind a fairy godmother, though the usual three wishes would barely suffice to scratch the surface. Her mother would have called such fruitless longing *wishing your life away.*

The clatter of feet down the stairs announces Colt, her brother's twenty-nine-year-old estranged son, staying with her, temporarily, for the past two years. Possessor of an unused BA in economics, begun part-time at the community college before moving on to a nearby SUNY, and earned with great difficulty balancing job, fatherhood, and a failing relationship, he works at Slam-Dunk Construction. Not in the office either, and happy to have the job.

"Morning," he says, moving to the counter.

Garnet's nephew is tall (it runs in the family) and has a killer smile. He is a good father, ex-boyfriend, nephew, friend, employee. He admits to not being an ideal son. His relationship with his father is fraught on both sides. His daughter, Meg, is the apple of his eye. Colt has his departed, sainted mother's gray-green eyes, and lank sandy hair that falls over his forehead when he needs a haircut. Like now.

"Time to get that mop cut, Colt?"

"What? And lose my outlaw status?"

She believes Colt exhibits many of his own mother's fine traits, while also possessing a sense of humor, something sorely lacking in both his parents. He evinces few reminders of his father, Garnet's brother Remington, who, she believes, had he been born a hundred years earlier would have made an excellent riverboat gambler. He is one of the very few people she knows who could convincingly manage a pencil-thin mustache.

Though he's twenty-nine, in his heart of hearts Colt feels as adrift, as unsettled as he remembers being at eighteen. He would like to be feeling that his real life's begun. Instead, he believes he lost his way somewhere between Rain telling him she was pregnant eleven years ago and today. Yes, he stuck it out, got an education, which truth to tell has not proved very useful. Yes, by working part-time during the school year, full-time summers and breaks at the construction job he still holds, he's debt-free. He's even managed to become and remain a part of his daughter's life and cobbled together a mostly positive relationship with her mother. But he'd hoped by now to have a partner, a term he despises for its business-as-usual implication, but the person it represents in his mind, this unknown someone, he thinks he'd like her. A lot.

He'd hoped to have a house, no, a home, by now. He loves his aunt, does not know what he'd have done without her kindness, but maybe it's time to free them both up, break up the current stasis? Colt does not have a girlfriend. He has not had a date in, has not had sex in, *what the hell*, he is not going to say how long. For either one. He'll be pinned down only to *it's been a while*. If nothing else, maybe he needs to actually do something about that.

"Remember, I'm organizing bookshelves today," Garnet says to her nephew, who is now standing meditatively in front of her open fridge.

She wonders why some people appear to do their best thinking while running up an already astronomical electric bill. One more example of multitasking gone awry?

"Colt. Please. Close that door."

"*Oops*," he says, taking out his lunch supplies and shutting the refrigerator door.

"By the way," he adds, "I did hear you, and I do remember that I'm responsible for boxing up and taking the rejects to their new home."

"Please don't call them rejects. But yes."

"Knowing how much you love your books, auntie, do we really even need a box for the three you decide you can live without?"

Garnet knows what that "auntie" means. Her nephew is finding her enormously amusing again.

"You'll see, young man. Be prepared for a couple hours of backbreaking labor when you get home tonight."

They smile at each other, appreciating a quiet relationship lacking any drama whatsoever. It has been a pleasant change for them both.

Garnet watches Colt assemble his lunch, same as always, baloney sandwich with mayo and a slice of American cheese—they both know how much willpower Garnet exercises every morning in not pointing out that it might be American, dear heart, but it is *not* cheese—two packages of Twinkies and a bag, not small, of Cool Ranch Doritos, all in a plastic grocery sack he will bring home, re-using it until it shreds—*my nephew the eco-warrior*, she thinks. Last but not least (in sugar content anyway), he adds a bottle of SunnyD.

When Colt first arrived, Garnet did attempt to convince him of the wisdom of healthy eating, but he is still young enough to take for granted that bad things are what happen to other people, despite no little evidence in his own experience to the contrary. Meanwhile, Vera has stationed herself by his side. Waiting. Colt sneaks the dog a slice of lunch meat while Garnet pretends not to see. He then fills his bowl with Lucky Charms and sits down at the table across from his aunt.

"Meg's here this weekend," he says, pouring milk over the pastel, marshmallow-studded confection.

Colt is a good boy at heart with many admirable qualities, Garnet has decided, even if she cannot bring herself to dignify his breakfast with the noun "cereal."

"We'll pick up a pizza on the way home, Gigi," he says, using the affectionate family nickname for Garnet. "You won't have to bother making dinner."

In his shared custody agreement, her nephew has his daughter, Meg, every other weekend from six on Friday night to six on Sunday evening. Garnet has no grandchildren. However, this little grandniece, who's just turned ten, more than suffices. Garnet sees in Meg both the grace of Monday's child and Tuesday's pretty face. She believes her grandniece to be one of those few that an unreliable and maddening universe occasionally grants temporary dispensation, sparing them not only Wednesday's ten car pile-ups on the freeway but all of its minor bumps in the road, flat tires, dead batteries, breakdowns, the smoky engine fires. Who knows why? And Meg, of course, will not even realize her good fortune until much later, when finally the wheels begin to come off, as they inevitably do. As with us all, Garnet knows her little niece's reaction to that will be the making (or unmaking) of her.

Colt is not the only single parent in the house. Garnet has a grown daughter herself; it's been almost three years since she last heard from Tommie. She tries not to think too much about it. Unsuccessfully. Garnet does not remember, well, she chooses not to remember, the weeks before Tommie left town, the ridiculous arguments—over her daughter's buzzed haircut, her new tattoo (an actually quite well-executed rose Garnet now concedes), even the way Tommie treated (mistreated, in Garnet's opinion) her fiancé. After all, Ben wasn't Garnet's own first choice for Tommie, but did that really matter? Not her first choice, she is ashamed but now willing to admit, because she thought Ben too good for her wild child.

Tommie, after all, was an adult, true, not a mature adult, but how to become one of those except by making mistake after mistake after mistake? That Garnet had been in the midst of divorcing Tommie's father as well had not helped her own behavior. Could Garnet have done things differently? And if she had, would it have made the slightest difference? She thinks not. Sometimes she wonders if she will ever see her daughter again. Sometimes she thinks it would be better if she didn't. Sometimes, although she abhors the current practice of reducing once-powerful Anglo-Saxon curse words to sniveling, repetitive, often adjectival status, she doesn't give a flying fuck one way or the other.

And what this means is that she pretty much thinks about Tommie all the time, her child, this gift of a late and unplanned pregnancy long after she and Bowie had given up all hope. A family at last, Tommie, a delightful little person at five, six, seven, and Garnet, in love with her husband all over again, and he with her, and Tommie, in love with them both, her mommy, her daddy. Experiencing unexpected motherhood for the first time at forty should have been a nightmare, stressful and overwhelming; it was not. It was heaven. Whatever happened, what changed? How did that small miracle become the hell of Tommie's teens, when more than once she thought they'd lost her completely?

Garnet remembers Tommie on her booster seat at age two eating spaghetti with both hands, the kitchen table looking like the scene of a mass murder, or something out of medieval literature, *Beowulf* perhaps, her daughter having apparently consumed her victims, leaving behind only gore. Or Tommie at thirteen, up in the branches of the oak in the backyard, arms folded, refusing to come down, staying there until long after dark; Tommie at eighteen, bringing her new thirty-eight-year-old biker boyfriend home for Sunday dinner with her father, who'd already met him the previous week—had in fact successfully defended him in court to his subsequent paternal sorrow. And most deeply strange of all, Tommie, throughout, acing her high school AP courses, being chosen valedictorian (true, there were three of them, but still) and finally, most unlikely of all, announcing she was going to be a teacher, a primary teacher; she was going to teach little ones. And, for a while, she did.

Garnet tells Colt to have a good day as he grabs his lunch, keys, and jacket and heads out the door, then for the second time takes her own winter coat off its peg. Vera's tail has been swishing back and forth on the floor in anticipation. Now she is up, tail wagging furiously. It's time for their walk.

The calendar in Garnet's kitchen features watercolors of dogs; March is a black lab asleep on an unmade bed. It reminds her of the Wyeth print in her bedroom, its old dog sleeping on an iron bed made up with a candlewick bedspread. (Her favorite part of the picture, strangely, is not the dog; it's the way Wyeth has painted the fringe on that bedspread, something she's never thought to share with anyone else.) According to this wall calendar, the vernal equinox has already occurred. Some three days ago. Supposedly, spring has arrived even here in western New York State. Even so, Garnet winds a thickly knit scarf around her neck, pulls on her peppermint-striped wool hat and zips the down coat all the way up. She puts the excited Vera into her halter and attaches the leash, then pulls on her insulated gloves. Actual spring itself is a most unlikely construct on an overcast late March Thursday in the village of Haven, where proximity to Ontario and its dreaded lake effect clouds has ensured there's no lack of seasonal affective disorder in the human population.

Vera, if she could, however, would beg to differ; it is perfect weather for a big, exceptionally furry canine to be out and about. Tiny ice balls pelt them as they walk, two perfect targets for this miniaturized snowball fight, the sky for variety's sake also spitting occasional splatters of almost-snow their way. Vera's coat is so thick the ice that collects remains unmelted until she is back indoors.

The dog loves this. Wind that bites Garnet flows through Vera's long coat, lays her ears back, and wags her tail. She's a good walker in her harness, not pulling, sticking close to Garnet's side, but it's she who sets the pace for two elderly females who need to keep moving. They march forward into the delicious, freezing world. The only thing that makes Vera happier is when it is Colt who suits her up (Colt needing no special getup, simply the leash clipped on to the collar) and she turns to see Garnet also putting on her coat. Oh, the bliss of having one's entire pack assembled, together facing down the vicissitudes of an unreliable outside world. There is nothing: cats, wind-driven garbage cans barreling down the street, cats, heedless boys on skateboards, cats, or yapping tiny (in her opinion) not-dogs, nothing that they cannot handle when they all walk out together. Especially cats.

Two hip replacements in the last eight years, one for Garnet, one for the dog, have made these trips relatively pain-free, easier for both. Any sedentary alternative is grim, unacceptable—she pictures herself, morbidly obese, in a motorized shopping cart, trolling the aisles of Walmart, Cheetos for her, Snausages for her hundred-twenty-pound dog. Then out of sorts and out of shape, they snap at each other on the sofa as they watch "Real Housewives of NJ" dropping f-bombs on their wide-screen, not-so-smart, potty-mouth TV.

It's the warm weather that's problematic, their walks taken earlier and earlier in the day as the season progresses, along with the odd midnight stroll when it's really hot. In the summer, walks are desultory; Vera's tongue lolls. The dog, while still happy to be out, lacks the sheer joy that cold weather grants her. There is more panting and considerably more drooling—on Vera's part, Garnet would likely wish to point out. Thus far, drooling has not been an issue for her.

Garnet thinks of Vera as her guardian angel; they are devoted to each other. When her marriage of forty-some years broke up a few years back, she got the house and this dog she adores, among many other things. It was not always so. Vera was initially brought home by Bowie after he was (for once) unable to get a client, at the time also Vera's owner, acquitted. The man had been Bowie's next-door neighbor growing up—their shared history (nine years old, he'd smoked his first cigarette with Wayne, a filtered, menthol abomination, he'd told Garnet, which put him off cigarettes for good; his first beer belonged to Wayne's dad, swiped from his refrigerator)—the only reason Bowie would take on someone who couldn't pay his fee. With nowhere else to turn, on his way to multiple years in prison, the broke, dog-loving felon gave Vera to Bowie in lieu of what he owed.

Her ex was a terrible husband but a faithful, affectionate, and responsible pet owner (Garnet has said more than once that if she'd been a golden retriever, they would have been very happy). It grieved Bowie mightily when he lost custody of Vera in the divorce. Garnet is aware he thought briefly of suing for alienation of affection after it became clear that in his initial absence (he prefers now to call it expulsion) from the family home, she had wooed and won Vera. Vera, who even now after all these years, can regard him with the cool, noncommittal gaze he might remember seeing from the bench when it became clear he was losing a case. Indeed, it is a familiar look that all the females Bowie has known, biblically and otherwise, seem to have visited upon him sooner or later.

And Garnet? She remains secure in the knowledge that, represented by her husband's fed-up partner—his law firm did not survive their breakup—she got the better deal. Her ex, Bowie, got Lily, the firm's legal secretary, said partner's daughter. Briefly. A knife, a gun—Garnet is not unaware of the amount of time she's spent in close proximity to men named for weaponry. Who now would name their sons thus? She's aware the answer to that question would be telling, addressing as it does the depth of our present divisions as a nation.

Moreover it's actually not quite true to say she married a knife. Garnet knows something her ex-husband has shared with few others. Though now spelled like the blade, his first name initially was Beau, shorthand for Beauregard. Bowie's mother, homesick southerner from Charleston who never got over the interminable eight-months-long, or so it seemed to her, northeastern winters, named her only son after the brother later lost to a chilly war in Korea. Called Beau, or even worse, Bobo by his family, he was teased often. Finally, after enduring a summer's worth of torment caused by a neighbor's new frou-frou poodle, also named Beau, a male but wearer of a pink hair bow; Bowie's days filled with so-called friends' *Sit, Beau! Stay, Beau!*; their fits of barking whenever he appeared; he was more than ready to declare himself Bowie in September when sixth-grade social studies offered the story of the man and the knife. The first thing Bowie had done on turning eighteen was the minimal legal work required by the state of New York to change his first name. One of the stipulations in their divorce agreement requires Garnet to keep his secret. Beauregard Delaney is not merely dead to Bowie; as far as he's concerned, he never existed.

In his prime, Bowie, the attorney, favored bespoke suits, starched shirts with French cuffs, designer ties. But time, aging, and its effects have taken their toll, and now he often looks a bit disreputable, almost homeless on his worst days, though still somehow, maddeningly and inexplicably to Garnet, attractive in a disheveled kind of way. Their history however has rendered her, though able to acknowledge its existence, immune to his charm.

He occasionally asks for a weekend with his former dog. Though she is wholly Garnet's girl now, Vera holds no grudge against her former love, having happily moved on. Garnet, stuck firmly in place, having forgotten and forgiven nothing, admires her dog immensely, at the same time despairing of ever equaling her achievement. Therefore, headed to the library on their walk this morning, ex-wife and ex-dog do not slow their pace one iota as they approach Bowie's elegant old house, Garnet determinedly marching eyes-front, down their shared street.

❧

Garnet's ex lives alone in a too-large, somewhat haphazardly rehabbed Victorian beauty with a wrap-around front porch, a porte cochere, and like many of his neighbors, a carriage house in back that has not held a carriage or a horse in almost a hundred years, and shelters Bowie's automobile. Until he bought the property, the small apartment that replaced the carriage house's hayloft had provided the owner with a nice little cash infusion each month. But Bowie can't, rather won't, be bothered with being a landlord. Today he sits in one of the porch's four Cracker Barrel rocking chairs, bundled up in a filthy down jacket, its hood pulled up, his bible the *Wall Street Journal* in hand, getting his daily quota of fresh air. Though the March weather is being predictably execrable, a little adversity has not made him alter his routine. Morning means reading his *WSJ* on the front porch from vernal equinox through the cold, bitter end of fall, and his newspaper says spring has duly commenced. The *Journal,* fair, factual reportage unclouded by suspect opinion, unlike its sister New York paper which shall be nameless, that's all he asks.

And, yes, he is capable of gratitude, despite claims to the contrary by Garnet. Thank the Almighty for down and fleece: how about that? Bowie knows what everyone in this place, his small town, thinks of him, not that he lets it bother him. Most people are fools, easily ignored by a man of substance like himself, a man who knows what's what. He's willing to admit having made the occasional miscalculation along the way—unwilling even now to call them mistakes—he's always had his reasons. Sometimes though, watching his wife, of course he means ex-wife, her lined, set, pretty face looking straight ahead, walking *his* dog past the house he lives in now, he forgets what they were.

Bowie, even in his seventies, and despite some deficits caused by the TIA's that have deviled him since the divorce, has kept much of his lady-killer good looks—he's maybe five-seven, eight, down from his original five-nine, even then a couple inches shorter than Garnet. His white hair, lately uncombed, has a growing bald spot on the crown. But his brows are still dark wings over the beautiful blue eyes just beginning to fade and cloud with cataracts.

And Bowie is not stupid. He may be slowly losing his mind, but he is not stupid he tells himself. Often. He does not quite understand now how he managed a law practice all those years. And some days it is an effort to make sure he has put on all the clothes necessary to appear in public without again being humiliatingly picked up on Main Street by that twerp, Officer Del Diller, and delivered in a squad car, lights flashing to Garnet, just because he'd remembered the socks but not the shoes on a rainy late February day.

His ex-wife had at least settled the moron's hash, saying, "Lights, Del? Really? Why not the siren? Why not handcuff the old man while you're at it?"

Del's face had turned a deeply satisfying crimson, as he'd scrambled to put himself back in Garnet's good graces by abjectly apologizing.

"Too little, too late, young man," Garnet had replied, shutting the door firmly, then giving Bowie a pair of Colt's wool work socks to replace his wet ones before driving him home and reminding him to put on a pair of shoes. One thing he never forgets is how sorry he is that his old life is gone, maybe even that Garnet is no longer his wife. Try as he may, he cannot seem to forget it was his doing that made it so. Lily was a controlled substance, one he was confident he could take or leave, until he couldn't. Until he was addicted and wanted only her. And once he had only her, she left and then he had nothing. At least Garnet occasionally talks to him now.

Bowie is also aware Garnet has a birthday coming up. A big one. Seventy. A milestone he's already passed. Some three years ago. During their marriage such occasions often slipped by, of no import to him, unworthy of his attention. He admits he was never much good at empathy, in fact kind of thought it ought to be classified a—what's the term they use: *fake?*—fake word. Now he's not so sure. He wonders whether he will be invited if there's a celebration. *If?* Who's he kidding, of course there's going to be a party. Everyone loves Garnet. He sometimes finds himself trying to figure out if that group just might still include him.

For a long time he thought the affair with Lily the high point of his life. Never having regarded himself as a passionate person, someone capable of being a fool for love, he'd surprised himself as well as everyone else. At the time, he thought he would be unable to bear it if Lily left him. Of course she left him. His divorce was finalized and the following day Lily was gone. Garnet was gone too. And of course he got over it, he tells himself. For a while afterward, he occasionally saw Lily on the street or in a car, but as soon as she caught sight of him she melted away. She was like quicksilver. He'd blink and she disappeared. Was it worth it? Even after all this time, he is unable to answer that question.

Bowie also sometimes thinks about his daughter and wonders what Tommie's reasons could have been for leaving so abruptly. The thing about people is you never know. Like fingerprints, each and every one their own little kind of crazy, he now believes. His daughter running off like that, leaving in the lurch a fine young man, one he thoroughly approved of, not even bothering to say goodbye to her own father. How sharper than a serpent's tooth, etcetera, etcetera. Now he's heard that Ben finally has himself a pretty new girlfriend. You never get too old to notice "pretty." Oriental, he thinks he heard. Though his young grandniece, Meg, has informed him you can't say that; you have to say Asian. He doesn't want to make anybody feel bad anymore, and loves Meg, he really does, so he makes an effort to use the new terminology, but the whole time he's thinking *Oriental*, you know? Old habits die hard. He knows this better than anybody.

Garnet, reconsidering, pauses their walk to call out, "Morning, Bowie," after all, as they pass, deciding a greeting would be way more annoying than simply ignoring his presence up there on that porch. Her aggravating ex. The mystery to Garnet remains what an otherwise intelligent, attractive, educated young woman like Lily might have found compelling here—yes, late thirty-something looks young to Garnet; at this stage in her life, anyone under fifty seems disconcertingly youthful, even childish to her anymore. Moreover, Garnet is not exactly proud of her own behavior during the time in question, though only one other person knows the extent of her moral turpitude, and he has proved to be most circumspect, thank God.

Going to Jake's office late one Friday afternoon, a few weeks after the whole imbroglio blew up, had been an impulsive decision, Jake, both Bowie's partner and Lily's father. If she'd thought about it, she'd never have done it. Garnet went, aware that for a while, years actually, he'd had a soft spot where she was concerned. Long-divorced, he'd also become more attractive to Garnet as they'd both aged, Jake, a member of that endangered species, a true gentleman—Garnet believes Lily must surely take after her mother. And as she'd figured, he was still there at his desk, working, everyone else gone home.

"Garnet," he'd said. "What are you doing here? I am so sorry. For everything."

He and Bowie were in the midst of dissolving their partnership, and Bowie was persona non grata in the building. Garnet, humiliated and beyond angry, looking for revenge wherever she could find it, offered—*no*, actually nothing so euphemistic, she'd out and out propositioned him. He'd paused for a long minute, then gently turned her down, saying it truly would only make matters worse. But in that moment before he spoke, Garnet saw something flicker across his face, something she took to mean that he'd momentarily considered it, that going to bed with her was not the worst thing he could have imagined.

And she has not forgotten, though it's been a while since she's run into him, the last time almost a year ago in Starbucks, latte in her shaking hand, slopping milky coffee onto his shoe as they exchanged brief hellos. Strange, she doesn't see him more often, not that she's saying she'd like to, but they do live in the same small town. Maybe he's embarrassed too. Though they'd managed to work together just fine—denial not just a river in Egypt (something Garnet wishes Mark Twain really *had* said)—after she hired him, for the time it took to divorce Bowie's guilty ass, and fixated as they were both were on a common goal, two pirates bent on plunder. She's since heard through the grapevine Jake's hired two young associates; the firm, Bowie's name no longer on its letterhead, is doing just fine.

I admit it, I am not a nice person, Garnet thinks. *Mean girls? Well, I'm what they turn into. My own sister and I, growing up, following a long tradition of familial selective blindness, of willful inability to recognize any elephants inhabiting our living space despite the significant resulting impediment they caused, thinking ourselves perfectly happy ignoring their existence—Ruby and I, it goes without saying, we no longer have anything in common with those two naive young girls.*

The sisters had been named by a mother who persisted in calling the two girls her precious jewels throughout their obnoxious teenage years. She'd dropped that hint of sarcasm once they became two quite lovely adults, if Garnet does say so herself. Nonetheless Ruby, her namesake a costly gemstone, a lover of same, also of diamond earrings, pearls, gold, and platinum, has told her husband, Harold, that if she goes first her jewelry will be his long-term care policy. Garnet, having seen Ruby's jewelry boxes (yes, plural) thinks this is spot-on. Garnet herself—her stone a semi-precious purported harbinger of thoughtfulness and commitment, qualities she thinks (immodestly) an accurate summation of her character—is very fond of cheap ornament (relative to rubies anyway). At this very moment, she's wearing a silver bracelet set with a turquoise stone, her favorite Timex watch, one showing the phases of the moon, and three rings whose provenance is unknown. None of it providing or requiring insurance of any kind.

Ruby is dress-up to Garnet's dress-down. She is a kitsch-prone collector—Beanie Babies (remember them?), Hummel figurines, pewter tankards, you name it—and addicted to the shopping network. She favors pantyhose and outfits, to Garnet's ad hoc socks and separates, and does not go out unless she has applied makeup and Giorgio. Each sister admiringly views the other as an exotic. However, Garnet sometimes regards Ruby's Rolex and finds herself calculating the musk oxen, goats, and flocks of chickens, Heifer International could have provided third-world families. That's what the timepiece represents to her. Then she is ashamed of herself. She loves her sister and is in no way perfect herself, in no way unsusceptible to the siren song of mammon. Their baubles simply differ.

Moreover, Garnet counts herself the lucky one in the name lottery, having never had someone she barely knows come up to her at a party and smirk drunkenly before warbling, "Garnet, it's you" in a very bad imitation of Mr. Ray Charles. And no one has ever felt the slightest compulsion to request she refrain from taking her love to town. Then again, Thelonious Monk chose "Ruby, My Dear" rather than any less valuable alternative for the title of music that moves Garnet to tears every time she hears it.

Ruby, older by two years, is, like Garnet's mother Grace, petite, charming, a babe. She shares a ribald, transgressive sense of humor with only a lucky few, among them her little sister—who in truth has not for a very, very long time fit that label. At sixteen, the height listed on Garnet's brand-new driver's license was five-eleven, but she was a lot closer to six feet, awkward and embarrassingly (to her) intelligent. Even now, at sixty-nine, Garnet is still almost five-ten. She is fond of black flats for dress-up and Birkenstock clogs for everyday, worn with colorful socks in winter. Ruby, in her Ferragamos, despairs of her.

Garnet now realizes that this close relationship, though not intentionally, left their ne'er-do-well brother out in the cold. Remington, who'd followed three years after Garnet, was named by their father, avid hunter who supplied his family's Thanksgiving turkeys the whole time they were growing up—the implication being their brother would be his sisters' protector for life? Not exactly the way it worked out, with Remmy so unlike her father, so unlike any of them. Her father, one on a very short list of people Garnet wouldn't mind seeing again, her mother one of the others, if eternity exists, if we somehow survive beyond death as individuals (which Garnet thinks most unlikely). And, of course, Garnet wonders whether they'd be happy to see her, blurter of inconvenient truths since childhood.

Garnet remembers her teenage self well, that youngster, occasionally even addressing her,

> Ha! I see from your sullen look, young Garnet, you are not happy being dragged out of our buried past today in order to have to listen to one more adult, your least favorite—yourself in fact—blah, blah, blah. It was such a bad breakup, the two of us. My finally growing up sometime back there in my twenties the final betrayal. I know you've never forgiven me for leaving you, my resentful adolescent self, behind.
>
> Yet here you are, summoned back, needy as ever, bad attitude and complexion intact, looking over this grown-up version of yourself with poorly disguised sorrow and hor-

ror, aghast at the damage fifty-some years have done to you. What can I say? Together we have somehow survived. Your stubbornness has stood me in good stead, your sarcasm not so much.

Who stands before you looks like a kinder, more tolerant person, looks like the grandma you might have liked to have had, in fact, even tries hard to be that kinder, gentler persona, all the while harboring the suspicion, little Shiva, little alien, that you are always there, readying yourself to burst noisily forth from her chest making a huge mess, appalling the locals who've had their doubts all along, wreaking widespread havoc and, preferably, killing your host (hostess?) in the process.

It seems detente is still not in the cards for us. Nor does my present almost-seventy-self harbor any desire to get out there, find some new and improved Bowie-replacement, or even worse, soulmate, though I'm pretty sure in my case any such exotic creature, if he ever existed, long ago became extinct. I have no wish to unload my long history on a budding relationship. Even worse, I don't want to hear another person's unhappy (boring!) story or alternately his (irritating!) tale of a wildly successful/happy life. Trust me, my dear, I promise that I won't be making that mistake.

Even so, Garnet has finally begun to realize that the resolve not to repeat a mistake often presages new, even more egregious errors. It's not that Garnet doesn't want to repeat or be reminded of the past. It's that the past will not let her go. It is a repeating tape, an unrelenting earworm, despite her efforts to silence it. Yet she loves memoir, wrenching tales of someone else's troubles, the worse the better. Go figure. There are at least two awaiting her in the stack of books she'd earlier requested on the library's website, books she is now on her way to check out. Logic has never been her strong suit.

Woman and dog continue down the street leaving Bowie behind, back there pretending not to have seen or heard her greeting or Vera's hail and farewell bark. The tall, old trees they walk beneath, looking dead, evidence not even a thought of leaf, though if anyone were to look closely, Garnet thinks, the buds are there seemingly dormant but quickening nonetheless, responding to the imperceptibly lengthening days.

Arriving at Haven's tiny downtown, after tying Vera's leash around a post, Garnet enters the hundred-year-old pile of stone that is their Carnegie library. Vera waits outside the entrance graciously accepting any and all attention and possible treats. There are multiple advantages for a dog living in a place where everyone knows her name.

Garnet's friend, Sylvie, calls out to her from behind the front desk, "Up for a walk on Saturday?"

"Yes. Walk. Meggie might join us," Garnet answers. "And breakfast?"

Sylvie, at seventy-five, is one of her dearest living friends, never married, now a retired head librarian though still working part-time, a collector of ephemera left in the books she checks in ever since she'd found a single orange notecard fifty-some years ago with the handwritten words, "I shall die without you," tucked into a picture book of Japanese gardens.

She enters the date, the book's title, then lists the item itself—which she refers to as an artifact—in her latest small spiral notebook. The one she's using now is blue, the kind in which homework assignments used to be kept before the advent of handheld electronic devices, or as Sylvie and Garnet call them, IODs, "instruments of the devil." Then she brings home what she's found, files it in one of her large, divided manila folders. There are pockets for grocery lists, to-do lists, for threats, the scribbles of the lovelorn, for food-stained recipes on torn paper, and for *miscellanea*: desiccated flowers, lengths of ribbon or colored string, the autumn leaf someone picked up and used to mark a place when nothing else was handy.

On rainy afternoons on her days off, Sylvie may empty one of these folders out on the kitchen table to study its contents.

White-haired oracle reading entrails, she considers each foundling a message from the universe. What do these scraps tell her? What does she then do about it? A mystery to Garnet who loves her friends' eccentricities. Sylvie has stated she never intends to fully retire. She hopes to be carried out feet first sometime after she turns ninety, although she acknowledges this may be stressful for any library patrons who happen to be present. *Not my problem*, she's decided.

Once home again, it is a day like any other. There's a message from Bowie on her voicemail asking if he can have the dog this weekend. Garnet has kept her landline because she's shared the new cell number with no one except her nephew and her sister. She decided, when Colt made her buy the thing, citing safety concerns—*What?* she'd asked. *Poor me, I have a flat tire and my car's surrounded by flesh-eating zombies? Yes, except maybe for the zombie part*, he'd answered—that she would not become one of the multitudes she sees everywhere, eyes glued to the virtual while the Fourth of July fireworks that are their lives explode unseen, unheard, unnoticed, all around them.

Procrastinating—talking to her ex not one of her favorite activities—her newspaper still damply unreadable, Garnet opens Facebook on her laptop. A semi-Luddite, she is a devotee of email, of Google—who doesn't love an answer, though not necessarily the answer you were looking for, always at your fingertips. But the blogosphere remains *terra incognita*. She does not text, is the source of no tweets, chirps, or whistles; she accesses no Instagram, Flickr, eBay, or Tumblr. She eschews them all as infernal life-devouring inventions. As far as Garnet is concerned, time is more and more an endangered commodity, both for herself and for her dwindling collection of friends, friends who keep disappearing around her, often with little or no warning—a blessing Garnet believes for them, though not necessarily for the ones they've left behind. Then again, what Garnet loves most about retirement is how time has also become elastic, like one of those stretchy garbage bags, able to contain whatever you stuff into it no matter how oddly shaped, no longer a week-long series of boxes into which she must sequentially fit herself.

Her Facebook account has thirty-five friends, which secretly appalls Garnet. Who has that many friends? True friends? Garnet counts maybe five over the course of her lifetime. Facebook should label the category "acquaintances," which would also serve to render less obscene all "friend" lists of five hundred or more. She pauses to peruse Ruby's latest sunset photos and resolves to check in with her sister later today. Her nephew has shared a post from some conservative website. Colt affectionately calls Gigi his *commie* aunt, she, only bleeding-heart liberal in the whole family, even her sister a libertarian—how is that even possible? Shouldn't some law of averages kick in here and result in at least one kindred spirit to be related to? Finally—guilty pleasure—she checks out the dogs that fill her newsfeed, photos of her friends' mutts, rescue sites, the dog-shaming site, though she thinks that one way too reliant on poop jokes.

At last, she calls her ex back on the yellow wall phone in the kitchen. His recorded message is classic Bowie, a man who's never met an imperative he didn't like. First some symphonic bit evincing there is no lack of culture here—currently the opening clarinet glissando from "Rhapsody in Blue," then, *You've reached Bowie Delaney. Leave a brief message. Speak clearly. Include your number and spell your name,* advances only as far as *Leave*...before he picks up. Screening his calls again—not that there would be many calls to screen, she thinks. Bowie is no Atticus Finch, admired by all (though Garnet has had to acknowledge recently and reluctantly the possibility that even Atticus may have had feet of clay thanks to an ill-advised, in her opinion, postmortem publication of Miss Lee's first draft of *Mockingbird*).

"Garnet, about this weekend," he begins with no preamble.

"You cannot have the dog, Bowie."

"But..."

"Meg is coming."

"And you were planning on letting me know when?"

"Never? She's not your grandniece, you know. She's mine."

Yet Garnet has to admit that Meg has an undeniable affection for her not-so-great uncle. And around her, Bowie is most un-Bowie-like. After a poor job as father to one little girl, he has turned out to be an exceptional uncle to another, perhaps a case of a leopard not so much changing its spots as noticing for the first time they are there and changing its ways instead.

"This attitude does not become you, Garnet. Please tell Meggie we have an ice cream date on Sunday afternoon."

Though the words, *Tell her yourself, you old goat*, or worse, are on the tip of her tongue, Garnet limits herself to slamming the receiver down, her version of anger management. One more thing she dislikes about cell phones, a whole generation growing up and old without ever experiencing the satisfaction of ending a conversation with physical violence that actually (ideally?) hurts only the recipient's feelings, maybe his ear. No wonder guns are such a problem—so many better alternatives have disappeared. Maybe she and Colt could design a hang-up app and become dot-com millionaires.

Garnet reads her finally dry newspaper as she eats lunch—a grilled cheese sandwich accompanied by dill pickle and a tall glass of kefir, the last third of which Garnet pours into an impatient Vera's bowl. Finished, she calls her sister. If not every day, they touch base often.

"Ruby?"

"Garnet. I called you awhile ago but your answering machine picked up. You really have to record a new message."

"Vera and I were out taking our walk. Why?"

"*Leave a message. Please!* It seems so...what? Curt? The attempt at *politesse* at the end so clearly an insincere afterthought."

"You didn't like the one I recorded before this one either."

"The only difference between the two, dear sister, is that the first one played that entire Gloria Gaynor song and left out the *please*. Mother would not have approved."

"Well, I did survive, didn't I? And it really cut down on my voicemail. I was lucky to have two messages a week. With this one, I'm back up to a couple a day. I'm thinking of maybe going with Bobby Dylan next."

"What? 'It Ain't Me, Babe'?"

"I'll surprise you."

"No. You'll never hear from me. Is that what you want?"

"Remember long distance, Ruby, how expensive it was to call, how careful we had to be about how long we talked?"

"Remember when there was that human being called an operator on the other end ready to take your call?

"We are old as dirt, aren't we?"

"Pretty much, I'm afraid."

Before Garnet starts winnowing books, she picks up her journal from the kitchen table and places it back in its cubby in Bowie's treasured birds-eye maple desk, one that originally belonged to his father. Garnet had moved it into the front hall right after the divorce so it would be the first thing she saw upon entering the newly all-hers house. It was a trophy, a shining, lamp-lit symbol of victory. But over time it has come to serve as a reminder that really there are no winners, only losers. In fact, one of these days, she just might ask Colt to put the thing in his truck, take it down the street and leave it on Bowie's front porch, out of the weather of course; it's such a pretty piece. Someday, but not quite yet, even though she accepts that time may be running out for her to become a better, less vindictive person.

To that end, Garnet tries to practice gratitude. Imperfectly, she admits. Just this morning she'd been working on a draft of a poem that had begun with her pleasure at finding herself here, thankful to be still in the world, alive, when so many friends and loved ones were already *poof!* gone for good despite this morning's dream—a poem that in its first drafts back in February had contained more than a little schadenfreude concerning her own good fortune and others' tough luck.

Even longevity, for which, don't get her wrong, she really is grateful, is not without its drawbacks. As if aging itself were not enough of a memento mori, there are birthdays, more millstones than milestones, their candles lighting one's way to dusty—well, we all know where Shakespeare's psychotic Scot was going with that. Birthdays like the one Garnet has coming up. True, it's weeks away, the sixth of May, but that makes it no less obnoxious. Seventy. Obnoxious not so much because of the number but because she knows already, though to the naked eye no evidence is apparent, plans are being discussed, plots plotted, a celebration is afoot. All of which makes her increasingly irritable, though it's too early to begin stamping her foot without seeming ridiculous, to start demanding she wants nothing special, a lopsided homemade cake, candle-free, perhaps her nephew's sinful chocolate version, a few gifts, preferably handmade and humorous, with volatile spirits available for adults, or more accurately—as far as her family is concerned—spirits for volatile adults? Or both? To be followed by a brief period of off-key singing.

She'd also prefer, on the birthday currently barreling down the track, to be turning thirty, as her daughter and nephew will next year, instead of the actual number that is her fate. A septuagenarian! The age at which, should she have the misfortune to mistake gas pedal for brake and wipe out the Honk 'n' Holler drive-thru, the newspaper account will refer to her as an "elderly female." No, she cannot pretend to feel thankful for that. Not a bit. This grateful-person project, just one more thing turning out to be a harder task than was initially thought.

In what Garnet refers to as her youth, she was reader, college student, English major, then an attorney's wife. But, despite the degree, in her working life, Garnet was not a librarian, a teacher, an editor, or a writer. After a few years, as it became painfully apparent she was probably not going to manage motherhood, she added employee—retail clerk, to her résumé, then manager of *books for all!* on Haven's Main Street. The job was perfect, giving an addict a crack house for her birthday, a drinker her own liquor store. She didn't regret any of it, leaving only for the first few years after Tommie's surprising arrival, returning once again after her daughter entered kindergarten, staying at the store till the big box at the mall, followed by Amazon, finally did it in a few years ago. Though, truth be told, she also hasn't minded a minute of the subsequent forced, and probably overdue, retirement.

Since she is already in the kitchen, Garnet fires up another pot of Sumatra dark roast, and decides to begin the day's project right here where her cooking and poetry books live, and where escapees have landed in small haphazard piles on counters, on a chair, one jumbled assortment, of cookbooks on a bottom shelf in the pantry. If only she loved the act of food preparation as much as she likes reading about it. If she'd felt this way about sex, there never would have been a Tommie, she thinks. And that? Maybe not such a bad thing? Happy to have assigned herself this task today, Garnet is sure it will prove therapeutic, resulting in a better-organized, if not a better, person. After all, one has to start somewhere.

It is a house of bookcases, from tall plain Janes with wood-grained paper covering their sturdy particleboard backs, lining the workspace in her bedroom/office upstairs, to the three gorgeous oak beauties in the dining room/library. Each is filled with books. Books on top of books. They are stacked on chairs, on the floor, her nightstand, on the kitchen table. It would be more efficient to list only the spaces in the house that have none, the two bathrooms excluded only because damp and paper are never friends. No wonder Garnet has decided it's past time to send some, no, many, to new homes, the senior center, Goodwill, maybe to the homeless shelter in the city. But she does not call it "rehoming," because she does not think that is a real word, or if it is, it's an unfeeling one–especially when heartbreakingly applied to a pet.

Garnet works steadily through the afternoon until she hears the back door open. Five-thirty already. Colt home from work. He calls her name, and she answers from the dining room where she is sitting on the floor surrounded by an untidy assemblage of art and history books. Her nephew enters the room, looks around, and raises his eyebrows.

Garnet says severely, "Do not laugh at me. I've been busy."

She points to the pile she's separated from the rest, fruit of her labors this day. On the chair in front of Colt are twelve books, three of them paperback mysteries in the advanced throes of decomposition.

Never ever one to say, *I told you so*, Colt says, "No matter what you said this morning, I did know when I accepted the job it was going to go something like this."

Then, unable to help himself, he begins to laugh. A full minute passes before Garnet joins in.

❧

It rains on Friday, an end-of-March rain, pouring out of the heavens like someone has unblocked a long-stuck spigot. Weather like this is the only time that Vera actually smells like a dog, and Garnet uses Bowie's prized outsized golf umbrella, another divorce trophy—she admits she may have gotten kind of mean toward the end of all the litigation—when she takes the dog out in a mostly futile attempt to keep them both dry. Why? Vera is perfectly capable, of course, of taking herself outside. The yard is fenced. But Vera, unattended, lover of foul weather, would stubbornly remain there gamboling in the mud and puddles until, satisfactorily matted, dirty, and soaked, she was good and ready to come in, her return accompanied by a vigorous shake or three, an asperges that would liberally anoint Garnet and her kitchen. Water and mud everywhere.

Like every other relationship in her life, the one with her dog is complicated. This animal is the reason Garnet knows she will burn in hell, if hell exists, which she (mostly after reading the newspaper some days) kind of hopes it does, though she has her doubts (also mostly after reading the newspaper some days). After all, Vera was Bowie's dog. He brought her home; the dog slept by his side of the bed; she followed him everywhere, bobbing along in his wake like a hirsute dinghy. In Vera's universe, Garnet was a tiny, cool, distant planet, Bowie the sun.

But when Garnet found out about Lily, things changed. She did not at first confront her distracted, straying husband, now seldom home. Instead, furious, hurt, she began to woo Vera, starting with food—chicken fingers, bites of raw steak, ice cream; then with privilege—the couch, her bed, until Vera's heart was hers. By then, Bowie had left the house for good, opting for a tiny apartment (above what had been *her* bookstore!) on Main Street.

What she hadn't planned on was falling in love herself, the big dog's devotion proving balm to a broken heart as her life fell apart around her. Too besotted with Lily to notice what was happening, Bowie was blindsided by Garnet's insistence she have sole custody of the dog as part of the divorce settlement. Her behavior had been sneaky and mean and manipulative. She was glad of it then. She is still glad. She feels not a single smidgen of remorse. (That is why she's going to hell. Where she will burn. Happily.)

Back inside—water rivering off Vera, despite the umbrella, and puddling onto the kitchen floor—Garnet takes the beach towel she keeps on a hook by the back door for just this purpose and dries her darling off. It's true, she sighs, no one is ever going to mistake her for Mother Teresa.

Garnet decides there's nowhere she has to be on this Friday and spends her day reading the library book club's next selection, Annie Proulx's querulous account of building an unlikely house in an unfriendly place using only bags of money. Garnet takes a break in the afternoon to make an apple pie, baking being her version of air freshener. No plastic, no petroleum products involved, smells great and then you get to eat it for dessert, or breakfast if so inclined, and therefore environmentally friendly.

Daylight saving time having begun a week ago it will not quite be full dark when Colt and his daughter arrive, but Garnet's lamps have been lit since early afternoon. The kitchen table is set, and the pie awaits on top of the refrigerator, Garnet having learned long ago that Vera, her breed known for being large and in charge, feels she has first dibs on anything left unattended on *her* counters.

❧

The rain has finally stopped and Colt, early, is waiting outside the school for his daughter, truck idling, heater turned up. He feels bad for the carbon-choked earth *but you know what, it's cold out there!*

Colt's conscience, guilty as always ignores his protest, and as usual has the last word, "God*dammit!*" he says and turns the engine off.

Meg has joined some kind of after-school club. He'll hear all about it soon enough, all the way to Garnet's probably. Meg, hers the only normal name in his whole abnormal family, his aunt and her sister named after stones, though valuable ones; himself, his father—guns; his mother, Grace, after a spiritual condition, Bowie, the knife; even his child's mother, Rain, a weather event. Rain has said many of the girls she grew up with, their parents suffering from sixties hangovers, were also named for meteorological events, as well as seasons, summer and autumn especially, for months of the year, for days of the week, for pop stars, jazz greats, even alcohol, Brandy, Tequila, names that to Colt seem more likely to enable, though not ensure, a choice of future employment as stripper rather than Supreme Court Justice.

Perhaps their own decision to name their daughter Margaret, okay, Rain's decision—he was too busy being pissed about an event that has turned out to be the best thing that ever happened to him—itself signals a kind of sea change for the better. Colt now believes parents of daughters should have stapled to their birth certificates a printed suggestion that any name being considered should first be said aloud, preceded by *Her Honor, Senator, Chief Justice,* or *Madam President,* before being chosen.

"We're home," Meg announces, opening the back door into the kitchen, though Colt knows the dog alerted Garnet even before his pickup turned into the driveway, and Vera is awaiting them, tail wagging.

"As promised, we've got dinner," Colt adds, coming in, placing the pizza box on the table.

It is a measure of Vera's love that her eyes do not follow the food but remain fixed on Meg, who leans down and puts her arms around the big white dog, ensuring that the navy wool of her jacket will once again spend the weekend growing its own coat of Vera fur. Colt, watching the two, is aware neither Meg nor the dog much care.

This house, his aunt's and daughter's laughter, the dog, all fill him tonight with the usual tangle of contradictory feelings. He remembers his response when Rain told him she was pregnant with Meg. Not his finest moment by a long shot. *But I used condoms*, he'd said, the weaselly and insulting implication being that maybe this was her problem, not about him at all. And, yes, it was true, most of the time he had. But even then he knew "most of the time" didn't cut it. "Most of the time" resulted in his girlfriend of a year, this young woman he was beginning to think he was actually in love with, telling him she was pregnant with his child. Rain, the first and only girl he'd had real sex with, as opposed to middle school fumblings, or previous high school almost-but-not-quites, despite everybody seeming to think guys begin sowing their wild oats—kind of an unfortunate metaphor to be so popular, he thinks—early and indiscriminately.

He'd been one messed-up kid. True, role models had been pretty sparse—absent father, his mom on her long journey into the illness that took her—thank God for the ones who'd stepped up, his aunts, even his uncle, Bowie. And Rain, Rain, having inexplicably fallen for him despite his attitude, his ponytail, and the lame, not-Bruce soul patch. For a year, the last year of high school, they'd been a couple, Colt under the impression it was he who'd invented sex, the rest of the world having no idea, no idea at all, and not paying attention to a lot else. And Rain, being Rain, keeping his listing boat on an even keel, helping him fill out college applications and financial aid forms, since everybody else was otherwise occupied.

Then Rain breaking the news to him after graduation, he'd been eighteen, legally a man—though Colt believes there might be some discussion as to whether he's achieved that goal even now. Colt, not stepping up when he had the chance; he gets that he was young, self-involved, but he doesn't think he'll ever be able to forgive himself for turning then and walking away from her. *Every time I look at our daughter*, Colt thinks, *this beautiful child, North Star by which I navigate my fucking life, I, judge and jury, bang the gavel, finding myself guilty all over again.*

❧

Saturday morning. At least Tommie thinks it's still morning. She opens one eye and sees that actual sunlight appears to be leaking through the bedroom's blackout blinds. A good sign. She throws back the covers and pauses for a moment on the side of the bed. It's been days since the big light in the sky has made an appearance. She'd returned in February to western New York, land of perpetual overcast, of clouds and snow and fog and rain. Seattle East, in Tommie's opinion, without the cachet but with the added dubious attraction of real winter, the occasional blizzard, and huge snowbanks lining the roads from December to March like filthy recumbent polar bears. Having managed somehow to reach the age of twenty-nine without developing anything as potentially awkward as insight might prove to be, Tommie, prodigal daughter, has returned home after running away (really what else could you call it?) three years ago to California.

Tall like her mother, she has also inherited her father's thick wavy hair and brilliant blue eyes. She is curvy and possessed of many hang-ups, although weight is not one of them; she thinks she is just fine the way she is, which in turn, for the most part, means everyone else does too. She has size eleven feet about which she is not the least self-conscious and possesses an embarrassingly extensive and expensive collection of shoes, not unlike her aunt Ruby. Tommie has a childhood history of pitting her father and mother against each other whenever her wants and desires were in play, and in her almost-thirty-year-old heart of hearts feels more than a little responsible for their breakup. (Of course she is not responsible for her parents' split, but she has the only-child's unconscious conviction that she is the white-hot center of her universe and that everything that happens in it somehow concerns or is concerned with her.) Their divorce, despite occurring long after she putatively became an adult, shook her badly, though not badly enough to cause her to actually grow up. Tommie is a mystery to herself and to others, especially others who care about her, as some have discovered from bitter experience. And, incongruously, she is also an excellent, empathetic teacher of primary age children (perhaps because so many parts of her psyche remain at their age level).

Tommie leans down, pulls her sheepskin-lined slippers closer and slides her feet into them. She'd be the first to admit she's vain about her feet. Whenever possible she wears sandals, thin strappy affairs that leave them almost bare, something that was a lot easier to do when she lived in California, not so easily managed here in March. But winter or summer, she keeps a standing appointment for a pedicure. Her toenails right now are bright pink. On each big toe, the manicurist has glued a tiny blue star. She is the only member of her immediate family not afflicted with, if not actually crippled by fallen arches, bunions, hammer toes, her father telling her frequently when they were still talking, *Just wait, you're young.* But Tommie knows her feet will be perfect always. Just the fact that he tried to convince her otherwise is proof enough for her. She also realizes that this, like so much else she believes, is ridiculous.

So far, Tommie is pretty sure no one knows she's back, though at this very moment, in this city, she's only half an hour away from Haven, the small town, village really back then, where she grew up. Didn't exactly turn out to be a haven for her though. She tells herself better job prospects, the lower cost of living, have brought her back—the apartment she's found is twice the size and half the monthly rent of her California digs, which required two roommates to afford. Unable to find a full-time teaching job out west, she'd been a barista, a waitress, a personal assistant, and a health store clerk. When she found herself, after her holiday temp job ended, seriously considering an offer to manage a medical marijuana venue, she'd decided maybe it was time to test Thomas Wolfe's theory. Though she suspects her mother turning seventy, her father on the fast track to seventy-five, and her seriously fucked-up relationship with them both, might also have something to do with it, along with that looming thirtieth birthday.

Unlike her sudden departure three years ago, bolting the ongoing Albee play that was turning out to be her parents' divorce, her engagement broken by a phone call from a motel room somewhere in Utah—she'd FedExed the ring back to Ben, uninsured, the next day—Tommie has decided it might be best to ease into the reacquaintance phase. She's decided to start with her cousin, Colt, with whom she's maintained contact despite the inconvenient identity of his best friend, the aforementioned ex-fiancé, Ben. After a protein shake and two cups of black coffee, and unable to further procrastinate due to the bleak contents of her cupboards and refrigerator—she draws the line at finishing off a jar of maraschino cherries—she picks up her phone.

"Colt? It's Tommie."

"*Umm.* I need to call you back. I'm in the middle of breakfast here with my daughter."

"It's Saturday; you're at The Cup with my mother. Sylvie's there too, I bet. Blueberry pancakes, Big Gulp Diet Coke, and a double order of bacon?"

We are, all of us, so predictable, thinks Tommie. This has been the weekend drill since Colt and Rain sorted out custody of the year-old Meg. And until she blew up her life, Tommie and Ben had been a fixture at these gatherings too. For that matter, so had her father before detonating his own life-altering bombshell. Family as Fallujah, though she does not want to make light of the troubles in the Middle East and has kept that thought to herself.

"Afraid so."

"Okay, call when you can. Just checking in."

"Everything all right?" Garnet asks.

"Fine," Colt says, wondering what his cousin is up to.

Until now he's been the one calling every couple months, making sure she hasn't found some new deep end to jump into, keeping both Gigi, and of course Ben, in the dark, the whole subject of Tommie too hurtful to visit. Ben, who has not by the way, in his humble opinion, gotten over anything despite the new girlfriend.

They are finishing up, the table a jumble of syrupy plates and half-empty coffee cups. Waiting for their check, Colt listens to his three breakfast companions discussing spirit animals, something Meg came across as she researched, with Sylvie's help, a school project on Native Americans. They have now narrowed their focus to assigning family and friends spirit dogs.

"I get to start," Meg says. "It was my social studies project."

"Let the little girl speak," Colt says.

In retaliation, Meg replies, "Daddy, a German shepherd, with all their good—and bad—qualities."

"Bingo!" says Garnet.

Meg turns, fixing her aunt in her gaze. "You're next, auntie—yellow lab, loyal, responsible, totally dependable."

"And your favorite librarian?" Sylvie asks.

"Golden retriever, of course." Meg smiles. "Best dog for the best librarian."

"My turn," Colt says. "Meggie here, a little beagle, but anything is possible in the years to come—corgi, Irish wolfhound, rabid maltipoo."

Meg rolls her eyes at her father.

Later Colt's thoughts will return to the subject, one he finds oddly appealing. He'll choose a feral border collie for his cousin, Tommie. Another lab, this one male, a canine Eagle Scout for Ben. For Rain, he picks a standard poodle, smart, independent, protective, despite looks that might lead one to think otherwise. Bowie? *Hmmm*. Pitbull? On second thought, *no*, the choice seeming to Colt to be most unfair to an already maligned breed. And his own father? Remington? Wolf dog? Maybe Remmy never really had a chance to become anything other than what he turned out to be.

The checks arrive. As usual, Colt notes, Sylvie takes hers, matter-of-factly placing a 50 percent tip on the table, her way, he figures, of protesting the way serving staff are, or rather are not, paid.

"So, Meggie, I will see you later?" Sylvie says.

Meg's weekend visits to the library are a routine begun when Colt, clueless teenager still living at home, trying to figure out what the word *dad* might mean when applied to himself, began taking Meg as a toddler to the kiddie room on her Saturdays with him. It was more for something, anything, to do than from some deep love of literature. His little daughter played at the block table while Sylvie had helped him amass a pile of picture books to check out, to take home and read to his child when all else failed.

Today, Colt knows that Meg will collect her own stack of books, many inappropriate for fourth-grade level—last time her selection included F. Scott's short stories, de Saint-Exupéry's *Little Prince* (easy to tell that women of a certain age are acting as advisors, he thinks), and *Because of Winn-Dixie*, plus three Babysitters' Club titles—she is a kid after all, give her a break; barely enough to tide his avid young reader over during a week at home where, he thinks, there's too little time in her scheduled life for library visits.

"Yes, indubitably," Meg answers Sylvie.

His daughter likes using words she's picked up in her reading with this collection of adults who can almost always be trusted not to laugh at her.

Home again, his aunt and Meggie having departed for the library leaving him behind, ostensibly to watch basketball though a sports nut he is not, Colt is stretched out on the living room sofa contemplating a nap. Vera, having taken the initiative, is already asleep on the carpet when he remembers his cousin's call. He picks up his cell.

"So, Tommie, what's up?"

"*Uhhh*, I'm back."

"Back as in?"

"Back as in back, dummy. As in here, for now, maybe for good. I thought maybe we could get together. Touch base. Help me figure out how to break it to the responsible adults."

"As opposed to…?"

Tommie sighs audibly.

"You used to be so much fun, Colt. What's happened to you?"

They agree that after Colt takes Meg home Sunday evening, they'll meet up at San Remo for dinner. They both like Italian.

❧

It's the last Sunday in March, another cold, dismal, drizzly afternoon more suited to hot chocolate than ice cream. Nevertheless, here's Bowie heading down the street to pick up Meg. From the window, Garnet watches him ascend the porch steps, arrive at her door, check his watch, pause, and precisely at three o'clock press the doorbell. Garnet snorts and, Vera close behind, answers the door.

"Bowie."

"Garnet. Why, hello there, Vera."

The dog slips past Garnet out onto the porch. Bowie bends down, scratching his ex-dog under her chin, his expression softening. Garnet sees an unsettling glimpse of the long-gone young man she married. He straightens up, grasping Vera's collar. They both know the breed's independent spirit would soon impel Vera down the steps and away, "Born Free" playing loudly on her soundtrack. He hands the dog over to Garnet, who ushers Vera into the house, then steps back outside. She could ask Bowie to wait inside. She could but she won't. She'd rather stand out here in the cold. She would.

"Meg is…?"

"Running a little late. Colt called; they're on their way. Their movie ran long. Twenty-seven previews will do that."

"I wouldn't know," Bowie says.

It was the seventies; she'd gone with Bowie to see *Taxi Driver*. Give him credit, he'd sat through the whole thing. Too close to the misery he often saw played out in court, the film had undone him.

When they got home, he'd turned to her and said, "No more."

And that was that. From then on, she'd gone to the movies alone or with a friend. It occurs to Garnet this may be one of the longest face-to-face conversations she's had with her ex-husband since their divorce decree was finally issued.

❧

Sunday evening Colt pulls into Rain's driveway, delivering Meg to her mom after a weekend in which nothing special happened. He and Meg ate pizza with Garnet; they took Vera to the dog park, went to breakfast with their elders, and Meg to the library with Garnet. They saw a movie, its forgetful fish reminding Colt of something, of someone, finally realizing on the way home that it was Bowie. Meg then went out for sundaes with that same uncle, the crummy weather bothering neither one. Colt and his daughter played Monopoly with Garnet, one game each evening, Colt, winning big and sorely lacking in good-sport humility, christened a "bad winner" and "glory hog" by the disdainful ladies. In other words, it was perfect. He turns off the engine and glances at his daughter. He would very much like to have her remain ten forever, his life remaining in perfect equilibrium, no looming future to scare the bejesus out of him. Nothing says happy and afraid don't go together. That they don't march lockstep, holding each other up like the two wounded soldiers they are. Considering the fragility of happiness, aren't we always looking back, worrying, making sure something, anything, isn't gaining on us, on a mission to take it all away? *I know, I know. Stupid.* Serving only to make a person less happy, more afraid. Even so, Meg's sweet round face, that smile her grandmother's, all of it more than enough reason to startle awake in a cold sweat in the middle of the night thinking of all the things the world contains. Its arsenal of illness, violence, accidents. To recognize your significant powerlessness in the face of its criminal beauty. *How do you live with that? How does anyone?*

Rain and his daughter live in the city in a duplex not far from where he'll be meeting his cousin later. The owner, a widow, Mrs. (Not Ms., she's made very clear) Cabrera, Julitta, Julie to her friends, lives in the other unit. Colt isn't crazy about the shabby city neighborhood, but Meg's school, a magnet for the arts, where his friend Ben teaches, is only a block away.

Rain, despite her piercings and tattoo, the rainbow colors that often streak her short dark hair, is a fiercely protective mother. She's been seeing someone for the past few months, someone she recently introduced to Meg, someone Meggie calls Eddie. Colt takes this as a clue that things might be getting serious and marvels that after all this time, he still feels more than a twinge of proprietary jealousy when he thinks of Rain with someone else. Sometimes Colt wonders what would have happened if he'd stayed, married, or at least moved in with Rain. Skipped college, just gotten a job, probably one not so different from the one he has now. He's managed over time to become a pretty good dad, but husband? Even now he can't picture it. And it's not like he's been some kind of wild and crazy guy, leaving in his promiscuous wake a string of broken hearts. If anything, the heart that's been broken a time or two has been his own.

Colt and Meg together gather her belongings from the car—backpack, library books, schoolbooks, a Tupperware of lemon scones Garnet and Meg baked for Rain on Sunday morning. Meg runs up the porch steps and opens the door, calling out, "I'm home," same words she used when she arrived at Garnet's. *Nice*, Colt thinks as he follows her in, nice to feel you belong wherever you find yourself. Waiting for them in the hall he sees Rain and someone else. And there he is, the man he's been hearing about in passing, the famous Eddie. Fast Eddie, Colt's labeled him, also, Eddie the Interloper, Eddie the Extraneous, Eddie-Get-The-Fuck-Away-From-My-Family.

"Mom! Hi, Eddie! I made us scones," says Meg.

"We love scones," says Rain. "Got time for a scone, Colt?"

"Nope," says Colt. "Got to be on my way."

"Okay. *Oh*. Colt, Eddie. Eddie, Colt," Rain says.

Eddie steps forward, offering his hand. Colt, really, really wanting to be an asshole and ignore it—but, unwilling to do so in front of his daughter—dutifully shakes hands.

Colt tries to be a good father. If he cannot accomplish this, he thinks whatever else he accomplishes will not much matter. But throw Eddie into the mix, and what happens to his goal? This unknown quantity presenting itself in the person of his ex-wife's new boyfriend, this possible live-in, possible fiancé, husband, second father to *his* Meg, this Eddie, who, in the two-minute conversation he just had with him, seemed okay, but who knows, right? God, he *hates* change.

Colt is almost in the truck when Rain calls after him, "Your daughter is making dinner here on Friday for you and Eddie and me. Will you come?"

If Rain had asked for herself, his answer would of course have been *Hell, no!* Rain is no dummy. He is incapable of saying no to his daughter.

The restaurant is half empty; it's Sunday evening, a weekend winding down. Colt spots Tommie immediately, always the prettiest girl in the room, her face illuminated by a candle-stuck-in-wax-encrusted-chianti-bottle cliché. She looks up and waves him over.

"Colt."

"So, Tommie."

"Nice to see you too."

Colt hangs his jacket on the back of the chair and sits down. He is not happy. No surprise. Recent events have had their effect on his normally quite sunny disposition. He resolves not to take it out on Tommie. He fails.

"How's my niece?" she asks.

"Fine, and the one person you can be sure will be thrilled to see you. Maybe we should start your rehabilitation with her."

"And my mother, your landlady? Think she misses me?"

"You'd have to ask her. Ditto for your dad."

"Harsh, cousin."

"Tough love, Tommie. Go ahead, ask. I know you want to."

"Ben?"

"Moved on. And maybe consider not asking him anything. Maybe stay away from Ben completely."

"It's slowly coming back to me what a stinker you can be."

"Regardless, you're back. You know your mother turns seventy in May?"

"Give me some credit. *One* of the reasons I'm here."

"We're going to want to start putting together a party soon."

"We?"

"Never mind, this isn't the best time to talk about it."

"If I hadn't come back, would you even have let me know?"

"You, dear cuz, are not putting me on the defensive. We'll revisit this another day."

"Whatever," Tommie says.

Monday, Colt has the afternoon off. This is not a good thing, because he doesn't get paid if he doesn't work. But things are slow right now, and this is one way the boss deals with it. Colt pulls into Garnet's driveway and waves to his next-door neighbor. George is out hosing off his black Escalade on this forty-degree March day with (*Can it be? Sure as hell is!*) a power washer, determined, Colt figures, to wash away every last bit of the winter road salt. George is retired military, a widower who runs a tight ship despite a crew of only one, who may also have a little crush on Garnet by the way, though she seems oblivious, maybe on purpose, to any such possibility.

Colt knows he has a few quirks of his own, like the way he sets out the garbage on Tuesday. Biodegradable thirty-gallon bags from a website he found—Colt is a big fan of online shopping, even Vera's food is ordered via the internet—cardboard boxes broken down, wedged along with Garnet's newspapers securely into the recycling tub, which he sets back from the road between the two bags. Nothing of his is going to be blowing down this street, unlike others he could name if you asked.

And George—his two step-kids might as well be his own, the boys always stopping by to shovel his drive, bring in the mail, drop off a covered dish sent by one of their wives. Not surprising. He'd married their mother and raised the two of them with her, their own actual dad pretty much of a no-show. Having met Eddie, who may well be assuming this role in his daughter's life, it all feels suddenly very close to home. Rain has never before, and ten years is a long time, introduced someone she was seeing to Colt, nor invited that someone into her home when her daughter was there, so what else is he to think?

❧

Ben knows he's perceived as a nice guy with a nerdy, even if in the best possible sense, streak. Of average height, he habitually dresses in casual Friday mode, khakis, loafers with socks, without when he wants to be edgy, a button-down solid color, long sleeve, perma press shirt, sleeves rolled, and an analog watch that requires winding. He wants to set a good example, show his third graders that they are worth dressing up for.

And it's not as though everyone else doesn't believe he's over Tommie. Ben is convinced he's successfully fooled them all, even his girlfriend who he knows holds a very low opinion of Tommie, viewing her, thanks to him, as not a serious person, as someone who goes through life breaking other people's things, a significant character flaw in her estimation. Moira, who if he has a lick of sense, he should be crazy about; Moira, tiny, pretty, with her straight black hair cropped short, a gamine haircut giving her an Audrey Hepburn look.

A nurse at the local children's hospital, a caretaker, Ben knows, who takes terrible care of herself. Her last mammogram and pap smear were five years ago. She patronizes Urgent Care rather than go to the trouble of finding a primary care doctor. She does not exercise, or watch her salt and fat intake, and still smokes the occasional cigarette, sometimes even where she should not. In other words, she is a healthy woman in her twenties who on some level believes, if she thinks about it at all, that she will not only live forever but never get old doing so. She will grant that karma exists, but at this point in her life, mostly for others. Ben is her first serious boyfriend. A virgin, she slept with him on their first date. She was ready. She told him it had come to seem like a cumbersome weight she was tired of carrying. He'd been happy to relieve her of the burden.

Distractible as ever, he wonders again what possessed conservative Asian parents, émigrés from Hong Kong, to give their precious first-and-only-born a venerable Gaelic moniker despite their own limited command of English, a fact that means, more often than not, that Moira must employ her fluent Cantonese to communicate or explain. He loves how unpredictable, even irrational, human beings are, though he has to admit that it wasn't exactly a plus in Tommie's case. Tommie. How is it possible to still be missing someone who treated him so badly? He isn't over her at all, is he? Nope! *Nope, nope, nope!*

Moira knows all about Tommie (except maybe that he's still in love with her, something he tries to ignore like some low-grade fever, debilitating but, alas, not fatal). In her practical, no-nonsense way, which is one of the things he loves about *her*, she does not worry about the past, something she can't change.

And now—thank goodness for small towns—he's been forewarned, hearing from at least three of his buddies his ex is back in town. Ben already knows if he gives in to feelings he believes he's been so successful in hiding if not obliterating, it will not end well. Forewarned is forearmed, right? But he has the sneaking suspicion he's capable of caving anyway. Knowing it will not end well? Well, that's just a given.

Ben is not the only one tipped off. The woman who rented Tommie her apartment is the daughter of a childhood neighbor, one Garnet played with every single day until the family moved three streets over sometime in her second-grade year. They'd recently reconnected on Facebook. She'd messaged Garnet the news last week. So when Tommie calls, if she calls, her mother has also had time to get used to the idea, lessening the probability of the coronary she thinks she might otherwise have suffered. Garnet is pretty sure Colt is also aware of his cousin's presence. She thinks he may be trying to protect his aunt. But from what exactly?

❧

Tommie has signed up to substitute, with an eye toward getting a job next school year. She's specified K-3 because that's where she wants to wind up, otherwise she knows she'll be at a middle school every single day, facing a pack of feral, puberty-fueled children sizing her up and judging her satisfactorily small and defenseless. In other words, prey. She believes teachers of this age group, even if they're lucky and don't wind up actual martyrs, are true saints, holy ones among us. Substituting however means five-thirty a.m. calls.

"Ms. Delaney, central scheduling here."

The voice is male, bored, all-business and very awake. Obviously some kind of vampire action going on. Casket awaits. Must finish calls before first light.

"Are you able to sub today at (she doesn't catch the school's name). Second grade?"

Despite the obscene hour, Tommie's heart lifts. Her favorite grade, age. It's going to be a good day.

"I'm sorry, what school?"

"Rosa Parks Elementary."

Ben's school. *Shit!* Maybe he's moved on. When they broke up, he was thinking about trying something more challenging. Somewhere he could truly make a difference. *Mister holier-than-thou. As if.* Well, just in case, she'll bring her lunch. Eat in her room. Slink out the door at three. On the plus side, she remembers that it's also Meg's elementary school, a magnet school at that. Maybe she can catch a glimpse of one of her favorite relatives, one with whom she has no issues whatsoever, her behavior always, as far as Meggie is concerned, impeccable.

"I'll be there," she says.

Of course, as Tommie exits her car (she's left extra early to have time to look at lesson plans and avoid possible Ben sightings) there he is. Ben. Standing in the early morning gloom in the school parking lot, a lot edged with mounds of cinder-pocked snow hanging on after a winter's worth of plowing. He's lugging his bulging, now rather ratty-looking, leather briefcase, the one her father (who, she believes, loved her boyfriend a lot more than his troublesome—okay, she'll allow she never made it easy for him—daughter) gave him when he got this teaching job. The dirty snowbanks behind him are almost as tall as he is. Moreover, he doesn't look nearly as surprised as she might have expected.

"Tommie. Thought I might run into you but didn't think it would be here."

He looks good, even with the lot's sodium lights casting an unflattering glare. She is painfully aware of the circles under her own eyes, the faint lines she's begun to notice around her mouth, her pallor, lack of makeup, her hair pulled back out of the way with a scrunchie—why take the time when second graders are reliably nonjudgmental about physical appearance, always inclined to love first, their opinions forming only later.

How could she ever have thought she was somehow excused, immune from the ravages of age?

"Hello to you too, Ben."

The teacher has actually left decent plans and the materials needed are organized and ready. It's a nice class, only twenty, and when they tumble in at 8:30, it looks like a little UN in session. At the end of the day, the principal, Ms. Jackson, tall, no-nonsense, African American, stops by her room. She is someone Tommie remembers seeing at district meetings, before she'd cut and run, leaving behind her life and job.

"So, a good day?"

"Always a good day with these little guys," Tommie answers. She'd almost forgotten how much she enjoys the company of small children.

"Ms. Pepper called this afternoon. Her doctor says they need more tests. She'll be out the rest of the week. Are you up for it?"

"You bet."

Knowing she'll be back, Tommie starts to organize things for the next day. There are, miracle of miracles, plans written for the entire week. As she's stacking egg cartons and cups of beans for tomorrow's math lesson, she hears a familiar voice at the door.

"Tommie! It's me! Meg."

Tommie looks up at her little cousin, not so little anymore. The last time she saw Meg she'd just turned seven, younger than some of her charges today. Now what is she? Nine? Ten? Leggy, dark hair like her mom, but with Colt's eyes and contagious grin.

"I thought it was you, so I asked Mr. Brown. He said yes, you were substituting today."

When Meggie was little, she'd called him Brownie. Ben Brown, how white bread is that, how Wonder Bread-boring. Could Tommie ever actually have written out, more than once, just to see how it looked, felt, *Mrs. Ben Brown*? And why? Of course she'd have kept her own surname. As she hugs her niece,

Tommie realizes the cat is out of the bag, or soon will be, the jig is up, how many more clichés can she think of to put off the inevitable? Unless she wants even more trouble than is already coming her way, she needs to get in touch with her parents before the news gets back to them.

Tommie has no further interaction with Ben, which is fine with her. More than fine, really. Two more ill-suited people you could not find, she thinks, on her way out to the parking lot at the end of the day. Once home she intends to pour herself some liquid courage, a large glass of white wine from the box that now resides in her refrigerator next to two cups of out-of-date pomegranate Greek yogurt, a package of non-artisanal bologna, first name Oscar, half of a very stale loaf of on-sale, white, no-fiber, not-Wonder, bread and a lone bottle, all that remains, of a six-pack of craft beer, plus of course those maraschino cherries. Wait. Maybe a quick stop for supplies at the gas station mini-mart is called for. Then she's absolutely going to go straight home and call her mother. Her father will just have to wait.

But back at the apartment after unloading twenty-seven dollars' worth of snacks from her bright orange eco-sack made from recycled something-or-other, Tommie, ripping open a jumbo bag of vinegar chips, decides it would be even better, much less stressful, to slightly delay her call, just until the end of the week, a mere three days from now. Leaving the whole weekend to recover from whatever emotional trauma speaking to her mother might—who's she kidding—*will* inflict.

Friday. The week has gone well, the principal promising before Tommie left today that she would ask for her by name when calling Drac at central scheduling, leaving Tommie feeling pretty good about herself for a change. Once home, not even waiting to change into her weekend uniform of sweats and woolly socks, Tommie decides now or never, pausing only briefly to wonder if *never* might possibly be a viable option. She picks up her cell.

"Mom?"

"Hello, Tommie."

From the sound of Garnet's voice, it's clear to Tommie her call was not unexpected, which really in itself should not be any surprise, knowing from long experience how fast news travels in Haven. That, plus her history here of never having gotten away with a single thing, no rebellious act so small it did not get back to her parents, and sooner rather than later. California had been a huge relief. Nothing getting back to anyone no matter what she did, a realization, oddly, doing more to settle her down than anything else that happened to her in those years. She is trying to hold on to some little bit of that personal growth now that she's returned to ground zero.

"I'm back in town."

"Yes?"

"So, I thought maybe we could get together, maybe catch up?"

The call seems to Tommie to go on for hours, though when she hangs up only minutes have passed. Her mom has suggested, in a faintly pissy tone, that they meet at the park and take Vera for a walk on Sunday afternoon. That at least allayed one of her fears. Vera is still around. (Wait, she thinks. Add Vera to that very short list of loved ones she's never let down.) And while Tommie really didn't expect a tearful welcome, *You're back! I've missed you soooo much. All is forgiven*—okay, maybe a little—her mother's cool reception has taken her aback. As it was meant to do, she suspects. There's going to be no easy way to do this, is there? She pours herself a very large glass of wine.

After seeing Tommie in the school parking lot on Tuesday and then avoiding her the rest of a very long day, Ben wound up going home and calling Moira, just wanting to talk, if not actually see her, touch her (if you want the truth), as though she was some kind of antidote to his ex, which now that he thinks of it, she is though she doesn't know it. He'd asked her to come over after work on Friday. Dinner, he told her, a nice break for them both, end of the work week, a chance to see each other instead of waiting until their usual Saturday night date. After all, she's fed him often enough. It's time he reciprocated. He's even remembered the recipe for mushroom pesto steak, torn out of the paper in February—six? seven?—weeks ago for just such an occasion, still up there on his refrigerator under a Snoopy magnet where it had subsequently been ignored, not looked at once until now.

But today, stopping on the way home from school, Friday at last, and oblivious to the packed parking lot, Ben is surprised once inside the supermarket by crowds surging up and down the aisles, only finally remembering, basketball, the big dance, the Final Four this weekend. Waiting in the checkout line, he watches as the huge order ahead of him slides beeping past the scanners. The clerk, finished, tells the man in a Tar Heels sweatshirt he owes two hundred dollars and change for the overflowing cart filled with salt, fat, sugar, and alcohol, its contents nicely summarizing, Ben thinks, Tommie's own favorite food groups. He then carries his own meager two-bags-worth out to the car, having picked up everything needed for a nice dinner for two, even shelling out twenty dollars for a bottle of a pinot noir that got good reviews.

Moira arrives at six after a day shift in the neonatal unit, bringing dessert, just as he does when he eats at her place, but not some quart of Cherry Garcia from B&J, his usual offering, instead, a small, perfect (much like her) Black Forest cake, something she herself put together. Moira is a talented cook. She's everything Tommie is not; her only flaw, she is not Tommie. Tommie, connoisseur of Twinkies, consumer of marshmallow fluff from the jar, fond of Fritos in bed, her mouth tasting of salt when he kissed her. *What is wrong with him!*

❧

Colt carries a six-pack of artisanal Wet Dog tucked under one arm—Rain is no wine drinker—picked up from the new brewpub off Main and chosen mostly because of the drenched dog photos on each label, one of which features a very soggy-looking Great Pyr. Hoping to kill two birds with one stone and trusting the clerk's assurance of a tasty beer, he knows Rain will drink it—*Eddie? who cares*—and the pictures will make his daughter laugh. He has a bunch of bright red tulips in the other hand, which have already dripped all over the front seat of his truck. So, confident he has two of three taken care of, and aware of a fervent wish the third had never been born, he checks his watch, one minute to five, and realizing how Bowie-like he's acting, ascends Rain's front steps and knocks on the door.

"He's here!" Meg calls out, hugging him and taking the flowers. "Tulips! Red ones! My favorite!" she adds.

"I know," Colt laughs, as Rain and Eddie appear behind Meg.

"Come on in, we're all in the kitchen as usual," Rain says.

Colt picks up on the *as usual.*

Eddie again steps forward to shake Colt's hand.

"Hey, Colt," he says.

Colt notices the colorful full-sleeve tattoo; Eddie, despite the chilly weather, is wearing a navy polo, its fit attesting to someone to whom the gym at the Y is no stranger. Colt reminds himself once again that appearances can be deceiving. This could be the nicest guy in the world. *Or not*, he adds again. *Or not.*

"Hey," Colt says.

They eat in the kitchen. Rain's little house has no dining room. There's lasagna—Colt's favorite, she's trying to make this work—and Meg has made her first solo apple pie.

"I asked Garnet to teach me when I knew we were going to ask you to come for dinner with Eddie," she tells her father, which also explains the surfeit of said pie her previous weekend at Garnet's.

Colt does not like this intruder's diminutive, its sound, *Eddie*, the name's kiddish aspect especially since he's pretty sure Eddie is older than he by at least a few years. He decides he will call him Ed.

"So, Ed," he says, having waited until Eddie has just put a

large forkful of salad into his mouth, "how long have you and Rain known each other?"

This is not who I am, he thinks, some bratty, scorned middle-schooler out to get even. But he waits for the reply, admittedly enjoying the sight of Eddie trying to chew and swallow so he can speak.

Rain laughs and says, "You don't have to answer that, and, Colt, you'd sound just like my dad, if I was still fifteen and he'd given a damn."

Colt remembers her father, gone now, departed, with no loving adjective appended, remembers meeting him for the first time after he'd begun dating Rain. She was right; he could not have cared less. It blows Colt's mind, watching Meg as she follows their conversation, looking from one to the other, like someone at a tennis match. He can see his future self, paying for background checks on any male showing the slightest interest in his daughter, setting nine p.m. curfews, maybe having Meg wait until she's in graduate school to begin dating. He also realizes that were he to indulge any of these fantasies of parental protective control, he could well wind up with the teen trainwreck that was his cousin, Tommie.

"I don't mind answering," Eddie says. "Rain brought the 'bucket' in…"

"One of my New Year's resolutions," Rain interjects.

"…in January," Eddie continues, "to have the tires rotated."

Her ten-year-old car may look like a worn-out wreck, thus the nickname, but it's dependable and Rain is religious about maintenance; the oil is changed on time, anti-freeze added, summer windshield wash replaces winter's in May. Her chaotic upbringing has resulted in someone who feels great comfort in taking care of all that is hers. Once again, Colt wonders how big a mistake not marrying this woman might have been.

"I talked her into buying new tires as well," Eddie says.

January. It's the end of March. Two, three months. Seems to Colt kind of like Rain may be moving too fast here. Two or three years, now that might be a tad more acceptable. He knows he's being unreasonable. It does not help. They finish off the evening playing Scrabble. They do not let Meggie win. She wins fair and square with "gelid." Sometimes his daughter scares him. Even though he considers neither Rain nor himself dummies, he still doesn't know where she got that big brain.

Rain walks him out to the truck.

"Meg says Garnet is turning seventy this birthday," she says. "Are you planning something?"

"I'd like to, but I could use a hand. I know Ruby will come, but she won't be much help. Her husband's not doing well. I'll just be happy if she can make it."

"Count me in."

This is great news to Colt. Rain is organized, a promise keeper. When she says she'll help, she'll help.

"Beer actually tasted kind of like a wet dog, didn't it?"

"Well, the labels were cute. Meg loved the Great Pyr. Reason you chose it, right?"

"Guilty," Colt says, getting into the truck, closing the door, rolling down the window.

"So that wasn't so bad, was it?" Rain says. "We can do this, right?"

"If you tell me what *this* entails."

"*This* means Eddie is, has, moved in with us. It means he's going to be part of this equation from now on. Okay?"

"*Son of a bitch!*"

Colt guns the engine and peels out, leaving Rain standing in the driveway. In his rearview mirror, if he'd stopped and looked, he would have seen that she remained there, looking thoughtful, for a full minute before turning and heading back inside.

April

You? You're a different story altogether—and here's
the problem:

how many times have I put you out with the trash,
dumped you into the recycling bin with the newspapers,
empty jug of
Tide, the wine bottles, only to find myself, once
again
at the curb, rooting through rubbish to find you, bring
you back inside

where, it has suddenly become clear to me, you belong?

The illuminated digits on the cable box next to her TV read two a.m. It's officially the weekend, also, fittingly, Tommie thinks, April Fools' Day. She's out of white wine, of wine period, with less than an inch of Jack left in the bottle under the kitchen sink. God knows, she's going to need that in the morning for her coffee, considering the drinking problem she seems to be working on here. Instead, she's scarfing down the last of a bag of ancient M&Ms left by a previous tenant and found in a corner of the cupboard over the refrigerator. Alone in the dark, under the influence, in the middle of the night, she's thinking about her mother, her father, and finally, Ben, finding herself at last willing to admit the possibility *goddammit!* that he has yet to return the heart he stole from her so long ago.

❧

Colt comes down the stairs on Saturday morning to find Garnet waiting in the kitchen, leaning against the counter, arms crossed.

"As you are no doubt not surprised to hear," she says, "my daughter called me last night."

Around his aunts, Colt finds himself, as usual, unable to curse. What would have customarily resulted in a *fuck, fuck, fuck!* goes not only unsaid but unthought. Garnet's tone makes clear to him what he already knows, had known, that he should have said something, anything, about Tommie to her. She sounds not so much mad as disappointed. He hates that most of all. She is the only one who can make him feel this way. His father, her brother, well, he'd stopped caring what that piece of work thought a long time ago; Remington—movie star handsome and knew it, never a problem getting what he wanted, the job, the girl, but as soon as he had it in hand, setting about to ensure its loss.

His father, his sweet aunts' reprobate sibling. How can members of the same family turn out so differently? But the girls, after all, had each other; Remmy, isolated by gender, had to find and make his own way in the world, choosing always the darkest, thorniest path, the least desirable alternative, choosing it every time. What his mother, another sweetie, saw there, what attracted her, he has no idea. Colt can't remember when he gave up hope, the first time he realized his father was never going to be a dad like the dads of his friends, imperfect every one of them, but like those on the sitcoms he watched with his mother, redeemed by their good qualities. It seems now like something he always knew. The man could be counted on for only one thing—he would always let them down.

For that matter, it's been almost eleven years since Colt has heard from Remington, since his mom died, in fact, her funeral. Much longer than it's been for Garnet here and Tommie. Eleven years ago, the year of his perfect storm, the year he turned eighteen, and the year it became clear how much of a man he was not.

Colt, able to vote, to die for his country, but, it seemed, incapable of stepping up to the plate—Rain, pregnant, his mother in the last stages of the cancer killing her, and Colt no use to either one. His aunts took turns staying with his mother, Colt's father—who he will never ever call dad—having departed for parts unknown soon after her diagnosis. It was the two aunts who had to make decisions, and they made it seem effortless; if it had to be done, one or both did it. Colt was no help, no help at all, but it turns out he was capable of watching and learning, though unaware at the time of doing either.

The first time he held his daughter—coming into the hospital room to find her in her mother's arms (no way was he ready to admit the reality of his situation by actually being present for the birth, insensitive shit that he was)—she was squalling, her little face cherry-red. Rain, exhausted, dark circles under her eyes, looked up at Colt and said, "Here. Your daughter. Take her." And with that, the furious little bundle was in his arms. For no reason, certainly not because he deserved it, Meg stopped crying and looked up at him. With what? It should have been pure disbelief such a sorry human being could be her daddy. But in that instant, Colt fell in love. *It saved me*, he thinks. Pure and simple. He knew right then he was not his father. He did not have to become his father. Instead, he could be Meg's dad.

And in fact, his father *had* finally showed up, coming into the church, late, for his mother's funeral. Brought up Catholic, she'd returned to the faith in her last months. Colt was seating the last of the stragglers, this assignment something his aunts thought it possible he could handle. The funeral mass had already begun. Colt had met his father's eyes. Remington did not look away but nodded, acknowledging him. He'd eased himself into the last pew, the seat nearest the doors, exactly where Colt himself would have put him, knowing his aunts would never have acquiesced to his real wish to usher his father out the door to sit in the cold rain on the wet church steps. When Colt joined the other pall bearers at the end of the service, he was gone.

Now, Garnet stands before him still awaiting his reply. Maybe he could play dumb.

"Tommie? You heard from Tommie?"

"Please, Colt. Do not treat me like an idiot. How long have you known she was back? And why did you not tell your favorite aunt?"

Colt satisfies these requests for information with "two weeks" and "I dunno," feeling not only Meg's age, but an immature ten-year-old at that.

"Not a satisfactory answer and you know it." Garnet sighs. "But I do understand. I wouldn't want to tell me either."

Then she adds, "How was the dinner with Eddie?"

❧

Sunday is cold but bright and breezy. It could almost be taken as a harbinger of spring, though, if so, as one more false promise understood as such by all, actual spring weather not expected to appear until mid, even late April, and then only after one more snowstorm and a few minor freezing rain and sleet events. Something, Vera, if she could speak, would say she looks forward to with great anticipation; her owner, not so much.

Garnet, with Vera, is rounding the corner onto the walking path that leads into the park when she sees her daughter coming toward them. Vera, usually perfection on a leash, lunges, jerking the lead from Garnet's hand, and tears off, a white blur headed for Tommie. Looking back, Garnet is grateful once again to her dog for saving the day, Vera, as usual her teacher, her Buddhist lesson if only she were a more attentive pupil.

Instead of the awkward meeting she'd anticipated, begun with a stiff, insincere greeting filled with resentment and not-so-hidden anger (hers, not Tommie's, by the way), there is chaos: Garnet fruitlessly calling Vera's name; Tommie, crouched on the blacktopped path, arms opened wide; Vera, hurling herself into Tommie's arms, knocking her flat on her back; Garnet, out of breath, arriving, looking down at the tangle of girl, okay, woman, and dog, fearing concussion, maybe worse; the dog covering Tommie's face with wet, slurpy kisses, erasing any evidence of tears. Where in this picture is there room for anything but joy, with tears if there were any (and Tommie is admitting nothing), tears of happiness. Maybe all is not forgiven, on either side, but a possibility has nevertheless been revealed, a path filled with pitfalls perhaps, but for all that still a way forward for the two of them.

"Have you informed your father of your return?" Garnet asks, after Tommie and Vera sort themselves out and things have calmed down enough to resume a walk through the park with the dog as fearless leader.

Informed. Your father. Tommie can tell by the stiffness of her mother's diction that her impulse to talk to her first was a good one.

"What do you think, Mom?"

"I think you should give him a call. The sooner the better."

"I was kind of hoping you'd help me with that."

Garnet and Tommie decide it best if Tommie calls her father before the news reaches him by other means and Tommie resolves she will call Bowie this very evening—as soon as she finishes baking a batch of Toll House chocolate chip cookies (a.k.a. peace offering)—and inform him she's back if he'd like to see her. As further instructed by her mother, under no circumstances will she mention Garnet's name or the fact that they have already spoken.

Tommie is beginning to feel like one of those early Christian martyrs who went around atoning for non-existent offenses (*okay*, so maybe her own sins are not totally non-existent) in hair shirts—although exactly what's so awful about a hair shirt except for the *ick* factor?—whipping themselves bloody, her own penance here consisting of one excruciating phone call after another.

Like everyone else who calls him, Tommie gets Bowie's voicemail first, this time the *da-da-da-dum* of Beethoven's Fifth followed by his instructions. I used to be crazy about this man, Tommie thinks; age does none of us any favors, just makes who we are more and more obvious to those around us. Not something she's looking forward to, by the way.

But as soon as she says, "Dad?" Bowie picks up.

"Tommie?"

His lack of surprise and instant recognition point once again not so much to loving paternal intuition as to the speed and efficacy of a small-town's communication network.

"Yes, I've moved back. I wonder if I could come over?"

"When are you thinking? I have to check my calendar. In fact, give me a couple dates to work with here, Tommie."

That does it. Tommie is through catering to aggrieved, withholding, passive-aggressive old people. She cannot stand one more minute as the guilty party, even if she is.

"Are you crazy, Daddy? I am coming over. I am coming over tomorrow after school, and I am bringing cookies."

"Well, cookies? Why didn't you say so to begin with? Save all this needless palavering."

"Palavering? Really? Speak English, please."

So quickly has she slipped into their old ways. Truth be told, she's always gotten her father better than anyone else including her mother.

"School? You say you're going to school? Finally decided to take your old dad's advice and join the legal profession, huh?"

"No, and no. I do not want to study law. Not now. Not ever. And I am not back in school. Or rather I am. Just wait. I'll tell you all about it tomorrow."

As they're about to hang up, her father states (it is not a question), "You've already seen your mother and talked to her."

"Good night, Daddy. I love you. I will see you tomorrow."

Despite everything she does and she will.

It's beginning to look like Tommie has a job until the end of the school year. The principal calls her Sunday evening, telling her Ms. Pepper's tests have resulted in surgery being scheduled, surgery requiring an eight-week recovery. Tommie really feels for Ms. Pepper, as much as a healthy twenty-nine-year-old is capable of feeling empathy for someone in her sixties, someone a year or two away from retirement, someone as distant from her ken as a visitor from another planet. Tommie still harbors the notion that she is immortal. She is aware this is possible only because she has been lucky enough not to have had any close calls herself. Yet. None of this lessens her happiness over her own good fortune.

❧

Monday afternoon, Tommie packs up, turning out the lights in the classroom, readying to leave as soon as the buses depart. The cookies for her father, minus the two she had for breakfast, are in a tin in her car. She is ready to leave when Ben pokes his head into her classroom. Tommie and Ben have reached a kind of détente here at school. They are able to sit in on the same meetings, to eat lunch in the teachers' lunchroom, to smile and greet each other with civility in the hall, though encounters in which coworker witnesses are not present, as here, do not always go so smoothly. They kid themselves that most of the staff are unaware of any previous shared romantic history on their part.

"Bugging out early, are we?"

"Not that it's any of your business, I am going to see my father."

"Bowie? Haven't seen him out and about in weeks. How is old Bowie?"

"Nailed it once again, Ben. Bowie is old."

Tommie is still smarting and it shows—for her entire engagement the two of them, Ben and Bowie, making up a kind of faux father/son/mentor/mentee/mutual admiration society, leaving Tommie feeling left out in the emotional cold.

"Tell your old man I said hello?"

"No."

"No?"

"Yes, that is what I said."

Ben is finding Tommie, as usual, prickly, unforgiving and, he is ashamed to admit, irresistible—though, what the hell, she *was* the one who broke things off and not nicely either, she the one who should be feeling apologetic instead of his pathetic self. He cannot understand why his first thought, standing here looking at his pissed-off ex, would be how much he'd like to take her home, to have her back in his bed. Okay, so is some kind of self-defeating nostalgia thing going on here? He's willing to cop to that but it doesn't halt his reverie—the two of them out of breath in a tangle of sheets and pillows, books tossed aside, clothes on the floor. Realizing Tommie is staring at him, he returns from the idealized past to a most unsatisfactory present.

"*Hello-o-o?*" she says.

Is her tone sarcastic? Is the Pope Catholic? Though Ben believes there may at least be some room for discussion if the Pope is Francis. He likes that about him.

"Well, maybe I'll just tell your dad hi myself," he says.

"Excuse me," Tommie says, her tone curt. "I have to go."

She breezes past him and Ben gets a whiff of the scent she wears, Obsession. How fitting is that, he thinks.

Tommie proceeds down the hall to the main entrance, pausing only to call back to where he is still leaning on the doorjamb watching her, "Shut that when you're finished loitering."

"That went well," Ben says under his breath and, no pussy, not him, walks away leaving the door ajar (though on his way out two hours later, unable to help himself, and muttering *OCD anyone?* he'll check to make sure the custodian has closed and locked it).

What was that all about? Tommie wonders on the drive over to her father's new-to-her house. She adds it to an already long list. One more thing to think about. Tomorrow. Tommie Delaney—a Scarlett O'Hara for millennials, she thinks.

It's not the house she grew up in. That would be down the street where her mother and Vera live. But her childhood neighborhood of large Victorians, despite its changes, is still recognizable to Tommie. Though tarted up—what's the word, gentrified?—with new sidewalks, landscaping, the houses sporting au courant painted-lady color combinations, it nonetheless still feels like home to Tommie.

Even Bowie's house, once a sedate gray dowager, is now a buttery yellow, its trim a grayed blue with dark red accents, the big front door an almost-black charcoal gray, all of which sounds terrible yet looks like a million bucks, even though the south side of the residence appears to be still awaiting its trim coat. None of this is exactly news to Tommie, her cousin having texted occasional pictures to her as the work progressed. But she, of course, has not been inside since her father bought it, shortly after his divorce was finalized and Tommie already gone. She's looking forward to seeing what he's had done. She turns into the drive and pulls up under the porte cochere, gets out, walks around the house and up the front porch steps, past a spent cigar in a large ashtray and a couple days' worth of newspapers haphazardly folded and tossed onto a rocking chair. She hears chimes as she rings the doorbell, twice, even though she saw a curtain briefly drawn aside as she pulled in, and knows her father knows she's out here.

The door opens at last—one of her father's courtroom tricks, delay giving the other side what it is expecting, putting him in control and shifting the balance of power his way. It's been almost three years since Tommie has seen Bowie. Visibly aged, her father is heavier; he sports a tonsure—how does she even know that word?—its fringe so white it is almost translucent. Rosacea makes him look alarmingly jolly, not unlike Santa's depraved beardless brother. And most disturbing of all to her, he's looking kind of shabby. Disheveled. *How is it possible for someone to change so much in such a short time?* She realizes getting old is an incremental process, one day following another, one tiny change after another, none, of themselves, obvious, but over the course of ten or twelve hundred plus days? Well, she must look different to him too.

"Daddy."

"Tommie, it's good to see you." He pulls her into an awkward hug. "Come in. Come in. You say you brought cookies?"

When Tommie gets home, it's almost ten o'clock. It's been a strange evening. Before polishing off her cookies, Bowie had ordered a pizza—vegetarian, extra cheese *for the calcium* her father earnestly explained—*just trying to eat healthy*, he'd added. She'd stifled the hoot threatening to rise up and burst from her mouth, her own advancing age finally successful in teaching her that sometimes it's better to STFU, keeping your comments to yourself, especially comments you think are funny but everyone else finds sarcastic and hurtful. Even so, she'd found herself asking silently and, yes, sarcastically, *Really?*

They'd dined in the kitchen, uncushioned stools pulled up to the island, no placemats for their paper plates on the cold, expensive granite. Tommie noticed that the refrigerator, where she'd gone to find something for them to drink, was absent of fresh food of any kind, heavy on orange soda, cola, on mysterious leftover and takeout containers from China Seas, Arby's, and San Remo. But she'd withheld judgment, her own refrigerator not exactly a nutritionist's dream. And the room's newly replaced windows? Uncovered by blinds or fabric of any kind in this actually quite attractively remodeled space, had only the manufacturer's stickers on the glass for decoration.

"You need to scrape those off," Tommie had said, pointing them out. "The longer they stay on, the harder they'll be to remove."

"Well, I don't plan to be here for long."

"What?" said Tommie. "You practically just got here. Where are you going?"

"Your mother and I might be getting back together."

No way on God's green earth *that* could be true, Tommie is sure of it.

"Please do not mention this to your mother," Bowie had continued. "I haven't spoken to her about it yet."

Tommie was silent, effectively struck dumb, a distinctly novel experience for her.

"And by the way, should the subject come up," he added, "I would like someone to point out that nobody threw a party for me when I turned seventy. I didn't even have a cake."

Tommie, recovering her speaking voice, had said, "Might that have something to do with the fact that on that particular birthday you'd left my mother and moved in with your law partner's daughter?"

Her father, choosing another cookie, took a bite, chewed slowly, and finally swallowed, only then answering, "Just saying."

Finished eating, they'd moved into the beautiful parlor with its art deco wallpaper, its stained-glass lamps casting warm light on polished cherry woodwork. ("Five thousand dollars for the two," Bowie said. "Tiffany. I got a deal," which left Tommie again thinking, *Really?* and wondering which Tiffany—Tom? Dick? Harry?—and who it was that likely made out on this so-called deal.) They'd sat in two matching, brand-new, bright blue velour recliners with remotes that raised and lowered and adjusted at will, purchased from Odd Lots. ("I like to put my feet up. Good for circulation," Bowie had said, nodding sagely, then adding, "Buy one, get one; it was too good to pass up.")

They'd parked their cans of Dr. Pepper on handsome attendant Stickley end tables—each one, if actually genuine, probably worth the equivalent of ten recliners, though the tops were already marked by constellations of water rings. (Tommie, unable to bear adding another, went to the kitchen and brought back a paper towel folded into fourths as a coaster). Father and daughter ended up watching a ball game on the sixty-inch smart TV (*Smart, my ass!* Tommie thought, her Meyers-Briggs JJJJ kicking in), the TV looming over the scraped and sanded, but as yet unstained, mantel of the fireplace, its surround framed by expertly installed gorgeous teal Rookwood tiles.

It was as though Bowie had hired the best contractor, painters, and decorator money could buy and at some point, maybe three-quarters through, they'd all, including her father, lost interest and wandered away. Not like the Bowie she knew at all, the one who latched onto a plan and didn't let go until it was carried out, until every single last one of his specifications were met and satisfied, something that had caused her no end of trouble when he'd taken her teenage self on as a project. Her father seemed to her both himself and not himself. Talking to him was slightly disorienting, the old Bowie merging with this new version like an unpredictable hologram coming into focus, then fading from view. Was this not a worrisome development? Perhaps. Probably. Something else she would address tomorrow. Tomorrow for sure.

And that whole thing with Ben this afternoon? They'd been talking—maybe talking wasn't the right word—Ben had been attempting a conversation and she'd begun tossing vitriol at him like some verbal terrorist, when he'd disappeared. Well, physically, of course, he remained right there, but his mind had certainly gone somewhere else. The look on his face—she'd almost forgotten that foolish, fond expression she'd sometimes seen, his face over hers when they were making love. Having sex with your eyes closed, well, you missed a lot, and Tommie's goal in life is to miss nothing. Too late, way too late to start thinking about that, and Tommie knows she is not referring to the lateness of the hour. Maybe she could work on postponing any reckoning at all, putting it all off not just until tomorrow but ad infinitum.

Tommie stops at Garnet's on her way home from school the next day. She's been trying to make sense of the visit to her father the night before. Garnet offers tea. In the kitchen, Vera walks over to where Tommie is sitting and leans against her while also managing to sit heavily on her foot, a combination Tommie finds oddly comforting.

She watches as her mother assembles a plate of ginger snaps and cuts lemon wedges. She has not really had a chance to observe Garnet at length since she returned, and she's struck once again by how pretty her mother is. No Botox, no neck lift, no makeup that she can see, except for what appears to be a trace of lipstick still left from this morning. Her hair, like Bowie's, is now white, and its curls cropped short. It shines under the fluorescent light. She has aged in all the expected ways; she does not in any sense look younger than she is. Yet she might even be called beautiful, especially when she smiles. It briefly occurs to Tommie what a waste of precious time it is to be obsessing about turning thirty.

"You don't take milk with your tea now, do you?"

"No milk. Mom, what's going on with Dad?"

"We don't exactly talk every day. You do know that?"

Tommie decides this is not the time to share Bowie's plans to reunite and move in with Garnet, though she does mention some of the oddities she'd observed during her visit.

"Your father has always marched to the beat of his own drum. It's not surprising it would only become more apparent as he gets older."

This does nothing to allay Tommie's sense of unease. Indeed, to her it has the sound of someone whistling a familiar tune to hold back the dark.

❧

Colt has stopped on the way home, pulling into the Walmart lot and parking his truck. He needs to talk to Ruby and doesn't want to take a chance on Garnet overhearing the conversation.

He picks his cellphone up off the console.

"Hi, Ruby."

"I've been expecting your call, Colt."

"Sorry, I've been way busy. Since your sister's birthday falls on Saturday this year, whatever we plan will happen then. So go ahead and make travel plans."

"You've begun preparations, right? We're already into April."

"Oh, ye of little faith. Actually, Rain has offered to help. I'll be checking in with her on Friday night when I pick Meg up for the weekend."

This is a big fat lie. Colt doesn't even know if Rain is speaking to him after his little meltdown. But he's going to find out. She's the next call on his list.

"I've always liked Rain," Ruby says. "I think you missed the boat big time there, Colt."

Colt continually finds himself amazed at the correlation between advancing years and its apparent implied permission to say anything, anything at all. He punts.

"How's Harry doing?"

"You know no one calls him that but you, right? Though he seems to like it well enough."

"They should. He's a lot more a Harry than he is a Harold."

"To answer your question, good days and bad. Today is one of the latter. Agata is going to move in for the time I'm gone,"

"His favorite aide?"

"None other. He won't mind my absence at all."

Garnet's older—by two years—sister married late. She was almost sixty and Harold ten years older. They were over-the-moon happy. Then shortly after their first anniversary, Harry had a stroke from which he has never completely recovered. His health twelve years down the line is fragile, but he remains undeniably the Harold, or as Colt would have it, the Harry she wed.

"I'll call you once I have reservations," Ruby says.

"You telling Garnet you're coming?"

"That part doesn't have to be a surprise. I'm telling her I'm her birthday present."

Next, Colt calls Rain.

"I was wondering when you'd finally get around to calling me."

"You, of all people, Rain, know I hate change. It took me by surprise, Ed moving in like that."

"Not Ed. Eddie, Colt."

"Ed, Eddie, what's the difference? It's the same name."

"His name is Eddie and he likes it. I know what you're doing there, by the way."

"Doing? I'm not doing anything."

"So, since you didn't call to apologize, to what do I owe this call?"

"I am sorry, Rain. I shouldn't have flown off the handle like that. He seems like a nice enough guy."

"Enough? Really, Colt? Nice *enough*?"

He has to admit, Rain does know him inside and out, and she does know exactly what he's up to, though it does not seem to be working. Instead of making her think less of Ed, *oh, all right, fucking Eddie,* he's only succeeded once again in making her think less of him.

"Can we talk about Garnet's birthday when I pick Meg up on Friday?"

"Good thing I love your aunt, Colt, or I'd be ending this phone call right now. Yes, we can talk."

❧

Though Garnet waved aside Tommie's concerns yesterday, this does not mean she is unaffected by them. She's noticed the state of the house on her walks with Vera. Bowie at one time used a lawn service but now last fall's leaves, driven by the winter winds, have filled the corners and crannies all around the house and lie in sodden masses on the grass. Also, deadwood and unclipped blooms from last summer's perennials catch her eye every time she passes by, and there is a lone hanging basket with a very dead geranium, forgotten and forlorn, at the end of the porch.

She really, really does not want to get sucked into becoming a part of her ex-husband's life, especially in any kind of caretaker role. This morning when she'd spoken to her sister, who called to say she was coming for her birthday, Ruby had told her to step away.

"Not your problem, Garnet. As much as I love my husband—and Harold is a hell of a lot nicer person than your ex—if I'd known what was coming down the pike for us, I don't think I'd have married him."

Somehow Ruby also knew all about Tommie's return. Garnet suspects this may have something to do with communicating with Colt behind her back. She tried to elicit what if any plans were being hatched around her natal day, only to have Ruby shut down that thread of conversation, maybe a little too firmly.

"I don't know what you're thinking, Garnet. Nobody cares about birthdays anymore. I bet nobody even sends you a card. Thank goodness you have a sister who loves you enough to come. Otherwise, I fear, you'd be celebrating all by yourself."

She felt her worst fears confirmed. If Ruby, instead, had simply stated she'd heard nothing, Garnet might have found her more credible.

"You are to tell my nephew and my daughter that I do not want a party," she ordered Ruby huffily. "I do not want presents, but I am okay with Colt making me one of his chocolate bundt cakes, and a single chorus of "Happy Birthday," and that's it!"

Garnet's antipathy is not rooted in denial, in some reluctance to acknowledge the actual number of her years. She's always been upfront about her age, although she does find annoying the supermarket pharmacy's insistence that if she wishes to receive her blood pressure meds she must say her birth date aloud for any bystander to hear and, if so inclined, judge her. It also does not mean she's one of those people who go around saying, "I don't feel *name-their-current-age*. Inside, I feel just like a kid." Garnet does *not* feel like a kid. She has been through a lot in the past sixty-nine years, and it has left her feeling fully sixty-nine years old. She also has no wish to be returned to thirty if it means that nothing would change, her choices remain the same, no do-overs involved. There is so much she is perfectly happy to see receding to the vanishing point in her almost-seventy-year-old rearview mirror.

So, if she can't have eternal youth, what's left? She's always kind of liked the saying, "If you can't be a stellar example, what about a horrible warning?" But she's already surrounded by too many people of all ages who seem to have embraced that concept as words to live by, and Garnet has always hated being one more face in a crowd.

"I've said it before, Garnet, you really do need to get some help with these control issues of yours," Ruby said before she hung up.

Once again, nobody is paying any attention to what she wants. After all it's *her* birthday, isn't it? Her sister, heck, her whole family, can be so maddening.

Unsurprisingly, Garnet decides, much as she had when she was a child, to ignore the excellent advice given by her big sister. Instead she places the thrilled Vera into her harness for an unprecedented second walk, snaps on the leash, and prepares to go see for herself her ex-husband's state of mind.

April may have arrived. Spring may officially be here. With the return of daylight savings time, Colt has even unplugged and stored the window candles she sets on the sills every November as antidote to the coming season's early darks. But winter's back today remains stubbornly unbroken; Garnet zips up her long down coat and ties a scarf under her chin babushka style.

Outside, breath freezes immediately, and their progress is marked by the icy clouds of their twinned exhalations. They turn in at Bowie's house, walking up the flagstone walk to the porch where Garnet lifts the brass knocker on the front door and lets it drop twice. After a pause, the heavy door opens, its autumn wreath askew and looking bedraggled.

"Why hello, Garnet. What are you doing here?"

"We were out for a walk and Vera pulled me up here."

"You know you need to let her know who's boss."

"We settled that long ago."

"Then why do you let her pull you?"

"I'm afraid we decided that Vera is the boss."

"Do you want to come in? It's not very nice out here."

"Yes, maybe we do."

Vera is extremely pleased to have her pack together again. Though actual years have passed since this last happened, she has not forgotten. Another reason for the dog's happiness may be that she associates this place, where she spends occasional weekends, with forbidden snacks, with bacon, cheese, and scrambled egg sandwiches, half for her, half for Bowie, bowls of ice cream, and, occasionally, whole hot dogs. While Garnet takes off her scarf, tucks it in her coat sleeve, lays the whole thing over the back of a chair, before sitting down in that same chair, Vera looks hopefully at Bowie—some chips, a little dip perhaps to stave off the worst of her hunger pangs?—then collapses, panting, onto the floor when it becomes clear that nothing is forthcoming.

"Would you like a cup of coffee, Garnet?"

"No, I'm fine. Maybe some water for Vera. It's a little warm in here for her."

While Bowie goes out to the kitchen to fetch Vera's bowl and fill it with water, Garnet walks over to the thermostat on the wall. It is set at eighty. She moves the dial down to seventy-two.

The dog slurps up most of the large bowl Bowie sets down, after which Vera smiles her doggy smile at them both as excess water niagaras from her mouth and onto an oriental carpet that looks to Garnet to be an expensive antique.

"The rug…" Garnet says. "Let me get a towel."

"You are looking lovely, my dear," Bowie says, ignoring both the flood, the rug, and her distress.

Vera, now obviously bored, finds a dry section of carpet, lays down, and closes her eyes.

"Bowie, how are you?" Garnet says. "Are you managing by yourself here?"

"Why do you ask?"

"Look around. It's not like you to live like this. So many unfinished projects."

Bowie directs a mysterious look Garnet's way.

"I have a plan, Garnet. All in due time, all in due time."

❧

Thursday after work, Colt arrives home to find a strange vehicle in Garnet's driveway, a Jaguar the color of unpolished antique sterling flatware with Nevada plates. He quickly puts two and two together and is about to exit the drive when Garnet emerges from the house and waves. He lowers his window.

"Don't you dare," she calls to him. "Don't you dare!"

Colt thinks better of it and pulls back up behind the vehicle. Turning the engine off, he steps out of the cab.

"What the fuck," he mutters, his first slip ever in Garnet's presence.

"You are aware I can hear you?"

It occurs to him that Garnet may not be having any more fun than he is.

"Did you know about this?" Colt asks.

"Do I look like I knew about it?"

"What's he thinking? Nobody wants him here."

"Which may be the reason he is here."

"I have to come inside?"

"Only if you wish to continue to live in this house after today."

Colt slams the truck door and heads over to where Garnet is standing on the step leading up to the back door. As he does so, a lanky figure appears behind Garnet in the open doorway. It's not so much that Colt's father has not aged. Rather it's as though his beat-up cigarette-commercial cowboy good looks froze at some point in his late forties, maybe early fifties, remaining there unchanged. That he is the owner of a recently acquired Medicare card tucked into his wallet would not be anyone's first guess.

"Hello, son. Pretty raw out here. You folks coming in?"

Garnet gives Colt a sharp look and for the most part he restrains himself.

"Hello, Remington. What brings you back here? Somebody die?"

"As a matter of fact, I have some business in the city and thought it a good excuse to come out here and say hi to my big sister and my boy."

Garnet fears nothing in her considerable arsenal is capable of defusing what is about to happen.

"If I were you, I would not call me your anything," Colt says, coherence not at the moment his strong suit.

Remington studiously ignores Colt's bellicose tone.

"I was hoping maybe I'd have a chance to spend some time with my granddaughter."

"No way," Colt says.

"Think of me as water, Colt, yourself as rock," Remington says. "I will wear you down."

"Like hell," Colt says, his resolve to keep a civil tongue dissolving. "Like water, you'll run away. Just like you always have."

Colt turns and walks out of the kitchen where they've all gathered. Garnet and Remington hear the front door slam. Vera, who uncharacteristically parked herself in a far corner for the whole contretemps, has now backed up further, pressing against the wall, her safe place during thunderstorms. But she looks concerned rather than fearful. Not yet having made up her mind about the tall newcomer, she continues to cast a doubtful eye his way.

An explosion, for the moment, avoided, Garnet and her brother listen to the ignition grind, Colt's pickup start, the squeal of brakes as he backs out of the driveway and pauses at the road, then to the sound of sudden acceleration, of rubber being laid on road.

"He keeps that up, he's going to need a new truck sooner than later," Remington says.

"This should not surprise you, Remmy." Garnet falls into using their childhood nickname for her baby brother without even realizing she has done so. "What would be surprising would have been if it had gone any other way."

"Don't you want to know where I'm staying?"

"Not here."

Remington sighs. "No, not here."

"All right, I'll bite."

"My niece, your daughter, has invited me to crash on her couch."

Garnet is taken aback only for a second. "You're getting a little old to be using the word 'crash,' much less doing it. I will give you credit for not calling her apartment a 'pad.' You are aware, Remmy, that there are nice hotels in the vicinity. You give them your Visa or your American Express card and they let you stay as long as you want. They even make your bed and give you fresh towels every day."

"Well, right now, that presents a problem."

"They've canceled your credit cards, Remington?"

"Not really, but—"

"You don't have any money, do you?"

"I wouldn't put it that way. However, my finances are temporarily in flux because of a recent commitment," Remington says, looking at Garnet expectantly.

She takes in what he's just said, but she is not going to ask for more information. Experience has taught her that she does not want to know more about any "commitment" Remmy may have made. She just hopes it was merely a morally murky choice rather than something out and out illegal, a felony, say.

"What about that car you're driving?" Garnet says. "How can you afford that?"

Remington looks crestfallen at her lack of follow-up. "A rental," he says. "You only get to make a good impression once."

"Oh, enough, Remmy! What do you want?"

"You think I'm going to ask for a handout, Garnet; I'm not. I will say, you, big sister, are never going to get yourself in hot water because you think too highly of people."

Garnet is willing to admit she has become more suspicious as she grows older, taking very little at face value. And Remmy, despite his (many, many) (many!) faults, has always possessed a kind of ESP with regard to his sisters' vulnerabilities, able like his namesake to set up and then execute the shot perfectly.

"*Ouch!*" she says and her brother shrugs, making a gun with his hand, raising it to his lips and blowing on the barrel finger.

By seven o'clock, Remington has left for Tommie's; a chastened Colt has returned, and dinner has been made and consumed. Now Colt loads their few supper dishes into the dishwasher, and Garnet puts leftover meatloaf into the fridge. Vera supervises in case the meatloaf somehow winds up on the floor—it could happen—in which case it belongs to her. Garnet closes the refrigerator door, and Vera retires sadly to her bed.

"I let myself get sucked in every time, don't I," Colt says.

"Don't be too hard on yourself. He knows how to push all our buttons."

"Everything I hold against him happened a long time ago; I should have gotten over all of it by now."

"If you manage to do that, please share your method with me; I could use a little help myself. By the way, should you maybe warn Rain?"

"I'll tell her when I pick up Meg tomorrow."

"Speaking of moving on, I ask again, how goes it with you and Eddie?"

"I'm having a little trouble there too. I maybe need a refresher course on adult behavior. I got the three-year-old-has-a-tantrum down pat."

"Maybe start with a drivers ed class."

Colt has been alone a long time. After his conversation with Garnet, he thinks maybe he might better handle the Rain and Eddie thing, and for that matter, his father, if there were someone in his life again. He's been out of practice for so long, he hardly knows how to talk about exactly what it is he wants—girl friend? girlfriend? significant other? friend with benefits? He's sure only about the gender. Female.

What the hell! Admit it. He's looking for someone like Rain. Smart. Independent. And hot (because he is a poor excuse for a human being. Though whatever his admitted character flaws, he will cheerfully strangle any young man in the future who might choose his own daughter based on such a premise). Where to meet this someone? His contemporaries are pretty much married, with kids, or in LTRs. He doesn't go to church. It won't be at work; the boss's secretary is the only woman he sees there. Not that Nadine isn't terrific. But so is her husband Joe, who's part of his crew.

Tommie snorts and suggests the internet when he calls and asks if she has any friends looking for a date. Colt thinks, *Why not?* and decides to give it a try. He researches online dating sites. He finds a smorgasbord to choose from. There are Christian sites and subsites—Mormon, Catholic, Pentecostal; there are Jewish sites. There are sites for farmers, for accountants, and LGBTQ sites. If you're into S&M, there's a site for you. Whoever or whatever you are looking for it seems can be found on the web. He picks one that looks middle of the road, one featuring ordinary human beings, male and female, then spends an hour trying to craft an honest description of himself that is not so boring it makes his eyes roll back in his head. He chooses a photo Garnet took of him last spring with Vera; he is down on one knee, his arm around the dog, grinning at the camera.

Who wouldn't love to go out with a dog lover? He leaves out the part where he lives with the aunt who owns the dog; he keeps the part where he is a single father of a ten-year-old daughter. He pays for a month and hits Send.

He immediately regrets doing it. Then he finds himself obsessively checking his account for responses. His age preference spans twenty-five to thirty-five, and he eliminates all repliers who do not read directions, or ignore what they've read, like the nineteen-year-old who just loves, and wants to meet, his dog—though he is momentarily tempted, impressed by her obvious good taste in species preference. Or a great-looking fifty-three-year-old who assures him she looks and feels twenty years younger but whose photo, given the model year of the car she's leaning against, he's pretty sure was also taken twenty years ago. A couple possibilities fizzle out before an actual meeting is set up. He texts back and forth with Aleta until she shares that her five cats might prove an obstacle to bonding with a man and his dog. Plus, she adds, signing off, she's allergic—Colt notices she doesn't specify whether it's to the dog or the man.

He finally manages a coffee date with Elaine, thirty-two, separated, a Democrat of the bleeding-heart-liberal persuasion—Colt has kept political affiliation off his own profile. Even so, he wonders why there are no women attracted to him who identify as conservative and Republican. Elaine is employed in financial services, owner herself of three rescued Great Danes. (And what is it about him that attracts owners of pet multiples?)

They meet at The Cup. Elaine is pleasant looking and friendly until she elicits his voting record in recent elections.

"Except for the fact that you're better looking and appear to be far nicer—but who knows, right?—you could be my soon-to-be-ex-husband's twin," she says. "We are just not politically compatible."

She's zipping up her jacket, ready to leave, when she adds, "Just my luck. The way this usually works for me, I bet we'd be terrific in bed. Still, so not worth it."

Off she goes. When Colt goes to settle up, he discovers

Elaine has paid the tab. He leaves a big tip in an effort to salvage his dwindling masculinity.

On Friday, Colt arrives at Rain's duplex early as promised to pick up Meg. Rain answers his knock and takes his jacket. Once again, they head for the kitchen where his ex has made some fresh coffee and put a plate of brownies on the table. Colt picks one up. It's still warm.

"You didn't have to go to all this trouble."

"Ah, Colt, still suffering under the misconception that everything is about you.. Please don't eat them all. Meg will be hungry too when she gets home from school."

Colt feels like a bad little boy in Rain's presence. He knows this is his problem, not hers. It doesn't help his composure that Rain, in black turtleneck, leather skirt, leggings, and boots, is looking exceptionally attractive. He wrestles with untoward thoughts concerning his child's mother, this woman to whom he is not married, with whom he has not been in any way romantically involved for many years. He really, really does not want to start thinking now about her and Eddie. Together. Which means, of course, a particularly vivid image pops into his brain. He feels his face reddening.

I have to start getting out more, Colt thinks.

"Are you all right?" Rain asks. "There are nuts in the brownies. You're not going into anaphylactic shock, are you?"

"I'm fine, Rain." (He's not fine, of course, and they both know it.) "Let's talk about Garnet. The birthday. Okay?"

"So, what are you thinking?"

"If we do what Garnet wants, according to the call I got from Ruby today, we do nothing. I bake a cake. We sing. That's it."

"No presents?"

"Nope."

"Well, we can't have that, can we? The whole point of a birthday is to give the person what *we* want, right?"

"I can't tell anymore when you're being sarcastic. Are you?"

"Colt, Colt, Colt."

They leave it at a family gathering, a surprise party. The only place besides Garnet's big enough is Bowie's house. Colt will talk to him. After all, despite everything, he is still family.

"By the way," Colt says, "Remington has turned up."

"I know," Rain says. "He called last night. Asked about seeing Meg."

"*Shit!*" he says, his language continuing its recent nosedive into the gutter.

"Thanks for the heads-up by the way. A little tardy but better late than never."

"What are you going to do?"

"He is her grandfather."

"But—"

"I've invited him to dinner. Do you want to be there?"

"No, but I'm coming. When?"

During all the years they've been apart, Colt has never sat down and eaten dinner at Rain's house. Now suddenly in the space of a couple weeks, he'll have done it twice, neither a pleasurable occasion.

"Good," Rain says. "Wednesday. Six sharp. You're bringing bread and salad."

"What's my father bringing?"

"He's bringing himself."

❧

April. Still pitch dark when Garnet rises but, even so, when she takes Vera out into the yard these mornings, bird song fills the air. To Garnet it sounds like an orchestra tuning up—first a few odd whistles and chirps here and there, random sounds that grow and swell into full-throated symphony as the sky lightens and dawn approaches. She's morphed as she's aged from night owl into this morning person, daily following her dog down the stairs at five-thirty in the a.m., fully dressed and obsessing about her shrinking future.

The early hour suits Garnet in many ways. Because of it, her family has remained largely oblivious of her poetic endeavors, unsurprisingly focused mainly on themselves and their own concerns, thinking, if they think about it at all, that she rises early to record the events of the previous day, its weather, a special meal, some family celebration. This is fine, more than fine, with her (the squeaky wheel truly does get all the attention—there's a reason things become clichés—and it is Garnet's desire to remain as squeakless as possible). Although if that were true, it would make far more sense to write at the close of the day when all was fresh in her mind. Blessedly, her current writing practice imposes no need to be able to mentally preserve a previous day's details.

Coffee brewed and Vera fed, she retrieves her journal with its soft leather cover from the desk in the front hall, placing it on the kitchen table. She'll be needing a new one soon, and she doesn't think she can bring herself to buy it at the cavernous B&N in the city, or worse, from Amazon, an even bigger betrayal in her mind. At least the big box, despite ersatz tendencies, exists as an actual building—with actual books one can handle. The pre-dawn lamplight softens the marks age has made on face and body as she sits down at the table to write, her silver hair a nimbus framing her face. Vera's legs jerk, her nails making a scrabbling sound on the wood floor as she chases dream rabbits and squirrels.

Yesterday, she and Sylvie had gone to the art museum in the city to see a new exhibit on China. Garnet was taken with the watercolors of cranes she saw there and so she fires up her laptop to learn more. As much as she may complain, she loves this aspect of technology, the internet handing her the world, giving her access to the great libraries of the globe, to minds great and appallingly small—her choice, to answers for all of her questions, answers that often contradict each other like quarrelsome children.

Garnet seeks more information about these large, beautiful birds before beginning the new poem in her journal. She goes to Wikipedia, the National Geographic site, finally opening

YouTube where she's rewarded by a video of adolescent cranes acting like teenagers everywhere, awkward and loud, and from the looks of it, as capable of bad behavior as any other species. More suggestions follow. She watches those too. Finally, smiling, she begins to write:

A red-crowned crane draws up one leg
and tucks her head beneath her wing.
Her rivers are dammed, mudflats drying,
the salt marshes receding. My screen glows.
She sleeps. Tomorrow she will dance…

❧

At work, while hanging drywall, Colt relates his recent adventures in seeking adult companionship to his coworker, Booker. Booker is in his early twenties, at the moment girlfriend-free.

"No way, bro. You don't want to do this online," says Booker.

"Why not? I'm batting zero here in the real world."

"Because everybody's too dependent on everybody else's questionable honesty."

"You try it?"

"I gave it a shot. Found out I can't be trusted. It was too much temptation. First I used a photoshopped picture."

"Why? Nothing wrong with your looks."

"Yeah? When my buddy got done I looked like Brad Pitt."

"Brad Pitt?"

"The young Pitt. Then I decided I deserved a better job and promoted myself to site supervisor and gave myself a BA in economics and a big raise."

"I have a degree in economics."

"*No shit!* Anyhow, I put my phony profile up on Tinder and found I was also too cynical to trust the responses. More about me than them, I get that, but 'twenty-two-year-old redhead, ivy league grad, looking for good times, no ties'? I'd translate for myself, 'twenty-seven-year-old single mom, associate's degree from local CC, redhead only when she can afford it.' I never did follow up on any of them."

"So, if I don't want to become a monk, what do I do?"

"How about giving the real world a try. Come out with us on Friday night."

"I'm a little old for—"

"Too old to have some fun? What are you, thirty?"

This hurts Colt's feelings. He thinks he looks younger not older than his actual years.

"Come on, Colt! Come out with us, old man."

Friday night, Booker picks up Colt at eight, Colt having showered, put on clean jeans, and a new shirt he found still in its box from Christmas. He'd also shared his plans with a bemused Garnet, told her not to worry, he'd be late.

"Hey," Colt says, getting into Booker's pride and joy, a car so often modified, its original make is no longer identifiable. Painted-on flames lick its sides. The muffler grumbles. The bass rumbles; the words to the music pulsing from the outsize speakers are rhymed and filthy.

"Nice ride."

"Got it when I was sixteen. I'm never letting it go no matter how much I'm offered."

"That been much of a problem?"

Booker changes the subject.

"You'll recognize most of the guys. In construction like us."

The bar is loud and packed. A country-western trio plays on a makeshift stage in the corner. They're singing about losing the job, the girl, the dog, about dancing and drinking and cheating. Colt listens, bemused, as the singer drops every final *g* in the lyrics. At least with the no-smoking regs, the air is clear. Booker's friends are drinking beer from longneck bottles. Colt orders two at the bar and begins trying to catch up. The girls swirling through the crowd around them are young, early twenties. Very early. They remind him of puppies. Drunk puppies. He is not going to find what he's looking for here, that's for sure.

"Mr. Adams."

Colt turns. "Ms. Fisher?"

It's Meg's fourth-grade teacher. One more female he's been known to have deeply inappropriate thoughts about. She is someone he knows something about already thanks to his daughter. In the way children know more about their teachers than their teachers are often aware, Meg had informed Colt the very first week of school last September that Ms. Fisher, her new teacher, was a widow. He still remembers the conversation.

"Do you know what that means?" he'd asked.

Her reply had been a look, both scornful and a little hurt.

"Sorry," said Colt. "Of course you know what the word means."

"And I know a man whose wife dies is called a widower. Ms. Fisher's husband died five years ago in a motorcycle accident."

"You know this how?"

"Christina Alesso's mom is a nurse and she was working in Emergency when it happened. Christy heard her parents talking when they found out who her teacher was."

"Little pitchers have big ears?"

"What does that *even* mean, Daddy?"

"Good point."

"Ms. Fisher wears their wedding rings on a gold chain around her neck."

"She told you this?"

Once again, the look.

"What else have you noticed?"

"Her favorite colors are rose and cerulean blue. Do you know what 'cerulean' means?"

"Of course I do," Colt answers (he does not).

"And she wears contacts and loves peanut butter cups and gummi bears, and she drinks a lot of coffee."

"I'm impressed. You have a bright future with the CIA."

"CIA stands for—"

"I know, I know. So, you like this teacher who you know so much about?"

"I love Ms. Fisher. She has a master's degree and beautiful

handwriting, and she's going to teach anybody who wants to learn how to write cursive after school on Wednesdays, because she says it's a crying shame it's no longer taught in our school."

Because of Ms. Fisher here, his Meg now has beautiful cursive handwriting too.

"You look like you feel as out of place as I do," Ms. Fisher says. "Who talked you into this?"

"Someone I work with thought I should get out and have a little fun."

"Me too. So, are you?"

"I'm afraid that without my knowledge or permission, and contrary to everyone's expectations, at some point I grew up. So, not especially."

"Want to get out of here?"

"I didn't drive."

"But I did."

"Then, yes."

They wind up in a nearly deserted neighborhood tavern down the street from where Meggie's teacher lives. It has an ancient working jukebox filled with 45s and no digital anything, that for a quarter plays three songs. Colt orders a bottle of house cabernet, and they pick up their glasses, walk over to the lit-up multicolored anachronism, and Colt drops in a coin. They choose all Sinatra, one Nancy and two Frank, and when the third song, "Summer Wind" begins, Colt takes her in his arms. As they dance, he feels like someone who's been given a glimpse of an oasis, someone who had almost forgotten the concept of water. By the time their second bottle of wine is finished, it's very late. They've spent most of the evening drinking and slow dancing, doing very little talking. Neither feels up to driving so they leave the car in the bar's parking lot and walk back to her apartment. The April night is icy, moonless, clear. Who knew stars could generate such light. Tipsy, they bump into each other as they walk, holding hands to steady themselves.

Sun pours into the room. Ms. Fisher—could he actually have forgotten her first name?—is still asleep. Colt's head hurts, his mouth is very dry, and his stomach does not feel great. Congratulations, he says to himself, parent-teacher conferences are next week and you've just slept with your daughter's teacher. He hauls himself out of bed and looks around. Lots of books. A good sign. Otherwise kind of spare. Bed. Night table and lamp. A chair. Not a lot of furniture. Neat, except for their clothes on the floor. That part is beginning to come back to him. He grabs his clothing and heads for the bathroom. He seems to know where that is anyway.

His first impulse after he washes his face and gets dressed is to disappear, especially after seeing the two gold bands threaded on a slender gold chain hanging from the knob on the medicine chest door. In the years since his breakup with Rain, he admits, intentionally or not, he's successfully insulated himself from others' pain while numbing himself up pretty good while he's at it. But even the pleasure of the night before cannot lighten the weight of sorrow these rings represent, that will belong somehow to him too if he continues on with this woman. So tiptoe out that door? Pretend it never happened?

He'd love to cut and run and he surely would, except for the moral compass that governs his behavior in the world, has ever since he was a kid. No Jesus involved, *WWRD, What would Remington do*? Colt's answer to this question requires he do the exact opposite of whatever he might expect of his father in the same situation. In this case, would Remington sidle right on out that door? Of course he would. Therefore, Colt walks, not away, but into the kitchen, and finding what he needs in a cupboard next to the sink, begins to make coffee. The machine has just finished its strangled gargling and is spitting out the last of a pot of freshly brewed decaf, all he could find, into its glass carafe.

"Hey."

And it comes to him. Franny. Her name is Franny. She's barefoot, her auburn hair barely tamed by a brush. Colt notes her freckles and fair skin; bet she burns easily. She's put on sweatpants and a T-shirt. The word that pops into his head is *winsome.*

"Hey, yourself," he says. "Coffee?"

He fills two yellow cups from the mug tree on the counter. Hands her one.

"I need to call my aunt," Colt says. "She's going to wonder what the hell happened to me."

"Then we should talk," she says.

Colt takes his phone from his pocket and summons up Garnet's number. She, thank God, is not home. He leaves a message: too much to drink, Booker put him up for the night. He'll be home later.

Franny looks at him. She has a really nice face, Colt decides, among other things, one of the requirements he'd listed when he was trying to organize his thoughts about dating.

"Well, the first part of that was true anyway," she says.

"I could lie or I could say, 'Gigi, I didn't come home last night because I slept with Ms. Fisher. Please don't tell my daughter.'"

"Well, you've already passed my first test. I woke up and saw you were gone, your clothes were gone. But then I smelled the coffee and realized you hadn't gone far."

"I won't lie. I thought about sneaking out."

"I guess now we're going to have to figure out whether we like each other as much sober as we did last night."

"If we don't, it sure would solve a lot of problems. I have many undesirable qualities."

Franny ignores his comment and says, "How about we start by throwing out this pot of coffee. I have the real deal in the fridge. This stuff is for a few of my misguided friends who think it's still coffee if it doesn't have any caffeine."

"You keep your coffee in the refrigerator? Why?"

"Because my mother kept it there. Her mother kept it there. So I do too. We don't know why."

"Okay. Sounds reasonable to me."

By the time Colt leaves for home late in the afternoon, he and Franny have sensibly decided not to see each other again until the school year ends and Meg has moved on to fifth grade. Then somehow—maybe not "somehow," he knows exactly how it happened—they wind up back in Franny's bed. He hasn't stopped to wonder why she has a box of condoms in her bedside table drawer; he's just happy it was there. This relationship is going to require at least one adult, and he's pretty sure it's not going to be him. Franny lets him out a couple blocks from Garnet's and he walks the rest of the way home, thinking, for once, about a problem he is happy to have.

❧

Garnet didn't worry when Colt didn't come home last night. Correction, she didn't worry much, trusting Colt's levelheadedness as she does. Also, as she reminded herself at three a.m. (then once again at four), he is not her ward but a grown man. She did not believe a word of his phoned-in excuse, except maybe for the over-served part. She knew this was coming. And in fact, she's surprised it's taken this long. Time for Colt to move on, to meet someone, or more than one someone, to make some mistakes, maybe break a few hearts, to begin feeling something again. Garnet is not unaware what she's describing could apply to herself too. She does not want to think about it.

Instead, for her breakfast she separates a very large chocolate rabbit from its ears, a rabbit that arrived yesterday, Holy Saturday, sent for an exorbitant sum from two Oregon brothers named Harry and David, along with Easter greetings from Ruby. She takes another bite. By the time Colt finally turns up later this afternoon, the entire head will be gone. In a week the confection will have completely disappeared, Garnet, having shared none of it, harboring not a single regret for her sins of gluttony and selfishness.

❧

Spring has come to New York State at last. The air is mild,

the sun is out. The trees, beginning to leaf out, wear a veil of green. Colt is happy to be alive. He's just talked to Franny, who's still at school preparing for parent conferences at the end of the week. They'd decided not to see each other; nobody'd said anything about communicating by cell phone. He's on his way home after work, with a stop first at Bowie's.

"Hello, young man," Bowie says when he answers Colt's knock. "What can I do for you?"

"It's Colt, Bowie. Your nephew."

"I knew that," he says, but Colt could swear it's news to him.

"What do you want ?" Bowie adds.

"For starters, can I come in?"

"I wasn't expecting company."

"I'm here to ask a favor."

"I was just sitting down to eat when you knocked."

"Don't let me stop you."

They walk back to the kitchen where Bowie sits down in front of what looks like very well-done mac 'n' cheese in a singed, partially melted microwavable container.

"I like it crispy," he says.

"I can see that," says Colt, wondering whether he's referring to the food or the container.

Bowie gestures toward a torn open, half-finished bag of Oreos. "Help yourself," he says.

Colt leans against the counter. The faucet in the sink is not so much dripping as emitting a barely there stream of water into an overflowing saucepan that looks like it once, long ago, held tomato soup. The sound is soothing actually, a kind of white noise.

"Where's your toolbox, Bowie?" Colt asks, pointing at the sink.

"Oh, don't worry about that. I'm going to call the plumber."

"Let me fix it while we talk."

"Look under my workbench downstairs," Bowie says, inclining his head toward the cellar door, which Colt opens.

He flicks the light switch and goes down stone-slab steps to the old house's basement. Its walls are stacked stone and it has a not-exactly-dirt-floor, but not exactly *not*-a-dirt-floor. He finds the toolbox where Bowie said it would be and lugs it upstairs. Next, he goes out to his truck and gets a paper bag of washers from his own toolbox. He brings it inside in the hope one of them will be the right size. Bowie has finished eating his burnt offering and is working on the Oreos, dipping each one into an increasingly murky-looking glass of milk, then popping it whole into his mouth.

Colt gets to work.

"You sure you don't want one of these?" Bowie asks, holding up a damp, mangled cookie.

"No, thanks. Garnet will have supper ready when I get home."

"We're getting back together."

Tommie has already shared Bowie's plan with her cousin.

"So you say," Colt says. "You planning on letting Garnet know about this anytime soon?"

Bowie, silent, retrieves a last cookie and crumples up the empty cellophane bag.

"You know," Colt says, "Gigi's seventieth birthday is almost here."

"Gigi who?" Bowie asks, wrinkling up his forehead and squinting his eyes at Colt.

Since it was Bowie who first gave Garnet the nickname, Colt is ready to start freaking out and schedule an intervention, or an appointment with a neurologist, or both, when Bowie looks up at him and raises a bushy eyebrow.

"*Gotcha!*" He smirks at his nephew.

Ignoring his uncle's feeble, in his opinion, attempt at humor, Colt says, "Okay. All fixed," and begins to load the sink full of dirty dishes into the dishwasher. "This thing works, right?" he asks Bowie.

"Last time I used it."

This does not reassure Colt, but he turns it on anyway and is pleased when it appears to start and operate normally.

"Anyway, we're hoping to surprise Garnet, and we'd like to have her party here," he says.

"Fine with me; Garnet's the one who insists on holding a grudge."

"Maybe your cheating on her, lying about it, and then leaving her for Lily Wentworth has something to do with it?"

"You've got a mouth on you, you know that? No wonder your daddy left home."

Colt tries to decide which he'd prefer, throttling the old geezer until he turns blue or finishing him off with the wrench he just used to fix the faucet.

Bowie then says placidly, "You know your old man's in town?"

"And you know that, how?"

"Oh, Remington stopped by. We go way back, you know."

Colt decides to change the subject. They wouldn't charge him with manslaughter; it would definitely be first-degree murder. "If we're going to do this party," he says, "we only have a couple weeks to set your place to rights. I'm going to be stopping by here on my way home from work from now on. You've really let things slide, Bowie."

"I've been busy," his uncle says, peering up at him through a pair of filthy spectacles.

"You ever clean those glasses of yours, Bowie?" Colt says.

"I have cataracts. I don't see so good anymore."

Colt takes his uncle's glasses and using dishwashing liquid, washes, then dries them and places them back on Bowie's nose.

"Better?" he asks Bowie.

"I was going to do that. Like I say, I've been busy."

"Yeah," Colt says. "Sure you have."

When he gets home, Garnet does indeed have dinner ready. There's a pot of homemade chili on the stove, and she is cutting warm cornbread from a boxed mix into squares—she's told her nephew that the only reason to bake from scratch is because he loves it, and she does not. As Colt sets the table he tells his aunt about his visit with her ex-husband, everything but the reason for it. About that detail, he lies. He seems to be lying to Garnet a lot lately. He has yet to mention Bowie's reunification plans to her, an omission not due to any sense of loyalty to Bowie. He doesn't know why. The thought occurs to him that he really wouldn't mind all that much seeing these two get back together; he's surprised to find himself thinking such a thing.

"I stopped by Bowie's on my way home to let him know my father is back in town."

"Let me guess. Bowie already knew," Garnet says.

"How did you know that?"

"I imagine Bowie was one of his first stops. In fact, it was Remington who introduced me to your uncle."

"How did I not know that?"

"I came home for winter break my senior year. Remmy had just flunked out of Syracuse and brought his new best friend, a second-year law student, home with him. Bowie told me later he'd helped Remmy out of a couple scrapes he'd gotten himself into. I was infatuated, then engaged. That fall, after I'd graduated and Bowie passed the bar, I married him. Looking back, I swept myself off my own feet. If I'd been a novelist, Bowie would have been my first book, the one I got out of my system and locked in a drawer where no one else would ever read it."

"That sounds a little harsh, not like you at all, Gigi."

"I am not the person you think I am, Colt. Like me, you are guilty of making up narratives about those you love that bear little resemblance to reality."

❧

On Wednesday before he leaves for work, Colt tells Garnet he'll be eating dinner at Rain's with Meg and Remmy. Garnet raises an eyebrow.

"Really."

"I don't want to go but if Remington is there, I need to be there too. I'm bringing bread and salad."

"So as far as Rain is concerned, there's no free lunch for you?"

"Something like that."

"Would you like me to pick up some decent bread and make a salad?"

"I was going to get something at the deli on my way over there."

"Should I repeat the question or is your answer yes?"

"Yes…please."

"Good boy."

Colt stops home first to clean up—he's feeling particularly grubby after spending the day using a sander on the heart pine floors of a circa 1920s home-remodel. Garnet has a crusty baguette, and a green salad in a large, lidded plastic bowl, along with a bottle of balsamic vinaigrette, bagged up and ready to go. There are daffodils, their stems rubber-banded into a plastic bag with a little water in the bottom. Colt resolves to remember this. The front seat of the truck has only recently dried out from his last floral offering.

But he says, "Flowers, Gigi? Flowers?"

"Be a good example to your daughter. Show her how she should expect to be treated by a man even, God forbid, an ex-husband."

"But Rain and I were never married," Colt says.

"Don't be disingenuous. You know exactly what I mean."

"I guess I do," Colt says. "Thank you, Gigi," he adds and kisses her on the forehead.

Garnet's voice follows him out the door, "Tell my little brother hello."

The Jaguar is in the driveway, so Colt has to park on the street. What might the driver of something like this be compensating for? Colt decides he doesn't want to know.

Opening the door, Rain takes one look at the flowers, the Tupperware, the bread, and says, "I should be thanking Garnet, shouldn't I?"

"What can I say, she loves me."

"I'm trying to be the kind of person my daughter can look up to, so I will not be offering a comment on that."

"Please don't change," Colt says. "I like you just the way you are."

Rain takes his offerings while Colt hangs his jacket in the small front closet where Rain has stacked labeled, clear plastic storage boxes on the floor and on the shelf, using all the available space not needed for outerwear. He thinks of the jumbled belongings spilling out of the closet in his bedroom at Garnet's house.

"Well, come on," she says. "Remington and Meg are in the kitchen."

They are indeed together in the kitchen. Colt's father is following Meg as she sets the table, adding a paper napkin under each fork. Colt thinks of himself as pleasant looking—but definitely more Opie than James Bond. In that online ad he'd written, he began by calling himself a nice guy rather than nice looking. It's not that the female gender finds him unattractive; they do not. But even so, he can see his father belongs in a whole other category. Way out there among the one-percenters. A charmer to boot, full of implied promises he will ever be incapable of keeping.

Colt fears what Meg's reaction to her grandfather might be. Will she, too, be sucked in? Though he also wonders if Remington's looks and charm have operated more as a curse than a blessing, limiting and stunting his options instead of the reverse. From his own very limited experience of wild success, Colt knows it's a thirst that can't be slaked, the more you drink, the thirstier you're left. Meg looks up from her task and flashes him a mile-wide smile.

"You brought daffodils, Daddy! My favorite."

"I'll remember that," Remington says.

I bet you will, Colt thinks.

"Where's Eddie?" Colt asks Rain.

"Working second shift this week."

Colt feels a first-ever twinge of sympathy for his nemesis.

"Don't forget our P-T conference is tomorrow," Rain says. "I'll meet you in front of the school at 6:55."

No danger of that, Colt thinks.

"I love my teacher," Meg says.

He can identify. Yet, still way too soon for him to be thinking about the L word.

Meg has continued her baking exploits. Tonight's feat is a chocolate mayonnaise cake with cream cheese frosting, which at first sounds kind of disgusting to Colt—though he would never in any way indicate that to the radiant pastry chef serving up slices. But it turns out it tastes just fine. He has a second piece and even brings a slice home for Garnet.

He spends the next day worrying. He'd even called Franny on his way home from Rain's last night.

"You know, Colt, we haven't broken any laws. We owe no explanations to anyone."

"I'm just worried Rain is going to figure out something is going on."

"Not because of me, she won't."

"You're implying I'm the weak link? Because I am definitely the weak link."

"If you come by my place tomorrow night after conferences are over, maybe around eight-thirty or nine, I won't tell."

It takes so little, thinks Colt, to scuttle all his good intentions. This is the kind of man he has become.

Though he's five minutes early, Rain is already waiting for him by the front door of Meg's school. An understated streak of purple adorns her hair. She has put in her most conservative nose ring and is wearing a very nice, new black blazer. From Eddie? Maybe.

"You look great," Colt says.

"And you always clean up well."

A seven o'clock conference has given him time to go home after work, wash up, and put on the last of his Christmas gifts, a checked twill button-down, and pair of clean khakis. If he's honest with himself, he probably would not have bothered were Franny not the teacher and he not thinking about later tonight. He's already told Gigi not to worry if he's late, or even doesn't make it home tonight. His aunt, no dummy, knows something is up, but has refrained from inquiring what it might be. She merely nodded her head as she chopped vegetables for chicken soup. His aunt, Saint Garnet. He is not being sarcastic.

They enter the school, walking down a hallway lined with undersized kids' chairs filled by uncomfortable and often oversized adults waiting their turns. They stop outside Ms. Fisher's classroom, Colt glad to sit, feeling faintly queasy at the prospect of having to rely on his pathetic powers of deception, their history with Rain especially problematic. Franny's present conference is going long. Bits of the discussion leak out of the classroom's open door.

"...an enthusiastic learner."

Rain interprets for him. "Loud."

"...eager to share what he's learning."

"Talks too much."

Colt laughs, and thinks that in a perfect world, meaning one made just for him and by him, he would choose both women, the one next to him, the other now speaking in her classroom. He needs to think about something else. Colt turns to Rain.

"So, what do you make of the current version of my father?"

"I think he's trying very hard."

"Tell me you are not buying into his bullshit, Rain."

"You forget I was there the first time Remington walked out. Your mom had found out about her cancer, and we'd just started dating. You introduced me to him before he left for parts unknown, but I'd already gotten an earful from my mother. She told me to keep my distance, not from you but from your father, that he liked adding mothers and daughters to his scorecard, and as far she and I were concerned, he was halfway there. He'll have to do a lot more than try hard now to change my opinion of him. On the other hand, people do change."

"Add *seldom* before the word *do*," Colt says.

"And he is Meg's grandfather. I have no objection to him spending a limited amount of time with her."

"Where's Meg tonight? Please, please don't tell me she's with Grandpa!"

"Remington will not be around Meg unless I'm right there. Give me some credit, Colt. I asked Julitta to come over and keep Meg company tonight."

"We can't call it babysitting anymore, can we."

"Not any place within earshot of our daughter."

Meg has instructed both her parents that she is no longer a baby, and if she were, hiring someone to sit on her would be most inimical to her; she loves her words. At any rate, she is willing to tolerate a companion for the evening if Rain is absent, as long as those hired are referred to as such.

"I made her day," says Rain. "I said I was willing to acquiesce to her conditions if she could spell it."

"And…?"

"She spelled *acquiesce* and then for good measure *inimical*."

"I think we are both pretty intelligent people," says Colt.

"Oh, spare me," says Rain.

"Now wait. My theory is she got both our brains and we have wound up with a kid twice as smart as we are."

"This does not bode well for her teen years; you know that, right?"

A harried-looking woman exits the classroom, clutching a packet of papers. She smiles brightly at them.

"Two down, two to go," she says.

Franny comes to the door and smiles. "Ms. Nelson. Mr. Adams. Come in."

At their P-T meeting in the fall, Colt found Franny attractive enough to have her appear in a few subsequent "what if" scenarios but he never seriously considered acting on the impulse. His ten-year-old daughter's fourth-grade teacher? *Come on!* And now? What's that song? "What a Difference a Day Makes"?

Of course, the news is good. Franny shares Meg's packet of work and walks them through class projects displayed around the classroom, asking if they have any concerns.

She says, "Meg is gifted academically, but what I most value is her empathy. You two have done a great job."

Colt feels, thanks to Franny, and the fact that he has pretty much kept his mouth shut except for a few pleasantries, he's gotten off scot-free despite his misgivings. They walk down the hallway afterward, Rain holding their packet of papers, ready for Meg's inspection and her impatient demands of "What did she say about me?" followed by "What else did she say?" and "Then what did she say?"

At the door, before going their separate ways, Rain says, "You think Ms. Fisher's pretty cute, don't you?"

"What? Why would you say something like that?" Colt responds, determined not to lie, or at least not lie outright.

He can feel his face getting hot.

For the second time that night, Rain says, "Oh, please, spare me."

It is seven-thirty.

Colt spends the time he has to kill before seeing Franny at Bowie's. This evening when he rings the bell and his uncle answers, looking especially frowsy in a wrinkled flannel shirt, one arm of which is partially torn away at the shoulder, and raggedy denim overalls, Bowie at least recognizes him this time. The old man needs a shave. And a haircut, which Colt adds to his mental to-do list. Where has the dandy gone, the attorney who insisted on French cuffs so he could show off his collection of 14-karat-gold cufflinks?

"Kind of late for visitors, don't you think, Colt? I turn in early."

"Go to bed, Bowie. I'll lock up on my way out. Tonight, I'm scraping all those manufacturer's labels off your new windows."

"Why? I don't even notice them."

"Gigi will notice them."

"We are going to a lot of trouble for that woman."

"Not 'we,' old man. I don't see you contributing any effort to the cause."

"I'm volunteering my house for her party. That's not nothing."

"I don't know that 'volunteering' is the word I'd use."

Bowie, as usual, has to have the last word.

"Nobody asked you."

By the time Colt is ready to quit, leaving the kitchen windows not only scraped but washed, Bowie is sitting at the counter eating corn chips and drinking Dr. Pepper. He's regaled Colt with stories of his glory days as a litigator, stories his nephew is not unfamiliar with. It is also a fact that the stories are mostly true. Other attorneys would sit in just to hear Bowie argue a case.

"I thought you said you turned in early, Bowie."

"Figured I better supervise, make sure nobody's doing shoddy work or stealing the silverware."

Colt cannot understand why he is so fond of the irascible old fart, but he is.

Conferences end at 8:30. Figuring he'll give Franny time to get home and catch her breath, it's close to 9:15 when Colt parks his truck. Luckily, one of the two designated guest spaces is free in the small lot adjacent to the brick box housing Franny's apartment and seven others. Her unit, 1-A, is on the first floor, on the left front if he is facing the building. He enters the glass double door into a front hallway holding eight metal lockbox mailboxes along one side, a credenza against the opposite wall with a dusty artificial flower arrangement in a willow basket. There is a faded print in an ugly frame of Van Gogh's much-abused sunflower painting over the table and a fairly clean black-and-white checkered linoleum tile floor under it. Colt knocks on Franny's door.

Franny opens it, looking exhausted. There are dark circles under her eyes. But she smiles when she sees him.

"I'm glad you weren't on time; I just got home," she says.

"Almost every conference ran long. I never learn; they always do."

Colt takes her face in his hands and kisses her.

"You did great," he says.

"Well, I didn't feel great. I felt like a great big lying phony. And Rain knew something was going on. If she hasn't figured it out yet, she will soon."

Colt has to agree.

"I think," he says, "I'm going to have to make an honest woman of you. When I get home I'm going to call you up and ask you to go to the movies with me next Saturday night. Then I'll tell Garnet and Rain and Meg I've asked you out. If you say yes, that is."

"Yes."

"Not yet. Wait until I call."

"Yes," Franny says again, kissing Colt.

She's already left for school when he opens his eyes the next morning, but she's made coffee and left a box of blueberry pop tarts for him. He's late for work and Booker gives him a knowing smile and punches him on the shoulder.

"It's not what you think," Colt says.

"Oh yes, it is," he says, with a laugh.

Colt thinks back to high school. He has yet to go on a real first date with Franny and he has already rounded all the bases and stolen home. He can hardly wait to hit a couple out of the park again. Enough with the lame baseball metaphors, he tells himself. Whatever this is, it does not feel in any way, shape, or form like a game.

Later that evening Colt tells Garnet he's asked Meg's teacher to go out with him.

"Good," she says. "I had great confidence you were not one to sneak around."

It feels like this happens to him every time he's absolutely certain his secret, whatever it is, is safe, and has ever since he was a little kid. He's sure he would have made the world's worst undercover agent.

❧

Rain drops Meg off for the weekend after an orthodontist appointment on Friday. Colt catches her before she drives away. Telling Meg he needs to check on something with her mom, he tells his daughter to go ahead inside.

"Good news. Meg does not need braces," Rain says.

"I need to ask your advice," Colt says.

"Make it quick. Eddie's waiting. We are going camping this weekend." She gives him a wry look. "A romantic getaway."

"If I were looking for a definition of 'oxymoron'…"

Colt leaves the sentence unfinished.

They no longer have a lot in common other than the daughter they share, but a deep suspicion of the outdoors as a pleasurable place to lay your head has always united them.

"My condolences," he adds.

He then tells Rain about next Saturday's date.

"Meg is not going to be happy. You know that, right?"

"Why?"

"Because she's in fourth grade and she's in love with her teacher. The operative word here is *her*. She will not want to share Ms. Fisher with you."

Colt has not considered this.

Meg takes Vera for a walk after Saturday lunch. Colt takes the opportunity to talk to Garnet. He tells her what Rain told him.

"So what do I do?"

"I don't see that you have any choice, Colt. You tell Meg what's going on and listen to what she has to say. She will be a lot unhappier if you keep it from her and she finds it out from someone else. And she will."

"Should I break the date?"

"We are talking about a ten-year-old child. She should not have to be responsible for your happiness one way or the other. Don't place that burden on her."

Sometimes Colt thinks Garnet should have her own show like Oprah. When he tells her this she laughs.

"I give great advice, don't I? Too bad I don't follow it."

That is why Colt is sitting on the front porch steps waiting when Meg returns with Vera. The dog flops down on the brick pavers. Meg sits down next to him.

"I have something to tell you," he says.

Meg, who does not like surprises, looks worried.

"What?"

Colt tells her. He has been warned, she is not pleased. The storm clouds gather. Her eyes narrow, then look away from her father.

"Why?"

"Because I like her. She seems to be a very nice person."

"Why can't you ask some other very nice person? Why do you have to go out with my teacher?"

"She will still be your teacher. I wanted you to know because this is happening. I will be taking Ms. Fisher to the movies."

At least she no longer looks worried. Garnet was right. No way did Meg want to be the arbiter of his actions.

"Her name is Franny," Meg says.

"Good to know."

"What are you going to see?"

"I'll ask her to pick."

"Maybe she won't like you. Maybe she won't want to go out with you again," Meg says in a hopeful tone.

"Maybe I won't like her."

"Everybody loves Ms. Fisher."

Out of the mouths of babes, Colt thinks.

"Now, how about spending the afternoon with me at your uncle Bowie's?" Colt says. "We've only got three weeks to get a house ready for a surprise birthday party."

❧

Though there was frost on some neighborhood roofs earlier this fine Saturday, the green spears of daffodils, unaffected, are poking up through last year's soggy fallen leaves. Her house, for the moment empty of people, Colt and Meg off somewhere, Garnet is blissfully free of responsibilities. Wearing a fisherman knit sweater—it's not yet all *that* balmy—she's sitting on her porch with a mug of coffee, her third of the day, the one she knows she'll pay for tonight, staring wide-eyed at the ceiling until she gives up, gets up, and makes herself a glass of disgusting warm milk, forced once again to accept that actions have consequences—a bill that never gets lost in the mail or arrives at her door marked *paid in full.* But the coffee is excellent, and night hours away.

Garnet is watching her neighbor, George, in the driveway next door polishing his SUV.

Colt has dubbed it, out of George's hearing of course, the Beast. Car names! thinks Garnet. In this case, an American automobile company named for an early French explorer of dubious character, each of its cars bearing his phony coat of arms as a hood ornament, loonily chooses a Spanish noun, *escalada*, meaning ladder, for one of its high-end vehicles. Maybe it refers to the social climbers that are targeted? No—too subtle, she thinks. Not to mention attributing to an ad agency dependent on a huge account a most unlikely sly sense of humor. Still…*escalade*—such a mellifluous name for the large, carbon-belching, planet-destroying hunk of machinery gleaming in the sunlight next door. Not that she's judging her neighbor. She's actually very fond of George. Though not as fond, she knows, as he is of her.

"Hey, you over there," he calls. "Where's your dog?"

"Vera's inside. Napping in the kitchen. We didn't realize what a pretty day it's turned out to be."

She remembers George standing at her back door in the middle of the night three years ago, telling her Marjorie was gone, cancer had won. It was snowing. She'd stepped out the door in her nightgown, her feet bare, and put her arms around him, held him while he cried. Why didn't she pull him into the house, out of the weather? Strange it never occurred to her.

And that was not the worst part. Her neighbor, in tears, had just lost his wife to an insidious disease and she, there, thinking how nice it was to be in a man's arms again. She is not proud of herself, of having to admit once again, not that there was ever any doubt, that she is just one more imperfect human being. She knows Colt calls her "Saint Garnet." She hopes he's being humorous, sarcastic would even be okay, but fears that's not the case.

"Vera still fond of ice cream?" George says.

"What do you think?" she says.

"The Corner Cone opens today for the season."

George, remembering her kindness, had tried to reciprocate for the rest of that long winter as Bowie busied himself in divorce court blowing up the last vestiges of their marriage. She'd found her driveway and walk shoveled, her newspaper retrieved from the lawn awaiting her on the front porch outside the door, car brushed clean of snow, windshield ice-free, ready to go. She had been too distracted, miserable, to even notice half the time, much less thank him.

"Are you telling me you want to take Vera for ice cream?"

"I believe I am, yes. And her human companion. My treat, of course."

"Of course."

George occasionally initiates these interactions with Garnet, usually, as now, using Vera as go-between and excuse. Garnet invariably and gently turns him down. She has no wish to encourage this perfectly nice man. She'd been half of a not-very-happy couple for most of her life, and she likes her present single status just fine. She does not long for romance, no matter how much she enjoyed that embrace. However, it is such a beautiful day.

"I will go suit Vera up," she says. "We will be ready momentarily."

"I'll be right here."

The three of them walk the block and a half into the village. Garnet would like a little more space between George and herself, but Vera obviously thinks of them as her little flock, and, despite the leash, exercises her superior herding abilities. Garnet can tell George is getting a kick out of the whole process, including her discomfort.

"Vera thinks we make a great couple," George says.

"More likely, Vera thinks we are two bald sheep in need of direction."

"Anyone ever tell you that you have the soul of a romantic?"

"No. I don't believe so."

"Not surprised."

Ouch! Garnet again thinks.

The crowd around the Corner Cone gives it a festival-like appearance. People, their kids and dogs, mingle. Garnet and George join the long line. Vera's mighty tail swishes back and forth metronome-like. If a butterfly can trigger a typhoon halfway across the world, who knows what far-away disaster this happy dog's posterior may be fomenting right now.

Once served, they settle on one of the benches that surround the little cement-block building with its three-scoop giant cone on the roof. Vera does not snarf down her ice cream cone as one might expect. George holds the cone and the dog takes one tiny ladylike lick after another of strawberry swirl soft serve until it's gone. Then she finishes off the waffle cone in a single snap, somehow leaving George's fingers intact. Garnet feels a hand on her shoulder and turns to see her daughter standing behind her, next to Ben. Vera immediately deserts George and Garnet to sit on Tommie's foot and lean against her, big head lovingly pressed against her hip.

"Mom."

"Tommie, what are you doing here?"

Garnet leaves the rest of her question, "...with your ex?" suspended in the air like a semi-deflated speech balloon.

"It's the Corner Cone. We are getting ice cream."

"Hi, Gigi," Ben says.

Tommie and Ben. Ben and Tommie. Whatever's going on can't be good for either one of them, though Garnet knows it is officially and properly none of her business. These are two adults perfectly capable of making their own horrible mistakes without help from anyone else.

George murmurs as they walk away, "I didn't know they were back together."

"If I were to hazard a guess," Garnet says, "I'd say it was a very recent development."

"Trust me, I'll be getting an earful about this," Tommie says to Ben.

"Why? Your mom likes me."

"She does. All the more reason."

They silently spoon up their hot fudge sundaes. Garnet and George can be seen heading back where they came from, Vera again ensuring they are in tight formation.

"George have an invitation to the birthday party?" Ben says.

"I don't know but that's a good idea. I'll make sure it happens. At the very least it will make Vera happy."

They watch George take Garnet's hand. They watch Garnet retract her hand and tuck it in the pocket of her jacket.

"George and Gigi an item?" asks Ben.

"George would like them to be an item, and it's becoming harder for my mother to pretend she's oblivious."

"And what are we?" Ben asks Tommie.

A great question, Tommie thinks. After what transpired this morning, how exactly to answer that question?

Yesterday, Ben collared her as she was leaving school. She was already in the car, ready to turn the key and start the engine.

He knocked on her car window and when she rolled it down, asked, "Can we talk?"

Really? Now you want to talk? she started to say but he looked so stricken she couldn't bring herself to do it.

"Get in," she said.

"I broke up with Moira."

Tommie couldn't help herself. "You're telling me this because…?"

"She thinks I'm using her, and I think she's right."

"Using her how?"

"As a substitute for you."

"Why would she think that?"

"Because last week I called her Tommie at a very inopportune moment."

"Good grief, Ben, the foot finally heals. You've moved on. So, it must be time to go out and shoot yourself in the other one?"

"I knew you'd understand," he said bitterly and got out of the car.

Thinking about that conversation left Tommie sleepless last night. She was not over him. The same seemed true of Ben. She could be her usual snotty self, or she could allow herself some vulnerability and see what happened next. Just as she'd finally begun to drift off, her increasingly unsatisfactory roommate, Remmy, had returned after another late night, making himself noisily at home, opening and closing doors, flushing the toilet, running water, and crashing repeatedly into the coffee table as he made up his bed on the sofa. His one saving grace, at least he did not snore.

This morning Tommie steeled herself and went over to Ben's apartment to try to talk civilly about what he'd said. Of course, then they hadn't talked at all. She'd brought no protection, not expecting this turn of events, though the possibility should have occurred to her, and Ben, usually Mr. Responsible, had simply let nature take its course. Twice. Tommie resolves to pick up condoms before she goes home today and get herself back on the pill ASAP.

Ben is still waiting for her reply.

"I don't know what we are, Ben. You tell me."

"Well, I was clearer on that before today."

"Whatever our problems, they were never apparent in bed which still seems to be the case. That's what I know about today."

"You haven't changed."

"Yet you love me anyway."

"Love. Or something."

When Colt and his daughter arrived at Bowie's this morning after leaving Garnet to her own devices, his uncle seemed pleased to see Meg. Colt not so much. Meg began work by sweeping the front porch while Colt applied stain to the new mantelpiece. Around noon, Bowie announced his naptime.

"The doc says I should have a routine and stick to it no matter what," he said.

Colt had given him a look.

"Listen, buster," Bowie said, "I need a midday siesta. Out of my way."

Later, Meg is finishing up when Ben rounds the corner and runs up the porch steps. The hanging basket with its dead plant is now gone. She's bundling up newspapers to recycle, and a very large ashtray filled with cigars in various states of decomposition is ready to go inside to be emptied and washed.

"Hey there, Meggie."

"Hi, Mr. Brown."

"You can call me Ben as long as we're not at school."

Meg prefers her world orderly. Like her mother, she finds security in heeding standards for behavior and sets of rules. Therefore, it's unlikely she'll be calling one of next year's teachers anything but "Mister." However, this does not mean she doesn't appreciate the gesture.

"Thanks, Mr. Brown."

Ben knows to let well enough alone.

"Your dad inside?"

"I'll tell him you're here."

Meg opens the front door, and with an unexpected and impressive bellow, informs her father of company. Colt appears with a paintbrush and a can of #32 dark walnut stain in hand.

"Hey, where you been? We need all the help we can muster."

"You wouldn't believe me if I told you," Ben says.

Ben is put to work washing the kitchen floor and finds it

entirely possible to mop while carrying on a conversation with Colt who's working in the other room.

"Garnet still in the dark about her party?"

"We hope so," says Colt.

"You and the lovely Ms. Fisher, huh?"

"What?"

"You have to know that truck of yours is pretty recognizable parked outside her apartment building. More than one teacher lives in that complex."

"Well, *damn*."

The front door opens and Meg enters just as Bowie clatters down the stairs in the Berluti dress shoes he's lately favored, shoes badly dilapidated since their courtroom days. His once-white socks puddle around his ankles. He takes one look at the ashtray in Meg's hands and hurries over.

"Give me that. We are not throwing away any fine Cuban cigars. No way are they ready for the trash."

And Colt says to Ben, "Can we please talk about something, anything else?"

The porch has been swept, the kitchen floor shines, and Ben has vacuumed the oriental carpets throughout the house for good measure. The newly finished wood of the mantel, set off by its tile surround, glows. The small crew, ready to quit, says their goodbyes.

As he's closing the big front door, Bowie pauses to call out to Colt, "By the way, your father's going to be moving in with me. Seems he feels he's worn out his welcome with Tommie. My daughter, as you know," here he peers knowingly over his spectacles in Ben's direction, "is not an easy person to get along with."

Colt, taken by surprise, stands open-mouthed on the porch as the door closes firmly, the thumb lock turns, and the dead-bolt engages.

Ben shakes his head in disbelief.

"Daddy, your face is all red. Are you okay?" Meg asks.

When father and daughter return, Vera is asleep and snoring, sprawled on the kitchen floor and Garnet is finishing up preparations for Saturday night supper.

"Smells great," Colt says. "Chicken?"

"Roast chicken, mashed potatoes, peas. There's apple crisp for dessert."

"*Ooooh*, my favorite," says Meg, setting the table.

"I don't know," Garnet says. "Your father and I are going to have to somehow teach you to be pickier. You are entirely too nice to live in this world, young lady."

"That's the truth," says Colt.

"But it is my favorite. You don't want me to lie, do you?"

"I guess not," sighs Garnet. "Well, maybe a little bit."

"While we worked our fingers to the bone," Colt says, "what were you up to, Garnet?"

"I offered to help, you know, and I was pretty much told not to worry my pretty little head about it."

"You must have dreamed that. I would never—"

"What? Why? My head is not pretty…or little?"

"Garnet, I do believe you are avoiding the subject. What did you do today?"

"If I must. George treated Vera and me to ice cream cones. There, are you satisfied?"

"I told you, Gigi, he likes you. He *like* likes you."

"I like George," Meg adds.

As they eat, Colt tells her of Bowie's parting shot.

"I can't say I'm surprised. Or rather I am surprised it took Remmy this long to figure out Bowie, rather than Tommie, is the easier mark. I'm sorry; forgive me for being so cynical about my baby brother's motives."

"We are going to be keeping an eye on him."

"It's so nice of you both to give your uncle a helping hand. The house has really gotten away from him. I wish I could say that I know he appreciates it."

"Uncle Bowie went up and took a nap while we worked."

"That does not surprise me," says Garnet.

"I like Remmy so far," Meg says. "Is my grandpa a bad man?"

"See, this is what happens when you conduct adult conversations when a young audience is present," Garnet says to Colt.

"I am young," Meg says, "but that doesn't mean I can't understand things."

"Amen to that," says Colt.

"So is he a malevolent person?"

"God help us," Garnet says.

❧

Later, dishes finished and Meg upstairs puttering her way to bedtime, Garnet makes herself a cup of tea to the sound of heavy artillery from the other room where Colt is watching something on the cable channel Garnet has labeled "All WWII All the Time." She sits down at the kitchen table and thinks how she would answer Meg's question. Like the Facebook descriptor she sometimes sees, "it's complicated."

It amazes Garnet how differently people perceive the same set of circumstances. Garnet's father loved his daughters; neither Ruby nor Garnet ever felt slighted in that department. But Remington, as a child, was undeniably his favorite and it didn't matter. From the start their brother, gifted with looks, charm, and considerable intelligence but lacking any semblance of self-discipline, or perspective, any sense of humor for that matter, saw himself as always coming up short. He routinely tilted any full glass given him until he could call the contents half empty. His sisters had each other. Who did he have?

Remington seemed determined to disappoint. Family assembled for his high school graduation; he skipped the ceremony. Given a free ride to Syracuse, he flunked out. The term narcissist is thrown around so often that much of its sting has dissipated, but it does not make it any less true that when Remmy gazed into a mirror the only image he ever saw was his own. There was no room for others' reflections, say, those of a wife and child.

Remmy, Remmy, Garnet wonders, *what do you want this time? And will mischief or havoc be the end result?*

The sounds of exploding ordnance have ceased. The kitchen now fills with the drone of bombers, Allied or German? There's no way for Garnet to tell.

"Colt," she calls out, "please turn that thing down."

"What?" Colt answers, turning the sound off. "I can't hear you."

"Exactly," Garnet answers.

❧

The party is only two weeks away. And it's been a long time since he's baked Garnet's favorite cake, so Colt has asked Rain if he can do a practice run in her kitchen after he brings Meg back tonight. She's agreed. Eddie will be off with a friend who's restoring an Indian motorcycle he found in the back of a falling-down barn, so she's even made herself available to help.

Colt and Meg have stopped at the supermarket on the way home and Colt carries their paper sacks of purchases into the house—he'd forgotten his canvas totes at Garnet's and Meg forbade him to accept the store's ubiquitous plastic bags for their groceries, threatening to hold him personally responsible for the mid-Pacific garbage weir. Bad enough to be the cause of the destruction of trees.

"From scratch, huh?" Rain asks, watching him empty the bag.

"From scratch. My one positive childhood memory of my father. He taught me how to make this cake."

"That does not sound like the Remington we know."

"We call it an anomaly," offers Meg. "Do you want me to spell it?"

Two hours later, the cake Colt puts together is done. It smells great. It tastes just fine too, especially with the scoop of vanilla ice cream Rain adds on the side. However all agree it is not aesthetically (and, yes, Meg would spell this too if they let her) pleasing. It failed to come cleanly out of the pans and had to be spackled back together, and though frosting helped, the middle sags significantly. "We need to check your oven temperature," says Colt. "There must be something wrong with the thermostat."

"More likely, we need to look at your tendency to approximate measurements and elide instructions," Rain answers.

Meg rips a piece of paper off a notepad on the counter and writes down *elide*.

"Even when we were in high school," says Colt, "you were the grown-up, but that's the way it's supposed to be; men, after all, mature more slowly."

Rain snorts. Meg regards her mother and father. You can almost see her thinking, *Why are these two not still together?*

"But you'd figure by now I'd have caught up," Colt adds.

"You'd think," Rain says.

Meg takes her backpack and goes upstairs to unpack. Colt fills the sink with hot soapy water and begins to wash up the mess—plates, bowls, and implements covered with batter and frosting and crumbs. The kitchen is bright and toasty, the oven off but still radiating heat. Rain picks up a dishtowel and dries. Her face is flushed from the warmth. She's taken off the *New Yorker* Booth dog sweatshirt she was wearing (given her by Colt so long ago he'd bet she doesn't even remember it), leaving her in a thin, oversized white T-shirt (Eddie's?) and a pair of strategically ripped jeans; Colt tries not to wonder if, despite her still-slender build, she now wears the bra she deemed unnecessary in high school. He resolves not to check it out; he's way better than that.

Dishes done, Colt calls up to Meg, "Good night, sweetie," and turns to get his jacket. Rain watches him. She is standing under the fan light Eddie recently installed for her, the movement of air ruffling her hair. He glances over, callow promise-breaker that he is. No bra. For some reason this makes him inexplicably happy.

❧

Remmy has finished moving in with Bowie. He's taken over the third floor, a semi-finished attic, and made it his own bachelor quarters. Rather than use the perfectly serviceable interior stairs from the second floor, he prefers the simple outdoor metal fire escape on the back of the house, accessing his room by climbing in and out of the window as he comes and goes. The Jaguar is gone, repossessed for falling behind in rental fees. In its place, Remmy has somehow latched on to an ancient white Lincoln Continental, a boat of a car, its leather seats dried out and cracked but the body and paint job surprisingly intact and rust-free. He's parked it out back, next to the carriage house, which is now dedicated to sheltering Bowie's Lexus, any left-over space filled with boxes from the move here, taped shut, unlabeled and haphazardly stacked. The apartment overhead is unused and neglected.

Colt and Ben, with help from Tommie and Meg, are making significant progress readying the house for its imminent close-up. Rain has declared herself in charge of the party space, and she and Meg are crafting decorations, tacky ones that Garnet will love. George, sworn to secrecy, has been invited, as has Franny.

The four have established a routine, meeting at Bowie's after work as their schedules allow, with Franny pitching in when she can. Sunset a little later each day has been helpful, as has the increasingly milder weather. Tommie has cleaned dead leaves from the beds around the porch and planted reliably hardy yellow and violet pansies. It's too early for most annuals but not these. Ben and Colt have found the unused paint in the basement and will finish the trim on the remaining side of the house this coming weekend.

But tonight, middle of the week, everyone has finished up and gone home early. It's dark now and the house is at last quiet. Tommie has given Bowie explicit instructions not to mess up the newly cleaned kitchen so he is obediently putting the few dishes used for his supper into the dishwasher. To minimize even further their number, he'd had peaches forked out of the can for dessert. He alternates, fruit one night—never fresh fruit, he says it interferes with his digestion—and vegetables the next, usually canned peas or corn, varied occasionally by barbecued baked beans, for the fiber he says. He's cut out his standby Mountain Dew after Garnet said it was the caffeine from his six-pack-a-day habit that was keeping him awake at night—a big relief to Bowie who'd feared it was his guilty conscience. And he's been sleeping like a baby since. Virtuously, he's also switched to what he considers a more wholesome option—caffeine-free Diet Coke.

In the attic, Remmy has a hot plate and his own little fridge. Even so, Bowie has noticed his Klondike bars disappearing since Remmy's arrival and keeps meaning to talk to him about it. Bowie is closing the dishwasher when he hears Remmy come down the fire escape. He flicks on the back door light and steps out, seeing his new guest walk over to his car, a car Bowie earlier checked out down to the dashboard clock, its long-dead hands frozen at 3:35. Amazingly, Remmy tells him, the radio still works.

Bowie watches Remmy get into the front seat and start the Lincoln. Then, sitting in the running car, exhaust fouling the evening air, driver's-side door open to the mild night, Bowie hears him tune the radio to a country station. Johnny Cash sings. Bowie hums along, having forgotten most of the lyrics, employing words only when the refrain begins and he sings the song's title, "I walk the line," wishing he'd somehow managed to do that for his ex-wife.

Forbidden by Colt to smoke in the house, Remmy lights up, the flame briefly illuminating his face. Who'd have thought, he'd complained when he took Bowie to the grocery store this afternoon, that a pack of off-brand cigarettes would ever cost *twelve effing bucks*! Bowie, dependent on the kindness of others after getting lost three times in a row less than a mile from home, is no longer doing much driving himself.

He dries his hands on the dishtowel he's holding, hangs it on the doorknob, and goes down the little back porch's steps to join Remmy. The Carter family is singing "Wildwood Flower," as he opens the car door and settles into the back seat.

Remmy greets him with, "What are you doing out here?"

"Too clean in there," Bowie says, pointing to his house.

"It's your house. Tell them all to get lost."

He takes a pull at the silver flask Remmy passes back to him, one he'd seen earlier in the glove box during his *sub rosa* inspection of the vehicle.

"I'm going to ask Garnet at the party," Bowie says.

"Ask her what?"

"To take me back."

Bowie nods his head to the music until he falls asleep. Remmy has to nudge him awake, sending him indoors to bed before he himself goes inside. His vehicle could almost fit the description of those well-preserved antiques you read about on the streets of present-day Havana, though only one of its headlights works, the other flickering intermittently, and the car's muffler is shot—which of itself precludes the possibility, this time, that Remmy can simply sneak away unnoticed and unheard when he eventually makes his getaway, as inevitably he will.

❧

Garnet is spending Thursday morning preparing for her sister's visit; Ruby will arrive in a little over a week. She's putting fresh towels in the guest room when the phone rings. She makes it downstairs just in time to hear the voicemail message begin. She picks up the receiver.

"Hello, Ruby."

"Screening your calls?" Ruby asks.

"Trying to make it down the stairs to answer the phone without killing myself."

"You know you could add another one upstairs."

"I already have too many phones. I want less, not more, communication with a very unsatisfactory outside world."

"I hear you," says Ruby. "I've called to tell you Uber will be picking me up at the airport."

"You know you can carry not being a bother too far, don't you?"

"Have you detected any actual plans being hatched for your birthday yet, dear?"

"I am ignoring the whole subject. For my birthday, I am thinking about treating us to a little road trip and a weekend stay at a B&B. Niagara Falls maybe?"

"Have you shared this with anyone, say, Colt, or your daughter?"

"I have not and I want you to promise—"

"I won't make promises I can't keep, Garnet. You know that."

"How do you know what I was going to ask?"

"Forgive me. What were you going to ask me?"

"Never mind."

❧

"Colt."

"Hi, Ruby. What's up?"

"I'm afraid I have the role of tattletale here."

"*Uh-oh.*"

"My sister is planning a little getaway the weekend of her birthday."

"I thought you were coming here."

"I am. She's making reservations at a B&B for the weekend. For the two of us."

"Any suggestions?"

"Not presently."

"Well, thanks, Ruby. Guess I better call a meeting of the troops. See what we can come up with."

They all cram into Rain's kitchen. It's been cloudy, threatening rain all day, and now the flood gates have opened. Lightning flashes and thunder booms.

"Our first spring storm," says Tommie.

"What are we going to do?" asks Meg.

"We can't force Garnet to come to her own birthday party if she doesn't want to," says Rain.

"Maybe this needs not to be a surprise party. Maybe we need to let Garnet in on our plans," says Colt.

"And have her take off for Canada as a conscientious objector?" asks Eddie, getting ready to spend one last evening in his buddy's garage, the Indian now nearly rehabilitated.

"Who doesn't love a party?" Ben says.

Colt's phone buzzes officiously. He looks down at the small screen, then up at the others.

"Speak of the devil. Sorry, I need to take this," he says, and leaves the room.

When he returns, he looks shaken. "There's been a fire. At Bowie's," he says. "That was Garnet."

When they arrive, it's still a working fire, though it's not the house that's gone up in flames.

It is Remmy's Lincoln. There are flashing lights and sirens. And smoke. The rain, as much as the fire department's effort, is quelling the blaze. Garnet is standing next to Bowie, her arm around his shoulders, which are covered by the blanket she has wrapped around him. He looks particularly small, wet and confused.

"Where is Remmy?" Colt asks.

"Nobody knows."

The fire chief approaches Bowie and Garnet.

"Robin, thank you," says Garnet, who remembers this rather intimidating adult female as a five-year-old picking out a storybook about fire trucks at the bookstore, and handing over her birthday money to pay for it.

"Garnet. Bowie. The good news is no one was in the car," she says.

"Thank God," says Garnet. "How did this happen?"

"Bowie, you or Remmy smoke in that vehicle recently?" Robin asks.

"Me? Never!"

"What about Remmy?"

"I'm no rat. Ask him yourself."

A ghostly apparition walks out of the smoky, drenched night into the flashing emergency lights.

"Ask me what?" Remmy says.

❧

The fire finally out, Garnet walks Bowie back inside the house. She sends him upstairs to bed, wondering briefly if she should follow and tuck him in. He bears almost no resemblance to the Bowie she married so many years ago. That man, for good or ill, is gone forever, and anyway, she is no longer his wife. But Tommie remains his daughter. And it is she who will wind up making the hard decisions. Garnet does not envy her.

Remmy has followed them inside. "Guess it was a good thing I didn't get around to filling that tank today."

"Remmy, for once in your life you are going to have to step up. I cannot have two adults incapable of caring for themselves residing here," says Garnet.

But it is not the adult male Garnet sees before her, it is the boy, the boy looking as usual not one whit apologetic. The boy to whom rules do not seem to apply. Growing up, Garnet and Ruby viewed Remmy's escapades with a kind of awe. Good girls, polite, they marveled, wondering why the sky did not fall, why lightning did not strike him down. Karma seemed to apply to everyone else while casting only a fond eye on Remmy, giving him pass after pass after pass. It is one of the reasons, though she has many more, why Garnet no longer believes in God.

After they get home Colt asks, "Are you okay?"

"Not really," says Garnet absentmindedly pulling large clumps of hair from her shedding dog and adding them to the pile she's building beside her chair, while Vera leans against it in a proprietary way.

"We have a brush for that, you know."

"I find this very soothing, Colt. It's either this or a shot or three of whiskey."

"I doubt it would take three. You're a cheap date, Garnet."

"Alcohol has never done this family any favors, so I've stayed away from it. It's not my fault; I never really had a chance to build up any tolerance."

"Which is by no means a bad thing. Garnet, this may not be the best time to bring it up, but we are trying to put together a little birthday party."

"You're right. This is not the best time."

"We can't have you going off with your sister pretending the whole thing isn't happening. You know that, right? And, not to guilt you too much, your grandniece has made seventy blue Kleenex carnations as well as a purple paper chain with seventy links, and a poster that says—"

"*Enough!* All right, I will not try to run away. What do you want me to do?"

"You can be happy, Gigi. After all it's your birthday."

❧

The storms have rolled through. In their place a cold front has moved in. Tommie's taken a hot shower, put on warm flannel pajamas, ones with a top-hat-wearing dachshund print—who knows what she was thinking when she ordered them online?—and climbed into bed, seeking solace with a large mug of cocoa made using her little niece's recipe, one scant half cup of very hot chocolate, the rest of the space to be taken up by melting mini marshmallows. She is talking to Ben on her cell. Seeing Bowie with Garnet tonight, watching her mother take her father's hand and lead him away from the fire scene—he might have been a small child—has had its effect.

"He's my father, but I don't recognize him anymore, the man I was so mad at."

"He changed a lot while you were gone."

"And he's not going to get better, is he?"

"That's not usually the way it works."

"Stop trying to make me feel better."

"I'd like to make you feel better but—"

"You could do that, Ben. Make me feel better. You could come over here right now."

When he arrives the door is unlocked. Tommie's pajamas with their little dogs are tossed on the closet floor, and nothing else has taken their place.

❧

Back home on Friday, after school, Ben finds a cardboard box. It is not from Amazon but from his ex. Moira has put it on the floor squarely in front of his apartment door. It is neatly taped, and addressed using a permanent black marker, to "Ben Brown." He almost expects to see after it the not-so-honorific Moira recently bestowed on him, "Ben Brown, SOB." He even experiences a moment's trepidation before opening it. But there is no explosive device (that had turned out to be Moira herself). Inside is the depressing detritus of a failed relationship: his Aqua Velva Ice Blue, a toothbrush, a few more toiletries, his running shoes, the library book he was reading—a biography of Alexander Hamilton who was, by the way, no angel himself if anyone wants to know—and a pair of jeans, this last making him feel unutterably sad because they have been washed and folded with care. He prefers to believe this might have happened before he showed up and broke things off. But he knows it could well have been done after. For some people, all bets are not off when things go south.

It occurs to Ben that making life-altering decisions using a part of his body that is definitely not his brain, or his heart for that matter, might well not be in his best interests. Possibly, though he sincerely hopes it's not the case, his heart may not be involved here at all. He feels bad about Moira. Did he use her? Lead her on? After all, he didn't text her or leave a breakup message on her voice mail. He'd tried to be stand-up. However, she did not seem at all appreciative of this effort, using words he previously would have bet never passed her lips. Ben has run into Moira only once since. At The Cup. He knows she was not happy to see him, especially since he caught her looking less than her best—pale, tired, wearing sweaty exercise clothes from her evening Zumba class at the Y.

May

I've been smelling smoke for days.
Somewhere something's burning,
the air permeated with drifting ash
borne on the wind.

Somewhere the remains
of charred bridges smolder,
blackened, skeletal, no longer
spanning the torrent,

and on the other side,
if only I knew where to look,
you are waving
                waving
                    waving.

Bowie looks out his back door at the burnt-out hulk in the center of a large, blackened circle in which all vegetation has been incinerated. He is not a happy man. He closes the door and frowns at Remmy, who's sitting at the kitchen table drinking, slurping really, the surplus milk left in the bowl after finishing his third serving of Bowie's Cheerios.

"That is one big mess out there, Remmy. What are you going to do about it?"

"I was thinking about quitting smoking."

"Funny! My neighbors don't want to look at it. *I* don't want to look at it. Do you have any insurance?"

"Not really."

"Do you even have a license?"

"Of course. My suspension expired over a month ago."

"Suspension?"

"Just a misunderstanding. But I couldn't afford a lawyer."

"We have been friends for a long time, Remmy."

"You're going to tell me to get out, aren't you."

"No. I'm going to tell you to buy your own cereal. And milk. And suggest you stop being everybody's least favorite fuck-up."

Sometimes the Bowie of old makes an unexpected reappearance. This is one of those times.

Remmy makes a deal with a scrap-metal dealer in the city to haul away his car which puts a few bucks in his pocket. He tells Bowie he wants to use some of the money to buy his big sister a birthday present. He talks a reluctant Bowie into accompanying him.

"We're divorced, you know," says Bowie. "I don't have to buy her anything. Besides, she's using my house for her birthday party." (Sometimes Bowie forgets his intention to reconcile with his ex-wife. When he does, he refers to Garnet as *she* and *her*.)

"We are turning the page, Bowie," Remmy says. "You and me. Becoming better people. Together. A new leaf."

Remmy is now driving Bowie's car, his beautiful silvery-gray late model Lexus. He's managed this by promising to be Bowie's chauffeur, available whenever Bowie needs a ride.

"Where are we going?' Bowie asks him. "The mall?"

"We are going to the city. Second Chance Books. One thing I know about my sisters is that they love their books."

"Too bad some of that didn't rub off on you, Remmy."

"What? I love to read."

"You bet. The *Daily Racing Form*."

"You are one mean old man. I haven't bet on the horses since I got here."

"So what *are* you betting on? Sports? Baseball? Tennis? What?"

Right now, Second Chance Books is the only locally owned bookstore left in the area, housed in what had been a small brick shoe factory overlooking the river, one built in the early 1900s. It's now stuffed to the rafters with books of all kinds. No greeting cards for sale, no puzzles, T-shirts, or umbrellas featuring images of literary heroes, only books are found here.

"You're getting your sister a used book for her birthday?"

"Bowie, sit right here. Don't move until I come back."

Remmy wanders off to look for a birthday book, leaving Bowie in the store's reading space, a place defined by a worn maroon rug, some sagging but comfy upholstered chairs, and one battered ancient leather sofa onto which Bowie plunks, looking pretty ancient and battered himself. He is suddenly very sleepy and stretches out, closes his eyes, and falls asleep.

When Remmy comes back, a coffee table book featuring Katherine Hepburn and her leading men tucked under his arm, Bowie is no longer snoring, and one side of his face has gone strangely slack. When Remmy asks if he's okay, his protestations that he's fine are slurred and difficult to understand.

After Remmy's frantic call, Garnet and Colt reach the hospital only to run into Bowie in a wheelchair, being pushed by a nurse out of Emergency. They are headed toward the front entrance. Nurse and patient pause in front of Garnet and Colt before going outside and Bowie tells them Remmy awaits, having pulled the car up to the door. Declared okay for now, he's been told to see his doctor.

"Merely a little TIA," he says to Garnet. "A piffle. Nothing."

"A stroke, even a little stroke, is not nothing, Bowie," Garnet says.

In answer, he pulls out a cheroot from his breast pocket. They watch as he is helped into the car and Remmy gives him a light using his beautiful brushed-steel Zippo lighter, one possession he has never ever attempted to pawn.

In the confusion of the 911 call and the arrival of the EMS, Remmy has managed to walk out of the bookstore without paying for the oversized book now on the back seat. It would surprise no one if the thought of that cheers him immensely though he did not shoplift intentionally. He will probably (probably? who are we kidding) not be going back to make things right either.

"You trying to scare me to death?" he asks Bowie as he pulls away from the curb.

"Like I said, it's nothing. Can we go home now?"

"Yes. I think we've both had enough excitement for one day."

Back at the house Remmy and Bowie wind up sitting across from one another at the small kitchen table in the breakfast nook, playing checkers, trying to stay out of the way of the crazed party planners, who have only four more days to complete their work.

Bowie has just torn open a large bag of jalapeño tortilla chips which he offers to his opponent.

Remmy takes a handful. "King me!" he says.

They can hear Ben's and Tommie's and Meg's voices as the three put the finishing touches on the dining room.

"Kleenex flowers, *check*. Paper chain, *check*. We'll wait till Saturday morning to blow up the balloons, Meggie," Tommie is saying.

"I might have some company coming," Remmy says as they set the board up for another game. "Can he stay here?"

"I don't see why not," says Bowie. "Who is it?"

"My husband, Freddy," says Remmy. "Freddy D'Apolito."

"You're married?" Bowie says. "When did you get married?"

"January."

"*Huh*," says Bowie. "This is not the big city. We don't much like change."

"But I'm still the same."

"The problem is so are we."

When Bowie arrives to pick Vera up for the walk he requested earlier that morning, he delivers Remmy's news. It throws Garnet only briefly, as she begins to understand she's been looking at a picture for a long time not realizing that something important was missing.

"And when is Freddy arriving?" she asks as she hands over her leashed and haltered dog.

"On Thursday. From Las Vegas."

"Ruby is coming in on Thursday. Maybe we can pick them both up in one trip."

Vera is tugging, anxious to be on her way.

"Whatever," he calls back.

"Maybe this helps explain some of your father's behavior," she says later that day when she tells Colt what she has learned.

"Explains maybe but doesn't excuse," he says.

❧

On Thursday, to allow for traffic, Garnet picks Remmy up forty-five minutes before Ruby's flight is set to arrive. Freddy's is scheduled an hour later. They arrive at the airport early, only to find both flights delayed because of thunderstorms in Chicago. They sit down to wait in the café, Garnet with a latte and Remmy with a mocha macchiato, the extra whipped cream he requested drizzled with caramel. "Anything else you want to pile on top of that, little brother?"

"You don't know what you're missing."

"True in so many ways, I'm afraid," Garnet says, adding a packet of sugar to her coffee and stirring it with one of the skinny wooden sticks provided at the sugar and cream station. "Do you think we should tell them spoons were invented for just this purpose? Though I suppose that then adds to the plastics problem."

"Instead of decimating the forests?" Remmy says. "Are you sure you don't want to ask me anything, Garnet?"

"Like?"

"When did you realize you weren't straight, Remmy? Why weren't we invited to your wedding? Is it too late to give you and Freddy a wedding present, Remmy? Is cash acceptable?"

"Okay, okay, so tell me about Freddy."

"Oh, you'll see for yourself soon enough."

Garnet's sister will not be blindsided by Remmy's news or Freddy's arrival because Garnet texted her yesterday.

Thus, when Ruby's flight finally arrives, almost two hours late, Ruby hugs her brother, saying, "Remmy, I am so happy to see you. What's this about a wedding?"

Freddy's flight comes in twenty minutes later. Remmy's facade of composure had begun to develop cracks upon his arrival at the airport and the long wait has not helped matters.

"I'd kill for a cigarette," he says.

"Either of which would get us tossed posthaste out of this airport," Garnet says, but Remmy is already gone, having spotted Freddy walking toward them down the concourse. He drops his carry-on, kisses Remmy on both cheeks, and then sweeps him into an embrace.

Freddy is a bit of a revelation. He is a nice-looking man but not scarily handsome. Younger than Remmy but not unreasonably so; Garnet guesses maybe a decade. She notices that his wide wedding band looks like real yellow gold. And Remmy now sports its twin on his left hand for the first time since he came back to Haven. Freddy is polite. He drops a lot of French phrases into the conversation. He wears a beret, and not a green one; it is navy blue. He holds Remmy's hand as he speaks.

"Remmy has told me so much about you," he tells the sisters. "But his description has not done you justice. *Tres jolie. Vraiment!*"

Garnet catches Ruby starting to roll her eyes and pinches her hard on the arm. "*Ow!*" Ruby says. "Cut it out."

"So, Freddy, what is it you do?" asks Garnet.

"Oh, a little of this. A little of that. But mostly I play poker," Freddy says and grabs a large suitcase off the carousel.

"Freddy is very successful," Remmy says, coloring slightly each time he looks at his husband. "In fact, two casinos have banned him."

"I am cursed with a photographic memory," Freddy says.

"I play a little poker myself. Spit in the Ocean. Texas Hold'em, Omaha Hi-Lo," Ruby says.

This time it is Garnet who rolls her eyes. Freddy looks from one sister to the other. He seems enchanted.

"My husband likes older women," Remmy says.

"*Non*, we call them women of a certain age," Freddy protests.

"Well, he's certainly come to the right place," Ruby, who looks a little charmed herself, says.

They are by now in the parking lot. Remmy fits everything in the back of Garnet's SUV and they climb in. Remmy and Freddy in the backseat, Ruby up front with Garnet.

"Where to?" she says. "Anybody else hungry?"

They stop at Marie's, an old-fashioned, hole-in-the-wall family restaurant tucked away on a Haven side street and known for its homemade fruit pies, fish fries on Fridays, biscuits with sausage gravy every day, and a pretty good meatloaf. Everyone orders something different. When the food arrives, conversation ceases.

"I guess we were all a little peckish," Ruby says when coffee arrives and the dinner plates are cleared away in anticipation of pie and ice cream.

"Now, tell us your plans," Garnet says to the two men.

"Well, Freddy and I have spent more time apart than together—"

"The secret of our success," Freddy says.

"So Freddy's decided to take a couple weeks off."

"The cards have been very kind to me this year," says Freddy.

Along with the check which she places on the table, their waitress puts a cupcake with a lit little candle stuck in it in front of Garnet.

She then smiles at Freddy, who takes the check before anyone else can react.

"A little bird told me someone's birthday is coming up."

"Just a little *merci* for picking me up," he says.

"Well, all right, thank you very much," Garnet says. "But Ruby and I will be leaving the gratuity."

Predictably, the two sisters between them come up with their preferred exorbitant cash tip.

Garnet drops Remmy and Freddy off at Bowie's and continues home with Ruby. Colt, feet up on the coffee table, a hopeful Vera parked nearby, is eating a Hungry Man Salisbury steak dinner when she arrives, but at the sight of Ruby entering the room, he leaps up and gives her a hug.

"We should have come by and picked you up," says Garnet. "We ate at Marie's."

"There are leftovers?"

"No leftovers, I'm afraid," says Garnet.

Vera, taking her cue from Colt's expression, looks desolate, but perks up when he sets the remains of his dinner down on the floor for her.

"Colt, you are contributing to canine obesity."

"It's okay, we spent a half hour after I got home playing fetch with the tennis ball in the backyard."

"Let me guess, you threw the ball, chased after the ball and retrieved the ball. Vera watched with great interest."

"Pretty, much. Yeah."

Garnet sighs. "At any rate, you'll like your father's spouse."

"I can't tell you how deeply weird this all seems," Colt says.

"And you will not recognize the man you think you know when Freddy is around," says Garnet.

"I believe he's fallen in love for the first time in his life," Ruby adds.

"Just shoot me. Please," says Colt.

"You'll get used to it; Freddy's here for the month."

"What do you think he's after?" Colt asks. "Remmy has no assets I'm aware of."

"My nephew, a cynic. Who knew?" says Garnet. "If anything, I believe Freddy is supporting Remmy."

"Is it not possible that true love has found two deeply flawed, as are we all I might add, individuals?" Ruby says, giving her nephew a look.

"Not likely," Colt mumbles.

Vera has tipped over and fallen asleep, the conversation around her lacking any mention of her name, and therefore of no interest to her. She is a practical sort of dog.

The sisters reject an early bedtime to stay up and once again watch Fitzwilliam Darcy work his misogynist magic on Elizabeth Bennet. Ruby and Garnet are not big fans of the Hallmark channel's offerings, but they both love things British, and occasionally must admit to themselves that most of what they watch on the BBC could be fairly termed the Hallmark Channel's English cousin. However, they wind up doing more catching up than viewing tonight, only pausing their conversation, one or the other, or both together, to recite whole chunks of dialogue along with the characters. The literary version of karaoke, Garnet calls it.

"So how are Harold's spirits? Chronic illness is so hard."

"He's surprisingly sanguine. I guess once you accept that you really have no future, living in and for the moment actually becomes possible."

"You know I could come and help."

"Right now, things are stable. We have the support we need. And we so lucked out when we hired Agata. But when the time comes, don't worry, I will ask."

❧

Bowie sticks out his hand. Freddy takes it and they shake hands.

"Pleased to meet you."

"*Moi aussi,*" Freddy replies.

Bowie has many faults. He knows this because over the years Garnet has taken the time to meticulously point them out. However, intolerance is a notable exception, something that for a long time gave Garnet hope that the two of them might yet stumble into a way to be together. He has never been able to figure out what the big deal is. You're a man, maybe you're a man in a woman's body, maybe you love a woman, or you love a man. You are a woman, or you are a woman in a man's body. You love a man; maybe you love another woman. Maybe you decide you are not quite either. Nothing is simple. Why should love, sex, gender be otherwise? Love is love. Bowie believes the Almighty is much more concerned about the myriad ways we hate and hurt one another and does not give a rat's ass which bathroom (or pronoun) we deign to use. However, Freddy here? What's with Freddy here? Is he from France?

"Where you from?" Bowie asks. "You French?"

"*Non.* I am what you might call a Francophile."

Bowie is not impressed. For one thing that word is one he used to know, though the meaning eludes him right this second. He decides to be sympathetic.

"I'm so sorry."

Freddy looks at Bowie strangely.

"We've had a very long day, Bowie," Remmy says. "I think we're going to turn in."

"Old guy is losing it, isn't he?" Freddy says as they climb the stairs, Remmy for once using the more conventional indoor method of ascension.

When they reach the attic, Remington turns and kisses Freddy on the mouth.

"I missed you, *cher,*" Freddy says.

Tommie has not moved in with Ben. She wants to make that clear. Sure, some of her belongings can be found here. Those socks on the floor over there, for example, hers; also a few lacy items she'd handwashed and left to drip dry in the shower, which may or may not have slipped her mind and seem to be freaking him out—when did Ben turn into such a neatnik? The four-pack of out-of-date Greek yogurt in the fridge?—*Hey, it's yogurt, it can't go bad.* What is it with his obsession with *use by* dates? She will get around to eating it. Eventually. Maybe. Besides, Mister I'd-rather-take-a-pill-than-eat-real-food could use a natural source of calcium for a change himself. Okay, that *was* kind of mean, and sure, she spends the occasional night here. However, she has her own place if anyone's interested. And the rent is paid up.

Right now she's looking for some wrapping paper and tape. Garnet's birthday is tomorrow and they, she and Ben together, have assembled—well maybe he did most of the assembling—the perfect gift. After all, it was her idea initially, wasn't it? That ought to count for something. And she *is* the one wrapping it. If she can find some paper.

"Ben, where's the wrapping paper? I need some birthday paper."

"Why would I have paper? You were the one who said you'd wrap it. I figured you knew that would involve paper of some sort. You'll find Scotch Tape in my top desk drawer."

Yes, his desk, its drawers with their white plastic rectangular organizers, a place for every single fricking thing—paperclips, staples, rubber bands, pencils—and every single fricking thing in its place. Though she hasn't bothered to snoop, he probably has a special container for the condoms he takes out of a dresser drawer on those increasingly less frequent occasions they have sex. She would no longer call it making love.

"Who doesn't have wrapping paper?"

"Me? And, no, I am not going out at ten o'clock in the rain to look for what you should have picked up days, or at least *a* day, ago."

"If that's the way you feel, I'm leaving. I am going home, a place where I know there are at least three kinds of birthday paper to choose from."

"Hope you'll be able to find it in the chaos," Ben says.

"*Chaos?* Because I prefer to live my life rather than spend it cleaning?"

"No danger of that, is there?"

"Just so you know, I won't be coming back tonight! By the way, Ben, your presence is no longer required tomorrow."

Ben says, "Hold on just a minute."

Tommie waits for the apology she knows is coming and the offer to run out and get some paper. Maybe she should ask him to pick up a card too?

He comes back into the room holding a bulging black plastic trash bag.

"What is that?" Tommie asks.

"Your stuff, including the goddamn yogurt," he says, leaning over to pick up a pair of her socks and adding them to the bag.

"Are you crazy?"

"Apparently I was, but I'm feeling better by the minute," Ben says.

❧

Though it's Friday night, Colt has told Garnet not to expect them for dinner; he and Meg will be eating with Rain and Eddie tonight. This is at least partially true. However, the party is tomorrow and Colt's program for the evening also includes making Garnet's birthday cake here at Rain's. Even though the party itself is no longer a surprise, the cake, a dark chocolate confection made using chocolate pudding, might at least end up providing a bit of one. It's going to have chocolate frosting containing pieces of five smashed Heath bars. There were going to be six, but he and Meg have split one, judging the quality adequate for their purpose. His daughter had been made responsible for all measuring of ingredients after Colt's propensity for creativity in this area was deemed the cause of problems in their initial attempt. However, Colt *was* judged competent enough to demolish the frozen candy bars, securely encased in a gallon Ziploc, on the front walk, using a mallet belonging to Eddie.

Rain has just finished upending the cooled cake from its allegedly stick-free pan, a reputation that has miraculously turned out to be deserved, and Meg is now doing the actual frosting while fulsomely admiring the Himalayas of swirls and peaks she is creating.

"I believe it's customary for the artist to give others an opportunity to praise her work," Rain says, "rather than ensuring no one else can get a word in edgewise."

"But it is my best work ever. *Soooo* beautiful," Meg says. "Right, Daddy?"

"I am not going to be put in the middle here," Colt answers, then adds, "but, yes. Yes, I believe it is."

Rain looks heavenward—or at least at the ceiling—as if addressing some higher power (that she, like Garnet, does not believe in), *Just see what I have to put up with?*

Meanwhile Eddie, who worked a double shift earlier in the week to have this night off, is using a spatula to scrape the last remnants of batter from the mixing bowl, licking the same.

"That, moreover, *that* is disgusting," Rain says.

"You're not supposed to eat raw batter," says Meg, "because of salmonella."

"Sam who?" says Eddie, and he and Colt crack up.

As Meg finishes frosting the cake, Rain goes to the cupboard and brings back a large bag of chocolate kisses.

"I thought instead of all that fire, we could do seventy kisses with a candle in the middle for Garnet to blow out."

However, once they finish unwrapping all the pieces, it turns out there are only sixty-three kisses in the bag.

"It's not like Garnet is going to be counting," says Colt.

"But I counted these out last night," says Rain, fixing Eddie in her sights.

"*What?*" he says, his voice filled with wounded innocence.

"My God," says Rain. "It's true. I am the only adult in attendance here."

"What did you get your aunt, Colt?" Eddie asks, trying to steer the conversation away from his alleged kiss-napping.

"Meg and I bought Garnet a new journal."

"It has a violet leather cover," says Meg. "And we are taking turns writing reasons we are grateful for Garnet. So far, we have thirty-three."

"Wow!" says Eddie. "Even for Rain, who I am crazy about by the way, I could think of maybe twenty, tops."

"Maybe?" Rain says. "Maybe?"

❧

Garnet's birthday begins with a windy thunderstorm at five a.m. It's been raining all night. She takes Vera out, trying to shelter herself and some of her dog under Bowie's big umbrella. She stands, holding the leash, next to an ancient lilac bush that's surprised her some years with blooms on her birthday. Not this spring. The cold weather has left her favorite flowers still tightly budded. Vera, however, seems to be enjoying herself, sniffing here, squatting briefly there, repeating two or three, wait, four times, oblivious of the tantrum mother nature is throwing. The two return damply to the house, only one thoroughly pleased with herself and her performance.

Colt comes downstairs early, just as Garnet is finishing up the day's writing. She has been working on a kind of birthday poem, although it does not yet mention the actual word a single time, and she thinks she may at last have finished it. Vera, despite having been rubbed vigorously with an oversized beach towel when they came in, leaves a large damp spot on the floor when she gets up to greet him.

"Smells like wet dog around here," Colt says. "What are we writing about today, auntie? Could it be our party?"

Garnet has not chosen to enlighten her nephew about any poetic direction her writing has taken.

"Don't you mock me on my birthday."

"I would never—"

"Oh, *shush*."

"Seriously, you must wind up writing the same thing every day. Got up. Got dressed. Took the dog out. Had breakfast with my esteemed nephew."

"Yes and no," Garnet says, getting up to put her book away. "Yes and no."

Ruby wanders down around eight.

"Is my niece up yet?" Garnet asks.

"I believe so," Ruby says.

She and Meg are bunking together since it is Meg's weekend with her dad. Ruby pours herself some coffee, adding half-and-half until it resembles palely tinted milk. Then, because she has effectively erased the adjective "hot" from "hot coffee," she has to microwave it. "Dearest," Garnet says, "do you enjoy making such a simple task so complicated?"

"Watch it, or even at this late hour you may yet wind up with a delivery of a giant hissing espresso machine from Amazon for your birthday."

"Giving me something you really want—a classic case of narcissistic gift-giving."

"Not a case, dearest. Just one. What time does this gala start?"

"Colt will come back for us around noon."

Their nephew has already left for Bowie's where he and Rain and Tommie are attending to last-minute details.

"What are we to wear?"

"Well, Ruby, I can only tell you it is not clothing optional."

"Drat," says Ruby, as Meg, who makes a practice of eavesdropping on her aunts' conversations whenever possible, comes into the room.

"Then whatever will Vera wear?" Meg says.

"Vera is coming with us?" Ruby asks. "Do you think that's a good idea, Garnet?"

"It's my birthday, and if I must have a party, then I get to choose my guests. And, no, it is not a good idea. It may turn out to be very disruptive."

"Ah, not-so-passive aggression rearing its prickly head once again," Ruby says.

"Meg," Garnet says, "I am appointing you chief dog groomer and kerchief-chooser. We want Vera looking her most fetching."

"You made a pun, auntie," Meg says.

"I guess I did, didn't I," says Garnet. "Good for me."

"And I will be most happy to assist you, Meggie," Ruby says.

Bowie's house is a flurry of activity. Rain has brought the cake. The pizza has been ordered. Tommie has pinned Meg's seventy Kleenex flowers onto the sheer panels on the two floor-to-ceiling windows in the dining room. Seventy purple links of paper chain have been threaded through the chandelier, the two ends left to hang down and touch the table. And all seventy lavender balloons have been filled with helium and allowed to drift up to the ten-foot-high ceiling, the slightest movement of air setting seventy silvery strings swaying. A bouquet of real flowers is in the center of the table—lilacs someone forced which Remmy and Freddy found, bought, and arranged. A pile of wrapped presents fills one end.

"Well," Rain says to Colt, "your aunt didn't want a party. She asked there be no presents. Yet here we are."

"She asked for my chocolate cake, and she's getting that," says Colt.

"So, one out of three?"

"One out of three is not nothing."

"Speaking of cake, did you put it in a Vera-proof place?"

"It's in the butler's pantry, the pocket door shut, on a top shelf behind a closed cupboard door."

"All I know is we'll have to suspend the party and take Vera to have her stomach pumped if she gets into it."

"Oh, ye of little faith," Colt says.

It is still raining hard outside, though the thunderstorms themselves have moved on.

Colt arrives back at Garnet's to take the three, no four, ladies to the party. Garnet is ready and waiting. She looks lovely, wearing a lilac sweater and slacks, figuring one way or another, if only in hue, her favorite flower will attend her birthday party. Vera, Meg, and Ruby enter the parlor. Vera has been brushed, perfumed with Ruby's Georgio, and is wearing a Hermès scarf knotted jauntily around her neck.

"Oh, come on, Ruby," says Garnet, "your precious scarf?"

"I think it looks divine."

"You've never called anything divine in your life."

"Maybe it's time."

"If somebody swipes it, don't come running to me."

"You're expecting felons? Exactly what kind of people are coming to this party, Garnet?"

"Very funny."

Meg listens, rapt; you don't have to be psychic to see why she wants a sister of her own.

"No squabbling," Colt says and ushers them, one by one, out to Bowie's car, holding the umbrella over each as they leave the back door and enter the car. It's immediately obvious to all that Vera is not going to fit, so Colt leaves her. He will, of course, return after dropping his passengers at Bowie's but Vera does not know that and she is not pleased. She woofles plaintively as he closes the back door. The car's wipers beat wildly, barely keeping up with the deluge falling from the heavens, everyone happy they're only going down the street.

"You didn't think to request an ark as one of your gifts, old girl, did you?" Ruby asks Garnet.

Colt pulls into the driveway and parks under the shelter of the porte cochere.

"I just love old houses," Ruby says to Garnet, who only reluctantly admits to envying her ex's covered entrance. Umbrella-less, they exit the car and go inside.

"Don't start without me," Colt says. "I'll only be a few minutes."

He switches vehicles, figuring Bowie would appreciate neither the cloud of shed hair that Vera leaves in her wake, nor the marks her nails would leave on his leather upholstery. He backs his truck out of the driveway, heading down the street to retrieve the guest he left behind.

As she walks in the door, Freddy hands Garnet a glass of bubbly. "*Salud!*" he says.

"What am I drinking?" Garnet asks.

"Prosecco, elixir of the gods, for the birthday goddess."

"Aren't you glad you asked," Ruby says.

Meg seats Garnet in the parlor in what Garnet knows Bowie must consider *his* chair. He takes her usurpation remarkably well. She thinks the snifter of Drambuie he is holding may have something to do with it. The others are milling about. Franny is ladling non-alcoholic cranberry-ginger ale out of a borrowed punch bowl into plastic cups of which so far only Meg has availed herself, Bowie having opened his liquor cabinet to the adult assembly. Garnet catches sight of her neighbor talking to Sylvie. *What? George here? Why?* (Though Sylvie looks pleased to see him.) Remmy and Freddy are drinking beer and laughing. Freddy would say—and give him time, later he no doubt will—that the room brims with *bonhomie.* Rain and Tommie pull two side chairs up on either side of Garnet and sit down.

"Ladies-in-waiting! I feel like royalty," Garnet says.

"The pizza is on the way, Mom," Tommie says, holding her own glass of prosecco.

"Good, I'm starving."

"We are going to eat first, then open presents," says Tommie.

Garnet sighs.

Rain says, "I know. No one listens to me either."

"Come on, girl," Colt says as he re-enters the house. "Time to go."

Vera regards him with studied disinterest.

"Come. No sulking. *Now!*"

Vera sighs loudly and places her head on her paws and closes her eyes.

"Okay. You made your point. *Up*."

Vera turns her head and looks away.

The dog weighs a petite one hundred fifteen very stubborn pounds. No way can he pick her up, or drag her out to his truck. Moreover, she would never brook such disrespect. If he somehow succeeded in either endeavor, she'd never forgive him. He has no choice. It's bribery or stay here.

First, she turns up her nose—literally—at an offered handful of small five-calorie treats with which Garnet rewards Vera in a mostly successful effort to retain her dog's girlish figure. A cheese slice, generally a fail-safe offering, is also ignored. Colt resorts to rooting through the refrigerator until he comes across two slices of bacon left over from breakfast. Vera perks up and grudgingly gets to her feet. Colt, no dummy, gives her half of one slice and saves the rest, using torn-off pieces to coax her out the back door and into the pickup.

Back at Bowie's, Vera bounds into the house trailing her leash, heading straight for Garnet. Colt follows unhappily after.

"Did you miss me?" Garnet asks the dog.

"We thought you'd gotten lost," Rain says to Colt.

"We hurt the princess's feelings. She retaliated by being most uncooperative."

"Bacon—" Garnet begins.

"And how do you think I got her into the truck?"

"A little testy, aren't we?" Tommie says.

Remmy enters the room. "Lunch is served," he announces.

On the kitchen table and counter, arrayed in the boxes in which they arrived, are a fruit pizza, a breakfast pizza, two thin-crust pepperoni pizzas, and a vegetarian, though not vegan, pizza. All extra-large.

Freddy, wearing another beret today, a black one, is handing out plates.

"Help yourselves, *mes amis*."

Colt looks at Rain.

"Do you think he can really speak French?"

"I've also heard snippet or two of Italian. I bet he swears in Spanish."

"Just think, a citizen of the world here among the lowly suburban bourgeoisie," he says.

"Or bullshit artist?" says Rain, the single malt Scotch she's sipping possibly catching up with her.

"*Mommy!*" Meg says.

"I didn't see you over there, sweetheart," Rain says.

Colt and Rain find themselves together at the end of the pizza line.

"Great party, nice job," Colt says.

"Likewise," says Rain.

Garnet has moved into the dining room and is now seated at the head of the table. Vera has been lured into the kitchen by the sound of kibble being poured into her dish. However, as reigning champion of the ten-second inhale, the dog is soon back, comfortably situated on the floor under the table, muzzle resting on Garnet's foot, while Meg, having appointed herself her aunt's guardian angel, has left to get her pizza.

"Your favorite," Meg says, placing in front of Garnet one of the colorful paper plates she herself picked out at the Dollar Store, its riot of multicolored spring flowers obscured by two large pepperoni-studded slices. In the other hand, Meg carries her own plate with a piece each of fruit and vegetarian. She sits down at Garnet's left.

"Happy birthday, auntie!" she says, secreting a strawberry and a pineapple chunk in her hand.

"I can see what you're doing, Meg."

"What?" says Meg, not very surreptitiously handing the evidence to Vera, who now has her chin on Meg's knee. "I'm not doing anything. What happened to 'innocent until proven guilty'?"

She holds up her now empty, though sticky, hand.

"Is it possible," says Garnet, "that we have spawned a future defense attorney? Or possibly a criminal lawyer?"

"You're waiting for someone to ask what the difference is, aren't you?" Bowie, overhearing, says.

But, taking no offense, he refills her wine glass, then plunks himself down in the chair to her right.

"Yes, happy birthday, my dear," he says.

Garnet shakes her head.

Though it is now only one o'clock in the afternoon, everyone over ten years old is a little drunk. Their pizza has arrived in the nick of time, she thinks.

"A toast. A toast," says Remmy.

"*Hear, hear!*" says Freddy.

"To Garnet," everyone shouts, Freddy adding *Bravo!*

"Thank you very much," says Garnet. "Now I suggest everyone get some food in their stomachs."

Five very large pizzas prove to be just enough for the assembly. Then it's time for the cake which Colt takes down from its secure location, and after lighting the single candle in its center, bears into the dining room and sets it down before Garnet.

"Oh, just look at that," she sighs. "Thank you, Colt."

"Don't forget to make a wish," Meg says.

Garnet closes her eyes briefly, looks up, and blows. The flame goes out and everyone cheers.

"*Bravo, bravissimo!*" cries Freddy again.

The birthday song follows. There is enough alcohol still present in the assembled partygoers that various attempts at harmony are attempted, resulting in a full-throated howl-along from Vera.

"Thank you, all. I was very afraid I was going to have to blow out seventy candles. My, that's a lot of chocolate kisses."

Garnet cuts the cake and Meg plates and passes the pieces until everyone has one.

"Colt, you could start an online baking business and retire early," Freddy says. "This is one amazing *gateaux*."

"*Gat*-what?" says Bowie, who then stands and says, "I have an announcement."

Ruby, who is sitting next to him, pulls him back into his seat.

"Not now, old man, save your speech until later. Right now, we have to open presents."

"You have never liked me, Ruby. Never."

"I liked you fine until you cheated on my sister with that strumpet."

"What's a strumpet?" Meg asks. "Is it a musical instrument?"

Then she giggles.

"Good grief," says Garnet. "Please, yes, bring on the gifts."

First up, Meg and Colt read from Garnet's new journal. Meg begins, *Who doesn't love their auntie?*

Colt continues. *She had the good sense to keep Vera, even after she dug a crater the size of a Volkswagen in her backyard in the time it took Garnet to answer the door and tell the Jehovah's Witnesses she was an atheist and also perfectly okay with going to hell.*

They take turns passing the book back and forth, reading what they've written in Meg's beautiful cursive and Colt's awkward left-handed script. This makes Garnet cry.

And she gives me books for my birthday and Christmas and Valentine's Day and sometimes just because it's Thursday.

Me, too.

She dresses up as a different Star Wars character every Halloween, even though she's never seen any of the movies.

She gives excellent treats to trick or treaters—Snickers, Reese's, Twix. No granola bars or snack bags of carrots, no kale chips. Ever.

She says some things are worth the trouble. The trick is knowing which ones.

When they finish, Meg presents Garnet with the notebook.

"And it's purple," Meg says.

Garnet hugs her niece.

"Please don't cry again," says Meg.

"I am not crying. I'm allergic."

"But you don't have allergies, auntie."

"Today I have allergies."

Garnet's other gifts include a bottle of perfume from Ruby.

"Why, I haven't worn Chanel since college. I'd forgotten how much I loved it," she tells her sister.

Her brother presents Garnet with a large, flashily wrapped gift, the shiny paper topped by an exploding fright wig of violet ribbon. "Freddy wrapped it," he says.

"Thank you, Freddy," says Garnet.

"*Oooh!* Don't throw that out," says Meg. "I might need it for a project."

Garnet opens the gift carefully, handing paper and ribbon over to Meg. She sees the photo of Katherine Hepburn and Spencer Tracy in *Adam's Rib* on the cover of the outsize book, then smiles up at her brother.

"It's perfect," she says.

George gives her a card on which he has written that this very afternoon, despite the rain, a pink dogwood has been planted in Garnet's side yard. They'd talked about her plan to do this over the fence last fall. Garnet has not yet gotten around to it. But George remembered.

Rain has painted a lovely small watercolor of Garnet's house.

"That used to be my house, too, you know," Bowie says in a grumpy voice.

And Tommie? (Who knew she could crochet?) She presents Garnet with a gorgeous throw, its granny squares the vivid colors of stained glass.

"This is from Ben and me."

"Where is Ben?" Garnet asks.

"He said to tell you happy birthday."

"But where is he?"

"We're not speaking. We had a little tiff last night and I told him he wasn't welcome."

"Oh, Tommie," Garnet says.

Tommie folds her arms and frowns at her mother, looking approximately five years younger than the actual ten-year-old also present.

"You both made this?"

"Well." Tommie now looks very uncomfortable. "Ben actually crocheted all the squares and sewed them together. I wrapped the box."

Garnet is speechless, at a loss for any coherent reaction. Her daughter scowls at her.

Last, there is a miniature pearl-handled pistol wrapped in more shiny silver paper with a tag saying it's from Freddy. Garnet appears flummoxed. "I don't know what to say."

"It's not a *real* gun," says Remmy, taking it from her. "It's a candle lighter."

He helpfully pulls the trigger repeatedly until a tiny flame shoots out of the muzzle, licking the end of the paper chain resting on the table. The flame begins a quick ascent, traveling up toward the chandelier as people scream, the smoke alarm squeals, and Vera again begins to bark wildly.

The balloons nearest the light fixture begin to pop. Freddy grabs Meg's punch glass and tosses pink ginger ale onto the flames. George follows with his Bud Light. Then Colt returns with the small kitchen fire extinguisher and tragedy is averted.

Garnet sighs. "This birthday has turned out to be so much better than I imagined. Shall we start mopping up the mess?"

"No need," says Rain. "Let's remove anything that's a keeper, grab the four corners of this tablecloth and dump the contents in the trash."

"Save my lilacs," Garnet says.

Colt carefully cuts what's left of the paper chain from the chandelier and lets it fall as the Kleenex flowers nod in the breeze moving the sheers at windows opened to clear the smoke.

"What was it you wanted to say earlier, Bowie?" Ruby asks.

Bowie walks over to Garnet and takes her hand. "I have forgiven you, my dear. I am ready to move back to our home and resume our life together as husband and wife. Today, if you wish."

"Ummmm," Garnet says, turning away. "Somebody, help me out here. Please."

Bowie, looking bereft, drops his ex-wife's hand.

George gives the sisters a lift home. Vera commands the front seat, a dowager looking imperiously ahead, front paws on the car floor, rear snowily overflowing the bucket seat. The two women sit in the back, gifts and lilacs taking up the space between them. It is almost four o'clock. The rain has at last ended and a wan sun has emerged, lighting up the heavily budded dogwood.

"How did you know where to plant it?" Garnet asks.

"You told me last fall where you were going to put it."

"And you didn't forget. Thank you, George."

He blushes and says, "You're welcome."

How convenient, how easy, how right, how pleased everyone would be if she and this man became a couple. *Not gonna happen*, she thinks. And once again Jake, Bowie's ex-partner, slips into her thoughts. She's begun to admit to herself that it was not only simple revenge that prompted her actions three years ago.

Back in the house, Garnet trims the ends of the lilacs and arranges them in the vase she's rinsed and filled with fresh water. Blowing gently, she has been able to dislodge and disperse most of the ash that settled on the flowers.

Ruby watches, then says, "I'm so sorry I asked Bowie to speak up. I thought maybe he wanted to, I don't know…?"

"Deliver a birthday eulogy?"

"And then he didn't even get mad."

"He started to cry."

"Yes, and we left him there in his chair, weeping. I feel like such a bad person."

"Don't be so hard on yourself, Ruby. I handed him some Kleenex before we left. He's probably forgotten all about it by now. His powers of concentration are not what they used to be."

"I may be bad but you, Garnet, are a horrible person."

"But you knew that already, didn't you?"

"I may have had an inkling."

❧

After Garnet and Ruby leave for home, Freddy calls out to Remmy, "Anybody feel like going bowling?"

Freddy is himself unpinning Kleenex flowers from the curtains as Meg and Rain polish the dining room table, the only evidence of conflagration a single sooty patch on the ceiling above the chandelier.

Bowie, in his recliner, perks up. "It's been years since I was bowling." Then he blows his nose. "I could have sworn she'd accept my offer."

"You know the saying, Bowie," Freddy says. "Can't live with 'em, can't live without 'em. Instead come with us."

Meg turns to her mother. "Who's 'them'?"

"What's more important, Meggie, is to consider the source," says Rain. "What you just heard is the sound of the patriarchy talking."

"What's the opposite of patriarchy?" asks Meg.

"Us," says her mother. "We are the opposite."

Finished, Meg goes into the other room and hugs her uncle Bowie.

"I love you, anyway," she says.

"I'll remember that, my dear. Thank you."

Bowie gets up and goes out to the kitchen. "Colt," he says, "how about you go down to the basement and fetch my bowling ball and shoes."

"I would find them where?"

"You can't miss them. They're in a purple athletic bag."

"What is it with this family and purple?" Colt says, drying his hands with an already very wet dish towel.

"It was my favorite color first," Bowie says.

Colt finds the bag on a metal shelving unit, one of several that line the far wall of the cellar. The leather handles have pretty much disintegrated and the bag itself, faded to a violet-tinged gray, is covered with dust and cobwebs. But when he opens it, he finds the ball with its purple marbling looking brand new, as do the matching purple bowling shoes. He has to cradle the whole mess in his arms to bring it upstairs which means he, too, is dusty and cobwebbed by the time he sets it down in front of Bowie.

"Myself, I would have cleaned it off before bringing it up here," says Bowie.

Colt mutters something under his breath.

"Speak up, young man," Bowie says. "You young people need to stop mumbling and learn to speak clearly."

"I can bring it back downstairs and you can go get it yourself," Colt says.

"I can't understand a word he's saying," Bowie says to Remmy, who is now patting Colt on the shoulder with one hand and offering him a cold beer with the other.

"Call it a day, Colt," Freddy says. "We can finish up."

"That's imported beer there; I was saving it for myself," Bowie says, replicating in both pitch and volume the sound of Vera's whine.

Colt and Meg, home again, come in the back door into the kitchen.

"Did you bring my cake?" Garnet asks.

"There was not even a smidgen left. Not a crumb," says Colt.

"Wait," says Meg. "What have we here? I believe there may be a single piece left for the birthday girl."

"Where did you…?" Colt says.

"When Garnet was cutting the cake, I put a piece aside."

"No wonder I love you best," Garnet says to her niece.

At the bowling alley, the last one remaining in the county, the neon sign with its partly burned-out tubing, proclaims *The Lucky trike!* They have no trouble finding a spot in the pitted moonscape of a parking lot. Once inside, while Freddy and Remmy rent shoes, Bowie laces up his thirty-year-old pair—they fit just fine—and places the ball on the rack. Remmy returns first.

"Those shoes shout bowling team, Bowie. I'd love to have

seen your shirts. What was the name of your team?" Remmy says.

"Bunch of public defenders and defense attorneys. We called ourselves 'The Purple Pros.' Funny thing was, nobody else ever got it."

"Got what?" Remmy asks.

"You're just kidding," says Freddy. "Aren't you, Remmy?"

Bowie tells everyone he meets for the next week how he bowled three hundred. He does not mention it took adding up the scores from his four games to do it. Remmy and Freddy also stay mum which further endears them to Bowie, who by the end of that evening seems to have made peace with the fact that Garnet is never going to accept his proposal of reconciliation.

"I feel sorry for her, you know," he says as they are leaving the alley.

"Why is that?" Freddy asks.

"All that anger," he says. "Nowhere to put it."

❧

And in the way the universe operates, that is to say inscrutably, the Monday after her party Garnet takes her sister to the airport, a small to medium one in which it is entirely possible to walk—a long walk, but nevertheless—from one end to the other. She blows Ruby a kiss as she enters the security line.

Then, as she turns toward the exit to return to the parking garage, she hears, "Why, hello, Garnet."

It's Bowie's partner, rather, ex-partner.

"Jake."

"Was that your sister I just saw?"

"She's going home."

"Nice visit?"

"Very nice. What are you doing here?"

"I had to have back surgery in February—I'm fine now. Lily has come up a couple times from South Carolina to give me a hand. She's headed home today."

"I didn't know. When did she move?"

"She got married down there last fall. Nice guy. I like him."

Garnet wants to ask if the nice guy was already married when Lily met him but decides, though she is a snot for having the thought, she is not yet snot enough to voice the thought aloud. Sometimes she wonders what it would be like to have access to an alternate universe where our better selves still abided in the garden, every decision the right one, our behavior reliably admirable. Although she bets such enviable beings would themselves miss the fallen aspect we represent, feeling its absence like the sensation of a phantom limb.

"So, you're doing okay?"

"Better than I was. Back at work part-time but thinking about retiring. Still not driving."

"How are you getting home?"

"Lily used one of those ride apps on her phone to get us here. She showed me how to do it, and I was about to order my ride home."

"I'd be happy to drop you," Garnet says, detecting the slightest *frisson* of something in the pit of her stomach. Could it be butterflies?

In the incestuous manner of small towns, Jake lives three streets over from Garnet, in the beautiful Greek Revival in which he grew up, scion of a wealthy family, his father succeeding his grandfather as president of the local bank. The other side of that coin being that, mystifyingly, despite their proximity Jake and Garnet, or Bowie for that matter, seldom run into each other, which in Bowie's case is probably just as well. Garnet still remembers grade school recesses, dazzled by the big kids, watching Jake, fifth grader to her second, on the playground, chanting under her breath with his friends, "Red Rover, Red Rover, send Jake over."

"Actually, yes, I'd appreciate a lift," Jake says. "This is a new phone; I'm beginning to think someone confused smart with complicated. I was not looking forward to fooling with it."

"I know. I don't have any desire to text, take pictures, shoot video, watch films, listen to music, read books, or play games on my phone. Mostly, I just want to be able to make a call and then talk to the person I called."

"Do you think it's age that makes us such stick-in-the-muds?" Jake says.

"Not for sissies, is it."

"Bette Davis said that."

"Are you sure?" Garnet says. "I'm pretty positive that story is apocryphal."

"We could always ask our phones," Jake says, pauses, then adds, "How would you like to have lunch with me, Garnet, before we head home? An interesting vocabulary is hard to resist. It's been a while since I had a conversation of substance with anyone."

"I'd like that very much."

The new airport hotel has a restaurant that's gotten great reviews in the village's weekly newspaper, though Garnet admits she cannot remember it giving a bad review to any local business ever. They drive there, but wind up choosing a booth in the warmly lit café, rather than eating in a cold-looking, empty formal dining room. They sit across from one another, feeling a little awkward. Though of course, Garnet thinks, there's absolutely no reason to feel that way, is there? Finished, they linger, letting the waitress refill their coffee cups. Over the course of lunch, Garnet's hands develop an almost imperceptible tremor, one that she is not at all worried might mark the beginning of Parkinson's. She places them when not in use in her lap, one hand over the other.

After the check is placed on the table and they've argued amiably over who pays what, Garnet gives in, but only after Jake points out how much she's saving him by driving him home. He says, "A few years ago you asked me a question, Garnet. I want you to know that today, my answer would be a different one."

The hotel's pool with its grotto and waterfall is deserted (it is, after all, two p.m. on a workday). Garnet knows this because their room, with its small private patio beyond its French doors, overlooks the pool, a view she enjoys for the time it takes Jake to close the filmy inner drapes. Garnet has not spent an afternoon in a hotel room with a man to whom she is not married in many years. She expected never again to spend time thus, especially at this point in her life. Moreover, she cannot blame the lapse on alcohol. They'd had milkshakes and cheeseburgers.

Jake has had back surgery. Limber is no longer part of his vocabulary. It's been twenty years since Garnet has had the hormonal advantages estrogen lends sex. Yet, despite having lived as long as they have, or maybe because of it, there is much they can still do to please each other. They take their time. There is no reason to hurry. Some might think that one or both would be reluctant to share a naked, aging body in the ambient afternoon light that fills the room despite the drawn drapes, but they would be mistaken.

When Garnet says they need to think about getting back, Jake smiles up at her. "I wish we'd done this years ago, the first time you brought it up."

"Ah, but my intentions were not pure then. I wanted to hurt Bowie the way he hurt me."

"And now?"

"We're not hurting anyone, are we?"

"We are not."

That night Garnet lies awake in the dark for a long time. Jake said nothing about calling her when she dropped him off. But she is not sixteen and this afternoon was not a date. What's more, she's not sure she wants to see him again. The afternoon served to answer a question she's had for a long time and that in itself may be enough, more than enough. Besides, though Lily is in South Carolina, she'd still pose a problem difficult for the two of them to surmount were anything to come of this. It was a lovely afternoon, maybe the best birthday gift of all. She might be seventy, she thinks, but she is not dead yet.

The next morning when Garnet returns from her walk with Vera, however, she finds a bouquet of blood-red parrot tulips, blooms on the cusp of unfolding, laid carefully by her front door. The leafed stems are wrapped in a soaked newspaper and secured with twine someone—Garnet has a pretty good idea who—has tied into a neat small bow. There is no card. Vera, on the job, sniffs the flowers before Garnet has a chance to pick them up, categorizing them neither as food nor decomposing organic matter, and therefore of no interest to her.

Garnet carries the tulips into the kitchen, clips, slits and crushes the end of each stem, then places the bunch in her mother's blue Roseville vase—Ruby has the green one—and puts it on her desk. They look to her there like a small hot fire, albeit another one inadvertently lit.

Later, as she's running errands, she takes a detour past Jake's house and as she thought, the round bed in front, usually filled this time of year with spring flowers about to bloom, has been substantially denuded.

That evening, Colt remarks, "Two bouquets? Not bad. Who are these from?"

Garnet does not deign to answer.

At the end of that week, Jake phones and asks if he can stop by.

Garnet is not without vanity. She trades the ratty fleece she has on, old standby faded now to olive drab, for a peach cotton crew neck. She combs her hair and puts on some pink lipstick.

Vera knows the signs; someone is coming. She stations herself at the front door.

When Garnet opens the door to Jake's knock she says, over Vera's barking, "Thank you for the flowers."

"I tried to write something but gave up," Jake says and bends down to pat Vera, who is not having any of it, and turns her head away.

"Vera! What a rude girl you are! If you can't be nice, go to bed. Now!"

Vera slinks resentfully into her lion-sized crate in the kitchen. Garnet knows that as she and Jake talk, she will hear intermittent loud sighs and the occasional whine of protest from her bad dog. She can see Vera's head on her paws, looking not sorry but put upon and resentful.

"I thought you'd figure out who they were from," Jake says. "You know I feel like I'm seventeen again and not in a good way, in a clueless, zit-on-my-chin way."

"We don't have to do anything more, you know. Monday was lovely in and of itself."

Garnet allows Vera to come out of her crate before Jake leaves but the damage has been done. The dog wants nothing to do with this interloper, this not-George person who was the cause of her unfair incarceration. Jake ignores the dog, figuring correctly that the needier he appears, the greater will be Vera's scorn.

"As long as her owner still likes me, I'm okay," Jake says.

"Her owner likes you very much," Garnet says.

The second week of May already. Garnet loves this time of year, each evening's light persisting just a little longer. After dinner, she takes Vera for a twilight walk.

Coming back, George is sitting on his porch steps, smoking, and as they pass he calls out, "My two favorite ladies, good evening."

Garnet pauses and Vera takes the initiative, tugging Garnet behind her. Her tail wagging furiously, she pushes her big head between George's knees so he can rub her ears. He lays them out, one ear on each knee, stroking them. Of the two men in her life, there's no question that Vera prefers bachelor number one here.

"When are you going to quit those, George?" she says watching him drop his extinguished cigarette into the pop top hole of his empty beer can. "We'd like to have you around a while longer, you know."

"They're getting so expensive it'll be any time now."

"Promises, promises."

Her friend smokes; he drinks more than is good for him; he could stand to lose a few pounds. But Garnet is not his mother. She believes we all cope with impending mortality in our own way. George seems to favor throwing the gauntlet down, daring the motherfucker to come one single step closer. (Garnet does not censor George, even in her thoughts. He may be retired but his Marine Corps vocabulary is very much on active duty.)

"You had company this afternoon," George says.

"I did."

Vera is now on her back, eyes blissfully closed, tongue lolling, waving her legs in the air as George rubs her belly.

"My competition?"

"There is no competition, George. Moreover, I am no one's prize pig."

Though momentarily taken aback, he recovers. "Well, I know at least one of you is crazy about me."

Looking at the fool for love that is her dog, Garnet would have to agree.

❧

It's Friday night, and Ben, having burned the last of his bridges a week ago, is at loose ends. There is no way he can call Moira and smooth things over. There is nothing left there to smooth over. He has perhaps finally laid to rest his feelings for Tommie, who is not a bad person, has never been a bad person, but is, and will always be, simply oil to his water. He can however text his buddy, Colt:

what's up

missed u at the BD party

great gift by the way

didn't know u were so handy

would've come

tommie told us

yeah looks like thats over

sorry pal

(This last is followed by an emoji he knows is probably intended to show solidarity and sympathy, though without prior knowledge or any context, he'd be hard pressed to figure that out. It is, he thinks, like the rest of the emoticons on his phone, one ugly little fucker.)

Colt winds up inviting Ben to go to the movies with Franny and him. It makes Ben feel like some third—or is it fifth?—wheel. But he's got nothing better to do. They go to the art cinema in the city and see a western with English subtitles, made in the Czech Republic by a Serbian director, one of the big winners at Sundance this year. Against all odds, it's terrific.

"Who'd have thought?" Ben says.

"I picked it so we could make fun of it," Colt says.

"And who needed my Kleenex at the end?" Franny says.

"Hey, what can I say, I'm a sentimental guy. Where to next? The night is young."

The place is unfamiliar to them, a tavern close to the theater, a neighborhood favorite to judge by the clientele. They choose a corner table for people-watching. The food is simply prepared and good. Too late, Ben realizes that they are also close to the hospital where Moira works, and he almost chokes on his pan-fried trout when he sees Moira herself come in with three coworkers. She does not see him but it won't be long before she notices and…? Maybe kills him with a handy steak knife? It seems a perfectly plausible outcome to him.

Colt puts down his bacon cheeseburger.

"*Uhhhh!*"

"Tell me about it," says Ben.

"What?" says Franny, peeling and eating the crispy breading off a deep-fried onion ring, one that appears to have actually begun life as part of a real onion.

"You do know the whole reason for an onion ring is the onion," Colt says.

"But this is the part I like best," she says, adding the sheared onion ring to the pile on her plate.

Colt continues, "Ben's ex just walked in. They did not part on good terms."

Moira, never one to beat around the bush, walks up to the table. "Hello Ben. Colt."

She smiles at Franny, but she does not look happy.

"Moira, Franny Fisher," Colt says.

"Yes, Meg's teacher. I recognize the name."

"Sit down?" Colt asks.

Ben appears to have been struck dumb.

"No, thank you. I didn't want you to think I was ignoring you or pretending not to see you."

Moira returns to her table and her friends.

"That is one nice human being, Ben," Colt says. "But then you know that, don't you?"

Ben knows what Moira is. What that makes him. He'd finally fallen for a grown-up. Too bad she didn't have the same luck.

"That's kind of mean, Colt," Franny says. "Rubbing it in."

"Sorry. I just always liked her. You made a great couple."

"Tell me about it," Ben says again, pushing his plate away, both girl and appetite now having deserted him.

Ben, Colt, and Franny wind down the evening, settling the check, leaving the tip, Ben headed home, Colt and Franny to her place.

Tommie has just returned from her second trip to the all-night drugstore over on Montpelier with another pregnancy test. She watches the blue bullseye appear once again, lowers the toilet seat and sits down heavily. She's like clockwork every twenty-nine days; she's now three weeks late. It appears she is with child, with child and without plan, or partner with whom to share the news, with no clue how this could have happened. Okay, she knows how it happened.

Why did she depend on Ben? Why didn't she depend on herself for something this important? It's possible the time has finally arrived to take responsibility for her actions. She has decisions to make and those sooner rather than later. She stands, tips up the seat, and throws up. It's now 2:30 in the a.m. so she guesses what just happened could be called morning sickness.

❧

As all such calls do, the call very early Saturday morning comes out of the blue. Caller ID tells her it's Ruby. But it doesn't happen the way she envisioned it at all—Ruby ringing her up, saying Harold is gone, Harold, who refused to call his long history with illness a battle. He referred to it as his teacher, the experience a conversation, a conversation he hoped would be very long and very boring with many pauses in the dialogue. That's pretty much how it's worked thus far for him.

But when she picks up, it is not Ruby on the line.

"Garnet?"

"Harold?" Garnet says. "Hello."

"Garnet. Garnet, your sister's gone."

With that Harold falls apart. She then hears Agata's voice.

"I'm so sorry, Garnet."

"What? What's this all about, Agata?"

None of it makes sense to Garnet. She spoke to Ruby yesterday. She'd had no plans then. Gone? Gone where?

"It was an aneurysm. Ruby collapsed just before midnight. They'd stayed up watching *Casablanca.* Harold called me, and I called EMS. They got her to the hospital. I was with her the whole time. She wasn't alone. They managed a scan but she didn't make it into surgery. I just got back here. Harold, of course, is not doing well; don't worry, I'll be staying. She didn't suffer, Garnet. At least there's that."

Garnet may indeed have long ago composed a mental script for herself of how it would go, but as she had to have known, reality has played havoc with her plan, one in which Harold dies first, then Garnet and, finally, Ruby. Garnet is not prepared for this news. Is anyone? Ever? Yet, in the midst of her confusion and grief, she is already talking to her sister. *Just had to be first, didn't you? Show little sister how it's done. Here, then gone! Poof! Just the way we talked about, the ideal way: fast, fast, fast!*

Colt takes care of informing family and getting Garnet her ticket for a next-day flight to Ohio. He takes her to the airport.

"We'll all be along in the next day or two," he says. "Will you be okay, you and Harold?"

"We'll be fine. Agata will pick me up. Franny will housesit with Vera? She said yes?"

"She'll move in while we're gone. I'll bring Meg with me."

"Good. This is the first time someone she knows and loves has died. She'll want to be there to say goodbye."

The sisters both credited their mother, Grace, for most of whatever good qualities they possessed—gratitude, empathy, tolerance, a joy in doing for others—their mother, possessor of these and many other wonderful traits, also a secret drinker. Alcohol had threaded its way through her family, Grace's father, her brothers, her own mother—Garnet and Ruby's grandmother, like a poisoned underground stream. When Grace was drinking she was volatile, filling her family's life with drama, with fraught episodes of problematic behavior, most often followed by silence rather than abject apologies. The sisters happened not to inherit that curse in which one drink is too many and ten not enough.

But perhaps because of this history, as adults they both reacted to crises of any sort by becoming very quiet, acting out, hysteria of all stripes anathema to them both. Therefore, on the plane, Garnet—rereading her biography of Lincoln for its ability to give her hope that perhaps a fallen species is still capable of being, doing, good—makes as little small talk with her seatmate as possible without being outright rude. No one looking at her would guess she is like a glacier, a huge piece of which has just broken away, falling irretrievably into frigid seas, the outward calm she presents, its smallest part, and the rest below, hidden from view. She acts and looks perfectly normal. This, in some way, scares the hell out of her.

Agata is indeed waiting for her by the baggage carousel, just as Garnet knew she would be. They embrace, Garnet's agnostic heart persuaded that nonetheless angels occasionally dwell among us, and Agata, like Lincoln, is one of them. For her, no heaven, no hell, no God with its upper case 'G' unless it is the first word in the sentence. But winged spirits? Why not? Thanks to a martyred United States president and to Harold's aide, angels have her vote.

"I still can't believe it," Garnet says. "Thank you for picking me up."

"How could I not?" Agata says.

Harold tells Garnet that her sister will be cremated. He hands her a manila envelope with her name on it.

"It was supposed to be me," Harold says, sniffling.

"And then me," Garnet, in tears, says.

Agata brings a plate of cookies, a pitcher of cold milk, and three glasses on a tray into the room and sets it on the coffee table. Harold is in his wheelchair but he is capable of walking for short distances and doing for himself with a little help. He gets up, pours himself a glass of milk, and takes two cookies. Garnet sits down on the sofa and opens her sister's missive. She is not surprised to receive it.

Last fall, Garnet, feeling the effects of an approaching birthday freighted with intimations of mortality, had written her own letter to Ruby. Then she'd called her sister to inform her that Colt had been instructed upon her demise to place that letter in Ruby's hands. In it, she said Ruby would find everything she needed to know. It was not a will, she made clear. It simply addressed everything else.

Her sister had snorted, and then the line had become very quiet. "Ruby?" Garnet had asked. "Are you still there?"

"My bossy baby sister," Ruby had finally replied. "Are you telling me that you will pre-decease me, and I will be stuck with the arrangements and the headaches that entails?"

"Yes," said Garnet.

"And you believe this? Why? Don't you know the universe finds your arrogance amusing? That it will now make it a point of not following your orders?"

Yet, and this did not surprise Garnet at all, her sister had sat down, perhaps that very afternoon, and written her own letter, neglecting—perhaps in a futile effort to keep that pesky universe at bay—to inform her little sister she'd done so.

Darling sister,

I know it was your desire that I be the one here prostrate with grief, reading your last wish and testament, I, the one fated to then somehow pick up the pieces and move on. But if you are reading this...well, we both know how our human demands of the great unknown are met, don't we? Disappointingly, so seldom with obedient compliance.

Neither of us believes in an afterlife, but if it turns out we are mistaken, I want you to know you will find me nearby; that wraith glimpsed out of the corner of your eye? Me. In that case, I will not desert you, dear one. But if, as we suspect, the lights simply go out, I take comfort knowing I will live on in your head, your memories, your thoughts. No mean immortality that. I expect you at the very least to carry on a continuous one-sided conversation with me until you join me here or, more likely, nowhere.

Now for my requests. Demands? No, let's just call them requests.

Convince Harold to sell the house and move into the Quaker senior care center. There are birds and a golden retriever named Lucy, a tabby cat (how that works with the birds, I'm not sure), and a daycare program with small children. He will like it and Agata can have a life again. Tell him I have checked it out, even eaten lunch there; the food is not bad at all.

No funeral, absolutely no memorial service, no grace,

amazing or otherwise. Nada! Remmy will try to do an end run around this simply because I want it, and because in some respects he is still that disobedient little brother we remember so well from our childhood. Be prepared to head him off.

You get my ashes. Mulch your rose bushes. Release me into the wind, though I will make a point of making you sneeze. Put me on your mantel in a pretty pot. Dump me in the lake. Up to you. (I would prefer you avoid flushing me if at all possible for patently selfish rather than environmental reasons.)

I had such big plans for our declining years. Now, no pressure you understand, you will have to live for both of us.

Your loving (who else would it be?) sister, Ruby

Garnet hands the letter to Agata, who, by the time she finishes reading it, is again weeping. Harold waves it away.

"Ruby read it to me after she finished writing it. Once is enough," he says. "By the way, I'm not going anywhere, just so you know. If I want birds, babies, dogs, I know where to find them. And thanks to Agata, the food is not bad here either."

Here we go, thinks Garnet and meets Agata's eyes.

"So, no service of any kind?" Agata says to Garnet, choosing to ignore the ultimatum Harold has thrown down.

"No service. But my dear sister says nothing about a big bonfire and picnic out back, does she?"

"She does not," says Agata. "And this way we don't have to worry about Remmy, do we? Having taken care of the end run ourselves."

"We do not," says Garnet.

Colt, Meg, and Tommie arrive together late Monday, having driven the nine hours to southwestern Ohio. Garnet hugs each one in turn. George has lent them the Beast; he will be using Colt's truck until they return.

"How was the drive?" Garnet says.

"Did you know the speed limit in Ohio is seventy?" Meg says.

"Which means everyone is going at least eighty," says Colt. "It's a freaking Daytona 500 out there."

"I believe I did know that. I don't know what they're thinking," Garnet says.

"It was scary!" says Meg.

"But here we are, safe and sound," Tommie says.

They go into the house where Harold is waiting for them. Meg runs to him and bursts into tears.

Later, Garnet takes Meg upstairs to the guest room they will share with its white-painted twin canopy beds, made up by Ruby not so long ago with matching floral sheets and down comforters tucked into pale yellow duvets. Garnet helps Meg unpack her small suitcase and a backpack full of books.

While getting ready for bed, the young girl asks her aunt, "Do you think Ruby is in heaven?"

Garnet has thought about a moment like this and promised herself that she will not lie about her beliefs, or rather lack of them. But the temptation to offer this small comfort to her niece is very strong.

"What do you think, Meg?" is finally the best she can come up with.

"I hope she is. I liked your sister very much."

"I did, too," Garnet says, sighing inwardly with a relief that is short-lived. Meg has not finished her interrogation.

"Do you think Vera will go to heaven. Do dogs have souls?"

At last, something Garnet *is* sure of.

"Of course dogs have souls. And Vera is a very good girl. Where else would she go?"

Meg sighs happily. Though she is ten now and, in her own opinion, very grown up, Garnet tucks her in and gives her a kiss on the cheek.

"Sleep well."

Remmy arrives by Greyhound late that night with Bowie, and Colt picks them up in Dayton at the bus station; Freddy has already returned to Nevada to refill his coffers at the poker tables.

"This is not the best part of town, is it?" Remmy says.

"I've never seen a bus station that was," Colt answers.

"I don't know why," Bowie says. "We had a great trip. Bus was clean. Company was great."

"Bowie, are you okay?" Colt asks.

His eyes are red-rimmed, his face very flushed.

Remmy looks at Colt. "The fellows across from us had a flask, and I'm afraid they over-shared with Bowie."

The next day, neighbors are informed and invited as are Ruby's libertarian friends, and the ladies from the feminist book club. The Quakers and Master Gardeners are not left out. There is no need to ask each guest to bring a dish to share. It is part of midwestern DNA that death and casseroles, the occasional ham, are two sides of the same coin.

Ruby and Harold's home sits on five acres fronting the Little Miami River. Colt and company spend Tuesday afternoon collecting deadfall. Colt, using his Boy Scout training, constructs the makings for an impressive blaze using Ruby and Harold's fire pit as a base. There are already a couple of picnic tables on the site, its high ground overlooking the river. Stone benches surround the pit. Colt has even had the foresight to order a Porta Potty hauled in and set back near the trees.

Garnet comes out to inspect.

"You know that's going to make a huge bonfire."

"Wasn't that the idea?" Colt says.

"This is not Salem. There are no witches here."

"Oh, I think we have a few good witches, one of whom we've lost."

Garnet absentmindedly pats her nephew on the cheek.

Used to New York State's affinity for regulations, rules, prohibitions, exceptions, and paperwork, Colt and Remmy drive over and notify the local fire department of their planned blaze. Once the chief has ascertained that nothing is currently on fire, he suggests that Colt wait to contact him until something is burning that shouldn't be, instead of wasting his time as he's doing right now.

"*Whoa*," Colt says, walking out of the firehouse.

"You are not in Kansas anymore," Remmy says. "We want to get rid of those old tires in Harold's garage in this blaze, I bet we could."

"You saying Ohio's not afraid of no stinking air pollution?"

"Hell, yes! You set the woods on fire? Plenty more woods where those came from."

"You know what we're saying is terrifying not funny, right?"

"Hey, climate change? Fake news! Coal burns clean enough. Fossil fuels are good for the economy, *oops,* I mean environment."

"As your husband would say, *après nous le deluge*."

❧

Wednesday, Tommie and Garnet make a run for paper plates and cups, napkins, tablecloths. The grocery store has a stand of primroses out front and Tommie buys them all. Colt picks up beer and wine, soft drinks for the kids. It is a beautiful spring day. Mid-afternoon, Agata settles Harold into the golf cart that has sat in the garage since they moved here. Colt gets it started. They tootle down the path to the river. In the back where golf bags would go is a large, lidded glass jar with a spout, filled with sweet sun tea Agata has brewed. Meg skips along after.

The advance guard, the feminist readers, arrives at four with two large foil roasting pans, one each of baked beans and barbecued ribs. The libertariennes bring a chocolate marble cake, a red velvet cake, and three apple pies. There is a whole honey-baked ham from the Master Gardeners and the Quakers come with bags of homemade bread, rolls, and two large wheels of cheese. Otto, Ruby's nearest neighbor, head of Farmers for Trump and wearing his red MAGA baseball cap, has made sure there are makings for s'mores, and his group has taken up a collection and donated the proceeds in Ruby's name to the animal shelter.

On one of the picnic tables, surrounded by the pots of primroses, there is a glamorous color photo of Ruby wearing a slouchy dark green velvet hat tilted down over her left eye. Seeing it, poor Harold's eyes begin to water, but Agata is there to wipe away the tears and get him a beer.

The sun is getting low in the west when Colt lights the fire, which leaps skyward with satisfying speed, sparks rising up like a swarm of angry bees. It's getting chilly and everyone draws closer to the warmth. Harold, flying in the face of Ruby's dictate, as she had to have known he would, begins to sing "Amazing Grace." He has a lovely light tenor and the crowd listens, not joining in. But as he finishes, they begin the hymn a second time, this time everyone giving voice. The voices, the fire, the sunset, all seem unutterably beautiful to Garnet.

"Sorry, Ruby," says Colt, putting his arm around his aunt, "so much for no grace, amazing or otherwise."

❧

It will be a vessel that moves
not out into open water, but
always that hard left through
cattails and green muck
into the dock, the harsh sound
of piling scraping varnished wood,
a wound that might become a scar
if it were ever allowed to heal.

Colt is raking the coals, everyone else gone home, when Garnet walks back from the house carrying the box of Ruby's ashes that Harold has just given her.

She empties them among the glowing embers, telling Colt, "I don't know any other place she'd rather be."

They pause before returning, listening to the song of the river, swollen by May rains, making its way downstream in boisterous spring flood. The darkness that surrounds them—tonight's gibbous moon will not rise until close to midnight—is compromised only by the remaining live coals where Ruby rests, and by the cold light of stars and a few early fireflies sparking up out of the long grass.

They spend the following day with Agata and Harold, trying to figure out how things will work now that the linchpin that was Ruby is missing. There are no easy answers. Harold's illness is terminal and he is dying, but he is not dying today or tomorrow, maybe, though unlikely, not even this year.

What they come up with is that Harold will go into assisted living with the Quakers and the toddlers, the menagerie, and the not-bad meals. But he will return home each weekend with Agata, who will have her weekdays free and receive a hefty salary bump for her trouble, along with free housing.

"What else could I spend my money on that would give me even half as much pleasure as being able to spend time here at home?" Harold asks. "With Agata," he adds.

After dinner Tommie and Colt pack the car, preparing for an early start in the morning. Happily, there is plenty of room in George's Brobdingnagian SUV for Garnet to join them for the trip back. Tommie has not mentioned her dilemma to anyone so far and has decided she will not. Depending on what she decides, she thinks she may never do so. Thus far she's felt only faintly nauseated in the mornings and has made an appointment at the clinic after their return. Colt locks the car after they finish and then turns to her. "You okay, Tommie?" Colt says.

"Why would you ask that?"

"Because I'd like to know if you're okay. You've seemed a little off ever since Garnet's party."

"Well, maybe that's because I'm pregnant."

Tommie has always had a small problem keeping her resolutions.

"*Jesus God*, tell me I didn't just hear you say you were pregnant."

"Don't try to make me feel better about it, Colt. And let's not bring Jesus into this. He had nothing to do with it."

"I have to ask. Is it Ben's?"

"That is probably the most insulting thing you've ever said to me, which is saying something. Do not. *Do not* breathe a word about this to anyone else."

"Or what? Why would you want to lay this news on me? Why would I want to do the same thing to somebody else?"

"I don't know if I'm going to keep it."

Colt groans.

"Have you told Ben?"

"What do you think? And I have to talk to somebody or I'll go nuts."

"But why me?"

❧

Back in Haven, Vera and Franny are not getting along. Vera is miffed that her pack has inexplicably disappeared and this unsatisfactory stranger replaced them, even if said stranger regularly takes her out, lets her sleep on Garnet's bed, feeds her at the appointed times and gives her half of her breakfast bacon. The unpleasant look she gives Franny when she arrives after school says plainly, *Oh...it's you.*

George has stepped up during the day while Franny is teaching. He comes over and man and dog go for long rambles in the park. Sometimes he takes pity on Vera and lets her stay for the afternoon, following him around the house or napping at his feet while he watches a ball game. When four-thirty comes—Franny is trying to follow a consistent schedule, one Vera can depend on—George tells the dog it's time to go home and the look she gives him breaks his heart. *Why?* it says. *Why? My darling has disappeared. She is never coming back. I like you very much. Let me stay here.* (George, like many dog lovers, tends to flagrantly anthropomorphize.)

"Here she is, Franny," George says, ushering Vera in the back door.

"Is it time to eat, Vera?" Franny asks in a conciliatory tone.

Vera looks at her, the substantial tail *not* wagging, as though to say, *Shut up and feed me.* Franny sighs and fills Vera's bowl with senior lamb and rice kibble, a cup of no-salt, free-range chicken broth, and one teaspoon of fish oil. She then places the stainless food dish next to its twin, freshly filled water bowl in the elevated easy-feeder plastic "dinette" for large dogs Garnet found on Amazon. Vera, ignoring Franny, begins to eat.

"She simply does not like me, George. I've tried everything."

"She's a one-woman dog, Franny, and that woman is not here."

"You know, you'd think this experience would make me view having a dog of my own with a jaundiced eye, but just the opposite: I wind up thinking about what it would be like having something—"

George corrects her gently. "Someone?"

"Okay, someone love me as much as this girl loves Garnet. I'm seriously thinking about a trip to the pound after Garnet gets back and my responsibilities here are finished."

"Speaking of Garnet, Franny, any news?"

"Colt texted they'll be heading back tomorrow."

It's a long trip from Bonnybrook, in southwestern Ohio to Haven, almost five hundred miles. They say their goodbyes. Harold cries, Garnet cries. Meg, who'd been holding up well, breaks into sobs. Colt and Tommie, preoccupied by what Tommie this morning labeled their *terrible secret*, do not. They're on the road by eight o'clock. Agata has packed a lunch and tossed some unhealthy snacks into a bag for Colt.

On the road at last, Garnet wipes away Meg's tears and says, "She was my favorite sister."

"But she was your only sister," Meg, rallying, points out.

"Which doesn't mean she can't still be my favorite."

"It's okay to feel sad," Garnet adds.

They stop for bathroom breaks, to stretch their legs, for milkshakes. They pull off the interstate to pick up Dramamine for Tommie who says she's feeling car sick.

"Carsick my ass," Colt mutters under his breath.

Garnet hears him.

"Tommie's carsick, Colt. She is not hungover. I didn't see her have a single drink all week."

Tommie shoots Colt a murderous look and he shuts up.

They call Rain and let her know their approximate arrival time. Colt leaves another text message for Franny, who he knows faithfully turns off her cell phone at the start of each school day. And Garnet calls George to tell him the Beast will soon be back in its garage.

"We really appreciated it, George. It's a very comfortable vehicle," Garnet says.

"I was happy I could do something. By the way I got a friend of yours right here sitting on my foot."

"Tell her I'll see her tonight."

"Tell her yourself," George says. Garnet knows he is placing the phone near Vera's ear.

"Hello, Vera," Garnet says.

She is rewarded with an earsplitting symphony of barks which she—no less guilty than George of attributing human speech to non-human species—translates as *She's alive!*

"Maybe that wasn't such a good idea," George says when the noise dies down.

"I'll be home soon."

"She's not the only one who missed you, you know."

Colt drops Garnet off first. Although some canines express displeasure at their owner's absence by ignoring them upon their return, Vera is not such a one. Vera is beside herself with joy.

"I'll be back with your vehicle shortly," Colt tells George, who is watching the reunion bemusedly, some might say longingly, from his driveway.

"Take as long as you need. I'm not going anywhere."

Meg is dropped off next and Tommie is last.

Colt unloads her suitcase and carries it inside, brushing aside her expressed intent to do it herself.

"You better not start acting like this in front of other people," Tommie says. "You may as well hang a sign on me if you do."

"Saying what?"

"Fragile! Handle with care! Baby on board!"

"I doubt very much anyone watching me bring in your suitcase would intuit much more than the fact that they're seeing a perfect gentleman in action."

"You are so full of it, Colt."

"You, dear cousin, need to think about saying something to Ben. If you decide to go through with this, he's going to be liable for child support."

"I would hope if I decide to have his child, he'd contribute more than a monthly check."

"You know what I mean. He deserves to know."

"I'm not going to say anything to Ben until I've made up my own mind about what I'm going to do. By the way, will you go with me to a doctor's appointment on Monday?"

"*Christ*, Tommie, I'm not the daddy, you know?"

"I had no idea you were so religious. *Jesus God* this, *Christ* that," Tommie says and begins to cry.

Colt takes out the folded handkerchief he keeps in his jacket pocket in memory of the mom who, before she got sick, handed him his lunch and tucked a clean hankie in his jacket pocket as he went out the door every single day of elementary school. He hands it to his cousin.

"Okay, okay. All right, I'll go. Just stop with the tears. What time?"

"Many people would consider it a compliment to be chosen as a confidant by someone in the midst of a life crisis."

"*What time*, Tommie?"

"Four-thirty. I'll pick you up at four," Tommie says. "You're still working out there off 96, right?"

"*Yep*. Out at Havenly Acres."

"Havenly? Havenly Acres? Whose awful idea was that? But thank you, Colt. I really do appreciate it."

"If it's a boy, you better name him after me."

"My, my, that would set tongues wagging, wouldn't it."

Tommie's mood has brightened considerably.

Garnet and Vera resume their quotidian lives. Vera continues to hold no grudge against her owner for her disappearance, overjoyed simply to have her back. Garnet finds that it makes her feel less sad if she includes, as part of the day's writing, a brief entry addressed to her sister. Ruby was right; one way or another Garnet will be talking to her missing sibling until such time as she herself joins her. Today, she writes:

I can't put my finger on it, Ruby, the sense that things are happening around me, that somehow involve me, that I know nothing about. Kind of how I felt about my birthday party but there I had a pretty good idea of what was going on. I have no clue what this is about. And, no, I am not being paranoid. Colt and Tommie. Tommie and Colt. I wish you were here, Ruby. I need fresh eyes. Something is cooking, and Colt, usually so forthcoming, is not talking.

❧

Tommie picks Colt up at four on Monday. She's chosen a Planned Parenthood clinic in the city. "If I decide to do this," she says, "I will need a real job with health insurance, no more substituting."

"You don't think you and Ben might get back together?"

"I think the thrill is gone for both of us."

"Maybe it's time to let that whole thrill thing go, Tommie. It would solve a lot of problems for you."

"And maybe create a few new ones."

The doctor at Planned Parenthood who sees Tommie—young, Indian, female—confirms that she is indeed pregnant, and is sympathetic as they discuss her options. In the car afterward, she and Colt talk.

"If I'm being realistic, I do the sensible thing and end this pregnancy."

"I'm only here to listen," Colt says.

"But if I don't, there's a good chance I'll be offered a job for next year. The principal really likes me."

"Nobody has ever said you're anything but a terrific teacher."

"And what happens when I accept the job and show up in September great with child—"

"As is your right," Colt says. "You owe no one, except maybe poor Ben, any explanations."

"Please stop calling him 'poor Ben,' Colt. All I know is I need to decide soon. For one thing, I can't live like this."

"Amen to that," Colt says.

On Tuesday, Garnet writes in her journal to Ruby. *George saw Colt and Tommie in the city yesterday. He beeped his horn but said they didn't see him. I may just have to come right out and ask Colt what's going on and, Ruby, I do realize that would have been your first suggestion. You were always the smarter sister.*

By Wednesday, Tommie has made up her mind. She tells Colt.

"You're sure about this?" he says.

"I'm not sure about anything. Am I going to do it? Yes."

"And you're going to make me go with you, aren't you?"

"No, cuz. This is actually something I'm going to have to do myself."

Tommie decides she'll go to the clinic to make the appointment; she feels the need to be in the presence of an actual human being to do this. She has questions. She wants to know exactly what to expect.

Thank God there are no protesters outside when she arrives after school on Thursday, no one waving signs today, shouting at her, no one trying to show her photos of what she will be destroying, no one trying to talk her out of it. And, in her book the biggest missing piece, no one stepping up to say that if she changes her mind, they will help raise the child, or at the very least, take care of all her expenses for the next eighteen years (Tommie reacts with dismay at the feminine pronoun which has slipped so easily into her thought, the goal of remaining dispassionate about this decision not as simple as she'd first thought).

When she goes inside and makes an appointment for a week from Friday, the second of June, she is asked for an emergency contact. Without thinking, Rain's name comes out of her mouth. So much for going it completely alone.

Once home, Tommie gives Rain a call. She asks her if they can meet up this weekend at the Starbucks in the little strip mall near Rain's house.

"Colt and Meg are going on a father-daughter excursion with her scout troop on Saturday," Rain says. "So you tell me when."

"Ten?" Tommie asks.

"Ten is fine. Everything okay, Tommie?"

"Not really."

Colt arrives at Garnet's on Friday with Meg in tow. They need to meet the rest of her scout troop in the parking lot of Saint Adalbert's Church at 5:30 tomorrow morning, so she's spending the night even though it's not a scheduled weekend. Now Garnet will have to wait to quiz Colt about what's going on until after Meg's bedtime. Now that she's in fourth grade, she has pronounced herself "a *committed* reader," emphasis hers; that means nine o'clock in bed, and nine-thirty or ten for lights-out with nobody checking on the lights-out part.

This is so because a part of Garnet is convinced that the reason she's needed glasses since her teen years was all that flash-lit reading under the covers as a kid. Starting when she was seven, reading encompassed, in bed and out, one series after another, their titles having to be read consecutively, in the order they were published, each author's oeuvre having to be finished before she allowed herself to begin a new one, every single *Bobbsey Twins*, *Cherry Ames, Student Nurse*, and *Nancy Drew, Girl Detective*, and as she got older, Jane Austen in entirety, then Charlotte Brontë, Daphne du Maurier, various Russian blockbusters, James Thurber, her list went on and on. Authors of single titles she loved, like Harper Lee, broke her heart. She believes that, unlike Meg, she would have had to call herself, back then, more obsessed than committed. The flashlight was only finally retired when Garnet turned sixteen. These days, Garnet has become so insouciant a reader that she refuses to finish any book that has not managed to win either her heart or mind in its first fifty pages.

At last, the house quiet, Garnet takes Vera out for a final time. She still occasionally tries simply letting the dog out into the fenced yard, but the end result seems to be getting worse rather than better, despite Garnet's high hopes for the breakthrough in which Vera goes out, pees, and tail wagging, runs back to the door to be let in for the night. The last time she tried it, Vera, leash-less, lover of cool air and dewed grass, stayed out until two in the morning, ignoring all pleas and threats, ignoring even the nuclear bacon option of last resort, as she disturbed the peace in order to inform the neighborhood of kamikaze moth suicides, imminent firefly attacks, and (the horror!) a cat on the loose. George had called, concerned, at midnight and laughed when she told him her problem.

When Garnet and the dog return, Colt, having completed a final house check, locking doors and turning lights on or off, depending, is back in the kitchen finishing his nightly glass of milk and five Oreos, each one gone in a single bite, no dunking involved.

At the chocolate grin he gives her, Garnet says, "I hope you brush your teeth before you go to bed, or you won't have any left by the time you're my age."

Colt smiles even wider.

"Oh, grow up!" Garnet says.

Vera takes her last drink of the night, her blue ceramic water bowl the size of a dishpan. Colt takes the sponge mop and wipes up the lake and tributary streams of water the dog leaves behind. Then they listen for the sound of Vera plodding heavily up the stairs, gravity as usual proving the biggest challenge to a large, aging dog's ascent. Once upstairs, she will await her mistress, collapsed on the floor in the hall outside their bedroom door.

"She's getting old, poor baby," Colt says. "I remember when she'd be up those stairs in two seconds flat."

"We're all slowing down," says Garnet. "By the way, George said he saw you and Tommie in the city this week."

"Yeah?"

"So? What's going on, Colt?"

"I can't tell you."

"Something *is* going on, but you are not going to tell me what it is."

"I believe that's what I just said, Garnet," Colt says mildly.

"Well, I guess my next stop is my daughter."

"I'd hold off on that if I were you."

"But I will at some point be informed what is happening?"

"Maybe not. I'm sorry, Garnet, I can't say more than that."

Garnet retires to her room but does not fall asleep for a long time. She listens to the sounds Vera makes in sleep, her legs jerking on the carpet as she runs in her dreams, the odd whimper, a muffled bark, and Garnet worries. She wonders what kind of fix her daughter has gotten herself into now, a predicament in which she has apparently decided to involve her cousin.

Early and nervous, by the time Rain walks in Tommie has already purchased two lattes, two scones, as well as snagged a table in the far corner by the window. Tommie thinks that if she could choose to look like anyone else in the world, she would choose Rain, who today is wearing a black turtleneck, black capris, and gold flats. She has a purple streak in her short dark hair. a small shiny nose ring, and looks, if such a thing is possible, elegantly punk. Tommie waves and Rain comes over and sits down.

"Hope this is okay," Tommie says, handing her a coffee and pushing the plate of scones toward her.

"It's perfect. Thank you. What's up?"

Tommie explains her situation and decision and makes her request, trying the whole while to stop wringing her hands.

"Of course, I'll go with you," Rain says and covers Tommie's hands with both of her own.

She pauses for a moment before continuing, "I know how alone you're feeling right now. No one in your family knows what I am going to tell you. I had an abortion eight years ago. Meg was two. I was a mess." (Tommie can in no way picture Rain a mess. Rain, what? Serene? Yes. In control? Absolutely. But a mess? Impossible.)

"It was clear Colt and I were over and I did some, many, things I regret. One of those things was winding up pregnant again. It was a really hard decision, but I have no regrets about the choice I made."

Tommie does feel less alone. She does not wonder until later who Rain could have been involved with. Maybe, in fact, Rain has no idea who the father was. Maybe it was even Colt. At that thought Tommie feels unutterably sad. She might have had two little nieces. Somehow that sorrow does not translate to the life she herself carries, which in no way feels real to her. Her pro-choice mother—though Tommie knows Garnet thinks the term "second-wave feminist" affected and would never define herself thus—brought up her daughter on a female liberal's diet of *Our Bodies, Ourselves.* She would see no wrongdoing in her daughter's decision. But if she knew, she might try to dissuade Tommie for more selfish reasons, Garnet an aunt, while her brother has a grandchild.

June

what we pursue eludes us
what has been run to ground
taken home and tamed and loved
escapes
each breath released is lost

Friday morning arrives. Tommie is wide awake at five and finally gives up and gets out of bed at six. She hears Rain's knock on the door at eight, a full half hour early. But no matter, Tommie is ready. She opens the door.

"Tommie."

"Ben! Ben?"

"Rain called last night."

"What?"

Tommie feels blindsided and angry and confused.

"I've made up my mind," she says.

"I'm not here to change your mind, Tommie. That's why I'm early. Rain said if you still want her, I should call and she'll come."

"I don't know what I want. Everything was all set."

"And now? I'm putting out there that we could do this together."

"I don't see us as a couple, Ben."

"We don't have to be a couple to see this through. You have time, if you want to add what I just said to your options."

Finally, Tommie does cancel the appointment at the clinic. She also tells Ben not to contact her. She will call him when, *if*, she's good and ready to do so. She needs time to think.

When Colt comes to pick up Meg on Friday evening, Rain tells him, "We have to talk." She's sent Meg next door ostensibly to give Julitta a hand making cookies. "I'm figuring you already know Tommie's situation," Rain says.

"I wondered if she'd ask you to go with her. How is she?"

"Tommie canceled the appointment."

"Why? Sounded to me like she'd made up her mind."

"I called Ben."

"Holy shit, Rain. Good luck with that."

"And at some point soon, depending on what Tommie decides, you and I, Colt, are going to have to tell Meg her aunt is pregnant."

"Let's wait a little longer, see what my volatile cousin is actually going to do."

Tommie is beyond angry at Rain until she's not. Then she talks to Rain every day for the next week.

"How could you?" she asks Rain. "What if I called Colt and told him what you told me? How would you feel? How do I decide what's right for me?" she says. "Can I really do this? How do I know I won't regret it? Either way? Do you really have no regrets?" Tommie asks finally.

To each of these questions Rain answers, "I don't know."

Until the last.

Then Rain says, "I think of that little life often and I still don't know how I feel about what I did. Or maybe what I mean is that I feel many ways about what I did. I don't think it was some kind of sin. I would do the same thing again if my circumstances were as they were then. And I don't believe my choice is one that lends itself to regulation by a court of law. It was the hardest decision I've ever made. Does that help?"

"Not really," Tommie says, thinking instead how hard it is when you have postponed growing up until you are almost thirty years old. She would not recommend it to anyone.

In the end, Tommie calls Ben and asks, "Are you sure you want to be a daddy?"

"Yes," he says. "We can absolutely do this."

The two decide to tell Garnet together. They show up on Sunday evening to find her sitting on the porch with a glass of wine. Vera, attached to her by a long loose lead, is thrilled to have company and rolls over onto her back on the wood floor for a belly rub. When Ben obliges, her tongue lolls out of her mouth, such is her bliss.

"Nice to see the two of you talking again," Garnet says.

"We have something to tell you."

"All right," Garnet says, "what now?"

The news itself strikes Garnet dumb. Of all the things she might have expected, the news that Tommie is pregnant is one that was never on her radar, though knowing her careless daughter, she doesn't know why it should be such a big surprise.

She recovers enough to say, "Congratulations?"

"Yes," says Tommie. "Congratulations are in order."

"Maybe not an ideal situation," Ben says. "But we are one hundred percent ready to do this."

"You know you do have options," Garnet says.

"I know, Mother," Tommie says. "I do understand that. But Horton the elephant here has convinced me there will be two parents bringing this kid up."

"Faithful one hundred percent!" Garnet says and Ben sighs.

Then she asks her daughter, "Will you do this together as a couple?"

"I'm learning with great reluctance that you can't have everything, Mom."

"Well, you have a family who loves you. So two parents. With the ragtag bunch that is the rest of us as backup."

"I hope so," Tommie says.

The next morning after working on the new poem in her journal, Garnet writes to her sister. *Well, Ruby, I am vindicated, not certifiable. Yet. Things have been happening right under my nose. I am going to be a grandma. Tommie and Ben. They came, together, to tell me last night. Of course, not only are they not married, they are not together anymore. And they are perfectly okay with that. So, no, I am not crazy. But sometimes I wonder about everyone else.*

Colt picks Meg up on Friday for her scheduled weekend at Garnet's. Before they leave, the three sit down at the kitchen table. Rain has made coffee for the two adults and Meg makes herself a cup of instant hot chocolate, adding her baker's dozen of mini marshmallows.

"Really, Meg?" Rain says.

"The bag was open and they were only going to get stale

and we don't throw out good food if we can help it, right?"

"The key word here is *good*, Meg."

"I think marshmallows are really, really good."

"Enough with the marshmallows," Colt says. "We are here for a little family meeting."

"Well, at least I know you guys aren't going to tell me you're getting a divorce," says Meg.

"I wish I knew who to blame for that sense of humor," Rain says, looking at Colt.

"What? I'm not funny," Colt says.

"My point exactly," Rain says. "Meg, your dad and I want you to know, before you find out on your own, that Aunt Tommie is pregnant."

Meg knows the facts, how this might occur, though she has never had "the talk" with either parent. Instead, she has been part of an ongoing conversation. Rain has always answered Meg's questions honestly; she has matter-of-factly used the correct names for body parts and functions. When Meg gets her first period, it will not be a shock. Mother and daughter have assembled what she will need and placed it in a corner of her bureau.

And Colt has tried as best he can, which usually means awkwardly, to keep up his end of any discussion. Meg has told her father she is not looking forward to it. Too messy, and it sounds uncomfortable. But Rain has told her she only has to put up with it until she's fifty. For a couple days after she heard this, Colt noticed her eyeing her aunt speculatively, but he doesn't think she ever got up the nerve to ask Garnet how old she was when she stopped menstruating. Not that Garnet wouldn't have answered her if she had. Still, a little social restraint, learned and practiced at any age, is never a bad thing, he thinks.

"Wow!" says Meg. "Is it a boy or a girl?"

"I don't think they know yet."

"I hope it's a girl. Like a little sister, just what I always wanted."

Rain's face has the oddest expression. Colt wonders what

that's all about. Regret? She'd had her tubes tied, Colt remembers, a few years after Meg was born. "No more accidents," she'd told him. He remembered being surprised even back then by her use of the word *accident* to describe their daughter.

"Actually, Meg, you will be this little kid's cousin," Colt says.

"I want to be like Garnet! Can I be Aunt Meg?"

"Not technically. But I don't see why we have to get technical, do you, Rain?"

"We could definitely dub you Aunt Meg," Rain says.

Meg smiles.

Then she asks, "Are Tommie and Ben going to get married?"

"We don't know," says Rain.

Colt wonders exactly what they are teaching this child about adult behavior. At least Meg didn't ask who the baby's father could possibly be but took it for granted it must be Ben.

And, as it turns out, his daughter is not quite finished asking questions.

Meg regards her father seriously. "Are you and Franny going to have a baby too now?" she asks.

Rain looks at him too, eyebrows raised. She seems to be enjoying his discomfort.

"No, sweetie, we are not."

During the last week of school, Tommie's principal comes to her room, and tells her that Ms. Pepper will not be returning, and offers her the job. Tommie takes it. Time enough once school starts to disclose she will be taking a maternity leave in January.

Everyone knows. Everybody has adjusted to the idea. Anticipation has replaced disbelief; already there is talk of a baby shower, of setting up a nursery. So when Tommie has a miscarriage on the last day of June, there is more than enough sadness to go around. Meg and Colt in fact are eating dinner with Garnet when Ben calls and tells them the news. Meg bursts into tears when her father tells her.

"Tommie is going to be fine," he says, handing her a Kleenex.

"Please don't cry," Garnet says, though her own eyes are wet.

Meg gets up, walks over to her father, and plops down on his lap, putting her arms around his neck. She looks at him. "But I was going to be an aunt and now I'm not."

"There will be plenty of chances for you to be an aunt."

"There won't. Remmy is gay."

"Gay people have kids," Colt points out.

"They don't usually wait till they're over sixty-five to start though. And if he did have a kid, that kid would be *my* aunt."

"Or uncle," Garnet says.

"Or uncle," Meg agrees and continues. "And Aunt Ruby didn't have kids and Tommie is pretty old. Maybe she won't want to try again?"

"Twenty-nine is not old!" Colt says. "I'm twenty-nine."

"Then why can't you and Franny have a baby? I could have a real little sister," Meg says.

"I thought you didn't like the idea of your father dating your teacher," says Garnet.

"I'm getting used to the idea," Meg says.

After dinner, Colt calls Rain to let her know what has happened.

"How's Meg?" Rain asks. "She was pretty taken with her faux-aunt plan."

"We're working through it," he says.

July

ask yourself whether you would choose
if you could
to live without this
knowing the question to be unanswerable

On the plus side, since everyone knows, Tommie has lots of support. Her mother readies her old bedroom and Tommie spends the first week of July followed around Garnet's house by a concerned Vera, and waited on and catered to by her mother until, at the beginning of the second week, tempers flare, and the two women begin snapping at each other. The sound of their irritated voices sends Vera into fits of barking, which half the time culminate in her drinking all the water in her bowl and then throwing it up on the parlor rug. This is not a family that handles stress well; so it is that on Saturday Tommie packs up her belongings, hugs her mother, plants a kiss on Vera's head, and returns to her apartment to the great relief of all three.

There, on Sunday, Ben brings Tommie flowers, a bunch of orange lilies interspersed with daisies and ivy. She puts them in a green glass wine carafe and sets it on the kitchen counter.

"Thank you, Ben. They're beautiful," Tommie says.

"What are we going to do, Tommie?" he asks.

Tommie has never felt so old.

"You know I love you, Ben. But it's not enough, is it?"

"I don't think so. For either one of us."

"We're going to be seeing each other every day at school in the fall."

"I can live with that. What about you?"

"Maybe we can learn to like each other a little."

After Ben leaves, Tommie is as alone as she's been in a very long time. What feels strange is that it doesn't feel bad at all.

Since her return from Ohio in May, Garnet and Jake have been meeting for coffee at The Cup two or three mornings a week. Despite beginning as they did, or maybe because of it, they are tentative with one another, oddly shy. He does not walk or drive to the house to pick her up. Garnet is scrupulous about requesting two bills, paying for her own coffee though she treats them both to scones or muffins and will not hear of Jake kicking in for that.

Garnet and Jake prefer a booth if one happens to be free, and since they meet after the morning rush, that's often the case. Jake arrives first and by the time Garnet joins him he's drinking a latte into which he's emptied a couple more of the little half-and-halfs on their table, so the beverage, which is what Garnet calls it, has transmogrified into an excellent source of nearly caffeine-free calcium, a mystifying practice he shares with Ruby. Why have a gun without the ammo? They read the *Times* and eat the pastries Garnet orders with her own black coffee.

Ordinarily Vera, who is welcome at the little café, would accompany Garnet. But Vera's opinion of Jake remains unchanged. The one time Garnet tried bringing the dog, Vera spent the scant half hour she was there rumbling almost but not quite inaudibly, and directing a very beady fishy-eye in Jake's direction. "I'm afraid she just doesn't cotton to me, Garnet," Jake had said.

"Vera is not my mother. I will not let her dictate my friendships," Garnet replied, giving up anyway and preparing to take her aggrieved-looking dog back home.

As she was leaving, Jake said, "Garnet, I do believe she's trying to tell you she thinks I should be the one sent home."

"I wouldn't be surprised," Garnet said. "Somehow she's confused the dog-owner relationship and thinks of herself as the owner dog."

But for the week Tommie spends with her, Garnet, otherwise occupied, does not talk to Jake or show up at The Cup. When she finally joins him again, it is the Monday after Tommie has returned to her apartment.

"I missed you," he says. "Tommie doing okay?"

"Small towns," sighs Garnet. "Everybody knows everything. Tommie will be fine, I think."

"And Ben?"

"It's hard to give up the idea of something you thought you

wanted so badly for so long, and I'm not talking about Tommie's pregnancy here, but I think he's going to do it."

"Garnet, Lily is coming back for a week on Friday. To check up on me I think."

"So we won't be seeing each other for a while?"

"No, Garnet, I don't want Lily to keep us apart."

"*Hmmm.* Let me think about this. It won't be awkward? You, me, and the reason I divorced my husband?"

"Yes, and I don't care," Jake says and takes her hand.

At this, the equilibrium of the relationship they've so carefully established over the weeks since they had sex, its calm and measured platonic civility, destabilizes, and they walk hand in hand back to Jake's house where, on a perfect summer day in July, they become lovers once again.

"If you don't want to see me while Lily's here, I understand," Jake says, watching Garnet pull her pale blue-and-white-striped T-shirt over her head.

"I don't think we can do *this* while your daughter is visiting, but if we want to continue—"

"And we do want to continue."

"We do," says Garnet. "Then Lily and I need to somehow make peace with one another."

"I need to think how to do this," Jake says.

Garnet laughs. "Well, when you figure it out, be sure to let me know."

Jake climbs out of bed and comes over and puts his arms around the almost-dressed Garnet. Neither one has as yet uttered the fateful three words. In Garnet's case, she admits to herself that, really, she no longer knows what they mean when spoken in a situation like this, woman to man and man to woman. The words *I love you* fall from her lips easily when spoken to her reprobate dog, her little niece and, even now, to her lost sister, but here she's entered a foreign country with no map, a country whose borders she hasn't crossed in many years, and a place where it feels like a person might easily lose her way.

Later, walking home, Garnet can hear the unhappy animal inside her home from three houses away, Vera announcing to the neighborhood her displeasure at being left in the lurch. Coming closer, she also sees that Bowie is once again sitting on her porch swing. Since the birthday party, her ex-husband has begun turning up at Garnet's front door under the impression that this is where he lives.

She watches him get up and ring the bell, setting off a fresh volley of barks on the other side of the door. He's wearing his usual torn flannel shirt under worn denim overalls. She notices he's barefoot once again. At least now it's warm outside.

Bowie turns, and seeing Garnet walking up the sidewalk to the porch, he begins to complain. "I don't know what's the matter with this key," he says.

He is looking down at his own house key.

Even so, Garnet observes he has shaved today and his hair is neatly wet-combed. Always, always, her maddening ex refuses to be boxed in, unable even at this point to be pinned down, to be, as she fervently wishes, conveniently labeled like some euthanized fritillary.

"And why is my door locked anyway?" he whines.

Garnet takes him by the arm and guides him down the steps to the sidewalk.

"You don't live here anymore, Bowie. You live there."

She points down the street.

"When did I move? I don't remember moving. Why is my dog barking?"

He begins to shuffle down the street, looking for all the world like a character in a Beckett play, so caught up in his own drama he is unaware that others, some sorely lacking in empathy, might find him pathetic—Garnet reluctantly including herself in that number—or, even worse, amusing. What goes around has returned, as she so passionately at one time wished, and she is again surprised at how little satisfaction karma gives her.

When Colt arrives home from work, Garnet tells him it's happened again. That evening Colt calls Tommie.

"Houston, we have a problem."

"I wish you'd stop saying that every time you call me with bad news."

"What would you like me to say?"

"How about, 'Tommie, we have a problem.'"

"You, dear cousin, are no fun, no fun at all."

After Colt finishes describing Bowie's behavior, Tommie says, "You know this has been happening for a while, right? He's okay, better than okay, and then something like this crops up. It runs its course and then our Bowie returns from whatever planet he's been whisked away to."

"One of these times he's not going to come back. We need to start planning for that day, Tommie. It's not fair to put this burden on Garnet who, after all, threw him out of the house and then divorced his ass and has legally shed all responsibility for the man."

"We could start looking into assisted living."

"I'll help, Tommie, but you're the one with power of attorney."

"And, of course, we have to factor in that we'll get no cooperation from Bowie whatever we come up with. But you're right. We should at least start looking."

Lily arrives on Friday, Lily, product of a youthful marriage that ended in divorce when she was quite small, her mother soon remarried to another perfectly nice man who proved a perfectly adequate stepfather. Lily however, missing Jake, has spent her time ever since trying to get and retain his attention, sometimes in appropriate ways—graduating magna cum laude from Sarah Lawrence, for example, Jake paying the full ride. And sometimes—more often—in less admirable ways. Like her affair with Bowie which continued for over a year pretty much without anyone catching on, until Lily could not stand the anonymity one more minute and wrote a letter to Garnet asking her to step aside so that Bowie, who had no intention of doing anything of the sort, could marry her. (Though, truth be told, the idea of marriage to Bowie was not especially appealing to her either; *Homo sapiens*—a rational species, except when it's not.)

For a short time, she reigned as the Paris Hilton of Haven, lacking only a sex tape to seal her infamy. Garnet divorced Bowie, and Jake dissolved their partnership. Father and daughter were left irretrievably estranged, an unintended consequence—but how could it have been otherwise?—and a situation bitterly regretted by Lily who felt that none of it was really her fault, seeing how none of it would even have happened if Jake had not left her own mother all those years ago, something that still seemed like only yesterday every time she thought about it. And she thought about it all the time. Forty-five years old or five, sometimes it seemed there was no difference, no difference at all. Only with the advent of her father's health problems, have fences begun to be mended.

While out running a few errands, Garnet observes Lily's rental car, a Mitsubishi—appropriately scarlet, she thinks—parked in Jake's driveway. When she gets home, there's a message on her answering machine from him. "I'll be at The Cup tomorrow morning, regular time. We hope to see you there."

While Garnet listens, noting the "we," Colt sits, barefoot, at the kitchen table feeding Vera corn chips as he scrolls through his emails and texts. His dirt-caked work boots have been left by the back door in a cardboard box provided by Garnet and replaced often by her. His work socks are in his personal yellow plastic wash basket, also provided by Garnet. He does his own laundry on Sunday nights. This is an organized household. He looks up as the machine finishes speaking. "You and Jake, huh?"

"Too much salt and fat, Colt. No more corn chips for you today. Or Vera."

"We like them," Colt says. "And way to avoid the subject, Gigi."

"Yes, okay, Jake and I have been meeting up occasionally for coffee," Garnet says, taking the bag of chips off the table and putting them back in the cupboard as Vera looks mournfully up at her.

"Vera tells me she doesn't much like him. The obvious choice, she says, is George."

"Why is it that everybody has opinions on what I consider to be none of their business?"

"Whatever you say, auntie. You do know his daughter, Cruella, is in town, right?"

The next morning, Garnet changes clothes three times before finding an outfit she thinks gives the impression she wants to project, of someone who's tossed on a beautifully put-together but casual outfit without thinking about it (rather than the one whose bed and floor are now littered with discarded alternatives), someone capable of confidently heading out the door to meet a woman who'd slept with her husband (three? four? years ago. Could it really be that long?), the same woman who *snap!* like some witch in a fairy tale—no, she can't say *bitch*; there are no bitches in any fairy tale that she's familiar with—turned Bowie into Garnet's ex-husband. And then, most humiliating of all, walked away after the damage was done.

When she enters The Cup, their favorite waitress, May, says, "They're over in the corner booth, honey."

Garnet knows many, even most of her friends hate the *honey*, *sweetie*, *sweetheart*, *dearie* with which the young, and the middle-aged who putatively should know better—their turn so obviously rapidly approaching—address their female elders. But she rather likes it. There are so many much worse things they could be calling her, now that civility and good manners seem to have gone out the window with the advent of the current administration, Washington itself having morphed, behaviorally, from the idealized city on a hill back to a primordial, uncivilized state of chaos.

"Thank you, May," she says.

"No problem, sweetie."

"Good morning," Garnet offers as Jake stands to let Garnet slide into the seat she prefers, closest to the window.

"You and my father, Garnet? Really? Is this your idea of revenge?" Lily says, avoiding any pretense of beating around the bush, in fact pretty much incinerating the shrub. Jake looks appalled, but Garnet wonders how he might have anticipated anything different. Lily surely must take after her mother, she decides. Except for the green eyes, Garnet can see little of Jake in her.

"I'm fine, Lily. And how are you, dear?"

Sauce for the goose, she thinks.

"We have nothing to say to each other. I want you to know my father made me come today."

To Garnet, Lily resembles a resentful teenager. All she needs to complete the impression is a bad QuikCuts hairdo, and a less beautifully made-up face.

"And how did he manage to do that?" Garnet says.

"That's enough, Lily," Jake says.

To the surprise of everyone, possibly including the crier herself, Lily bursts into tears. Her mascara streaks, her face reddens unattractively, and her nose starts to run. Garnet begins to suspect for the first time that an actual human being might be sitting in front of her instead of what? a trollop? harlot? fallen woman? Garnet's angry imagination seems to tend toward faintly Victorian labels of opprobrium rather than current ugly epithets, the skanks, sluts, etcetera, up to and including the c-word she has never uttered, never will.

And there's no way this human being would have access to such a humble thing as a Kleenex in that expensive tiny (ersatz, she prays, but doubts it) alligator envelope purse lying on the table, a purse good only for holding one's platinum credit card and lip gloss. (Such a bloodthirsty species, Garnet thinks, killing intricate and beautiful creatures, not even for food, but for their skin. How can we even feign surprise at any of our other less-than-admirable behaviors?) As Lily reaches for her wholly inadequate paper napkin with its damp coffee ring, Garnet rummages in her own bag and finds a pack of tissues, pulls one out and gives it to Lily, then hands her the whole thing when it becomes clear one is not nearly going to suffice.

Meanwhile, May has hurried over to their booth.

"Is everything okay here?" she asks.

Garnet looks up at the waitress. "What do you think, May?"

"You can bring me the check," Jake says, and begins to get up. "We are leaving. I am so sorry."

What can Garnet reply? "Oh, it's nothing," "Never mind, it's okay," or worst of all, "Whatever." Plus, she's still trying to process what has just happened to her. We are not talking about Lily's initial outburst, but rather the effect Lily's mini breakdown is having on Garnet's own feelings. Her long-held judgment of Lily, the one that charged, convicted, and sentenced the defendant, no trial necessary, has developed a fissure and begun to crumble. In fact, later, she will wonder if the imaginary dust rising from that metaphorical collapse is what makes her begin to sneeze uncontrollably.

Both Jake and Lily look at her, alarmed.

"Are you all right?" Jake asks Garnet.

In reply, she sneezes again, three times in rapid succession, and Lily silently pushes the pack of tissues back toward her. Garnet, finally quiet, takes a deep breath, wipes her eyes and blows her nose, now Lily's twin, she thinks, red faced, runny-nosed, eyes streaming.

"Aren't we a pair?" she says to Lily and begins to laugh. "Oh, please sit down, Jake. You're not going anywhere."

"Can I get you anything else?" May asks, looking relieved.

"Anybody else hungry?" Garnet asks. "Bring us some menus please, May."

They wind up eating huge breakfasts. They order pancakes and little pork sausages, hash browns, bowls of The Cup's famous apple brown Betty with scoops of vanilla ice cream. Garnet and Lily are not suddenly best friends, or even especially convivial, but they find themselves capable of passing the syrup and commenting approvingly that it is real maple (Garnet) and complaining about the recalcitrance of the ketchup (Lily). Jake seems content to eat his breakfast, casting only the odd bemused glance at the ruined faces of two nonetheless quite lovely women.

"I know we usually pay our own checks, Garnet," Jake says when they are finished. "But today, I insist."

"And I accept," Garnet says. "As long as we each leave a tip. We gave May quite a turn, I'm afraid."

And thus it is that truce of a kind is achieved. Garnet continues for the duration of Lily's week-long visit to meet Jake at The Cup; his daughter does not accompany him.

On a few occasions Garnet runs into Lily, once with Vera, outside the library where Lily is returning a stack of DVDs and where Vera appears quite enamored, greeting Lily enthusiastically, nosing and licking her hand, tail wagging vigorously the whole while. (*Hmph*, Garnet thinks, finding herself disappointed in her faithless pet's lack of sensitivity, then murderously wondering if and when animal and woman may have met previously, before quitting that line of inquiry in the interests of her mental health and continued lack of a criminal record.)

They meet yet again at the IGA in the produce section. Nevertheless, both times they are able to exchange a few polite words before going their separate ways. Garnet thinks of this as their tiny contribution to world peace. At least one other time, Garnet, catching a glimpse of Lily getting out of her parked car a block away, turns around and walks the other way. She's not proud of it, but she's not going to beat herself up about it either, having recently bought into the whole radical self-compassion movement for just such occasions as this.

And then on Friday, once again on her way to the supermarket in the middle of the afternoon, Garnet drives by Jake's house (only slightly out of her way, after all) and the little red car is gone.

Bowie is incensed. He turns up on Garnet's porch again on Saturday morning, knocking loudly and ringing the doorbell.

Colt opens the door and takes in the disheveled elderly man standing before him in dirty sweat pants and a once-beautiful bathrobe sacrilegiously crafted from an antique Navajo blanket. He shakes his head and does not invite him in. Luckily Garnet has already left, meeting Jake yet again for breakfast.

"What is it you want, Bowie?"

"Nobody told me. Nobody told me until it was too late."

"Told you?"

"Remmy says that Lily was here and then she left."

"And?"

"And I wanted to see her and now I can't."

Furious tears are running down Bowie's face. He collapses onto the porch swing and begins pushing it back and forth rapidly with a grubby left foot.

Colt is glad Garnet is not here. And very reluctantly, he is also beginning to feel sorry for the old man.

"Did you ever think, Bowie, that if Lily really wanted to see you, she would?"

"What? No! I love her."

"I thought you loved Garnet? You asked her to let you move back here, remember?"

"I do love Garnet, I do."

Bowie is looking increasingly confused. His nose is also running now. Once again Colt finds himself taking out his handkerchief. He gives it to Bowie who swabs his face then blows his nose loudly.

"You can keep that," Colt says.

Colt takes Bowie's arm and walks him down the porch steps. As they walk together toward his house, Bowie begins talking about Remmy's impending departure this week, his mind already skittering from recent tragedy elsewhere. Colt regards him almost enviously. To have heartbreak fall away as easily as shedding an extraneous piece of outerwear, a jacket perhaps, is one advantage of the depredations of aging inexplicably too seldom cited.

"Freddy's bought a condo. He told Remmy it's too expensive

anymore to rent in Las Vegas. Like flushing money down the toilet."

"Nice image."

Bowie ignores him.

"What day is Remmy leaving?" Colt asks.

"Wednesday or maybe Thursday, I forget."

"You going to be okay by yourself in that big house? Maybe it's time to think about downsizing, Bowie."

"Me? I'll be fine."

Yeah, just peachy! Colt thinks.

"And Remmy wants me to come out and visit."

Riiiiight. What a great idea. Colt pictures Bowie navigating O'Hare. A Kingston Trio song he remembers from somewhere begins to play in his mind, the one about Charlie, who never returns, riding an endless loop on the MTA.

"Well, here we are, Bowie, back home."

Colt watches him unsteadily ascend the steps up to the porch. The front door Bowie then enters is not only unlocked but ajar. He waits until his uncle disappears into the house before going up the steps himself, and pulling the big door securely closed. Heading back to Garnet's, Colt has to remind himself that it's not all downhill all the time. Some days Bowie argues with Colt, finding himself quite able to cite legal precedent, usually about some topic having to do with the construction business, and once fairly recently they even discussed who actually gets to claim coverage under the Bill of Rights in present-day America. And who does not. But on other days, Bowie is foggy on what a Bill of Rights might be, and the pursuit of happiness, cited in another founders' document, sounds even to Colt like a race Bowie might have run as a much younger man.

Middle of the week, George invites Colt and Garnet over for a picnic. He splits and marinates two Cornish hens to barbecue on his state-of-the-art gas grill, a thing of dials and lights and digital readout, which looks to Colt, lover of both Star Wars and Trek, as though it just landed on George's patio in all its stainless-steel glory, visitor from some galaxy far, far away, his hope, expressed more than once to his neighbor, that it comes in peace. However, dinner is delayed because George, uncharacteristically, has forgotten to get the alien's propane tank refilled. Colt offers to make the run to Tractor Supply and on the way back picks up a quart container of actually pretty good red-skin potato salad from the grocery store deli as his contribution to the meal, Garnet already having furnished dessert, a key lime cheesecake. It's almost seven when they finally sit down to dinner.

When they finish eating, it's after eight o'clock, and cool enough for Garnet's purple cardigan or, in Colt's case, a threadbare though clean sweatshirt. Vera is on her long lead, clipped to the eye of a large shiny metal corkscrew, its base buried deep in the lawn. Having reluctantly abandoned all hope of an invitation to participate in her pack's chicken festival, she is on her side, eyes not quite closed, indicating to Colt that the dog is monitoring the situation, ready to spring instantly into action should, even now, a poultry malfunction, even one involving only bones, occur. The three humans sit at the picnic table in George's side yard drinking sweet tea, too full to feel like clearing the table, when Garnet spots Remington walking up her driveway.

"Over here, Remmy," she calls out. "I'm afraid all the chicken is gone, but there's a bit of cheesecake left. How about it?"

"Don't mind if I do," Remmy says, walking across the grass and sitting down next to his sister and across from Colt.

"I'm headed back to Nevada tomorrow and I came to say goodbye."

"Thanks for keeping an eye on Bowie," Garnet says, handing him a paper plate with the last piece and a fork.

"A little too tart for my taste," Remmy says, after polishing off the dessert in three bites. "And pre-made graham cracker crust, Garnet? Why?"

"I did notice how quickly you forced it down just to be polite."

"Well, there is that," Remmy acknowledges and sister and brother begin to laugh.

"Always was a critical little bugger, wasn't I?"

"Truer words," Garnet replies.

Remmy pauses, then continues, "He's not the Bowie I knew ten, even five, years ago, Garnet."

"I don't know that that's a bad thing, Remmy," Garnet says. "I didn't much like the Bowie of ten, even five, years ago. But you should be talking to Tommie about this, not me. She's pretty much taking care of things."

"I have talked to Tommie, Garnet, and of course she's aware of his situation. But, Garnet, he still loves you."

"I know he does, Remmy. I also know he still loves Lily. And sometimes he confuses the two of us."

"Well, I just thought I should say so. I also came to say goodbye to you, Colt. Maybe you'll come visit us sometime."

"Not likely," Colt replies.

"We can't let bygones be bygones, son?"

"I don't think you get to ask me that, Remmy. Or call me 'son.'"

Remmy sighs. George looks uncomfortable.

"Some tea, Remmy?" Garnet says.

"Thank you, Garnet," he says, rising. "But I have to finish packing. Tommie is picking me up at six tomorrow morning. My flight's at eight."

Leaving, he does not hug his sister. She does not appear to mind.

As Remmy heads back down the driveway, Colt looks over at Garnet. "You have something you want to say to me?"

Garnet says nothing.

"*I know*, all right?" he says. "Eat the poison. Wait for the rat to die."

"You carry both sides of a conversation so well, Colt. I wouldn't dream of interrupting."

"I will never let him off the hook, never," Colt says.

Garnet remains quiet.

"Gigi, you are making me crazy."

"Clearly," Garnet says.

It's now twilight and fireflies have begun to rise up into the not-quite-dark, their little lights winking on and off. The air is damp. Time to move indoors. But son, sister, and neighbor, even the dog, stay where they are, silent, watching Remmy walk away. The streetlights come on as he makes his way down the street toward Bowie's house, entering and departing one pool of light after another. Remmy is almost halfway to his destination when Colt swears under his breath. He abruptly gets up from the table to follow after his father, walking quickly to catch up.

"I wouldn't have predicted that at all," George says, finally beginning to clear the table, stacking dishes, collecting silverware.

Garnet wipes and folds the red-checkered, flannel-back plastic tablecloth.

"He's a good boy. He talked himself right into it. Remmy doesn't deserve it, forgiveness, but who does, really. If we deserved it, we wouldn't need it."

"And Colt will be a better man for doing it," says George.

"He will."

"Garnet, you're seeing Jake, aren't you?"

"I am."

"I can smell the coffee. Guess this means I don't have a chance."

"George, you and I were never going to be more than friends. But we are good friends, are we not? Good for each other too."

"You do know, Garnet, Vera prefers me."

"If it were up to Vera, she'd be herding me down the aisle to you, wearing her hideous bridesmaid's dress."

"Well, that's some comfort I guess."

"She does not like Jake at all, yet strangely is quite taken with Lily."

"And if not for that serious lapse destroying all your confidence in her judgment, we might well be together, yes?"

"Absolutely, George. Believe it. Yes."

The smile they direct at each other is barely visible in the darkness. George untethers Vera, handing Garnet the leash. Then George, with his dishes, and Garnet, with her dog, tablecloth folded over her arm, walk through the dew-soaked grass, each to their own back door.

Remmy hears Colt's footsteps behind him and turns around, waiting for his son to catch up. They meet under the streetlight in front of Bowie's house.

"What changed your mind?" Remmy asks him.

"Am I to believe you are a new man?"

"I make no such claim, Colt. I will admit to many regrets, especially regarding your mother and you."

"Hearing that does not make things better. It makes things worse. When it counted you were not around. But I'm trying hard not to hate you anymore. Have a safe trip. Tell Freddy hello."

Colt sticks his hand out, and father and son shake hands. He does not hug his father. It would be reasonable to assume that Remmy minds.

August

Leaf does not choose but inclines.
It is not the will of firefly
that ignites the darkness.

In this summer of momentous happenings for the Delaney family and friends, Rain flies under the radar. She and Eddie and Meg (Meg, ecstatic, filled with the importance of the secret she has kept for two whole weeks) take themselves to the courthouse. It is a beautiful day, the first Friday of August. Summer, that wily card sharp, is holding her cards close to her chest, promising the gullible that the dog days are soon to be only a memory, even though everyone here knows perfectly well what a liar she is, the rest of the month extending into September offering at least a couple more hellish blasts of heat and humidity, the worst preferably occurring the week school starts. But for today, her promise holds. The day is perfect, offering cloudless blue skies and a pleasant breeze.

Eddie, looking extremely uncomfortable in his suit, a 1950s blue-and-white-striped seersucker he will doubtless never wear again, and a tie, both of which he insisted on as only right considering the gravity of what they are about to do (and both found for him by Rain at Retro Treasures on Water Street). Rain and Meg wear long, pretty sundresses in complementing small floral prints made especially for them by one of Rain's friends. There is a heavenly smelling corsage of gardenia surrounded by violets pinned to Rain's bodice, and Meg sports a wristlet of violets, both provided by Eddie with no help from anybody else. When they depart the judge's chambers an hour later, having been third in line behind a biker couple, female, holding hands, with matching Harley Davidson tattoos on their biceps, and the stunned-looking, conservatively dressed middle-aged couple behind them, two have become husband and wife, the third remaining unchanged except for the addition of an extra father, one she will call *Pops*, to differentiate him from Colt's *Daddy*.

The three repair to the San Remo where Chianti and Pepsi flow (the soft drink usually forbidden, but as Eddie says, *What the hell, it's a celebration.* And Meg whispers, *What the hell* and smiles, tasting the words on her tongue and finding they tingle and pop much like the carbonation of her drink). The food is served family-style. There are no leftovers, matrimony like death apparently famishing to all concerned.

Instead of wedding cake, Eddie and his bride feed each other a bite of the tiramisu they are all sharing, neither even considering mashing the dessert onto the other's face, if only because both suspect the sight would horrify Meg, her life thereafter devolving into rabid single-till-death celibacy (using the original meaning, "never married," rather than its irritating current confusion with "chaste," as the embittered, future forty-year-old Meg would no doubt be happy to instruct you), the other thought also occurring to them both, though they do not realize it—how can they ever prepare this innocent to survive the real world in all its criminal, heartbreaking beauty? The following week, Rain sends out announcements intending them, barring post office screwups, to arrive on Saturday. Some, like Colt's, actually do.

"*Son of a bitch!*"

"Calm down, Colt," Garnet says, reading her own missive.

"How could she not tell me!"

"Rain or Meg?"

"Both! Either!"

"The same way you let Rain know you were going to date Meg's teacher before you did?"

"That was different."

Garnet ignores this and says, "You had to know it was a possibility. And you like Eddie."

"It's a huge decision. What about Meg?"

"What about Meg? I think you don't mind Eddie the boyfriend but are opposed to Eddie, Meg's stepfather. You hated to share even as a little boy."

"I am not that small-minded. And I have always shared just fine."

Garnet gives him a look.

"You would come over to play with Tommie," she says, "and the two of you would gather your toys around yourselves and glare at the other."

"Okay, maybe I am that small-minded, and if you want the truth, one father is all anyone needs."

"Like your father?"

"God damn it, Garnet."

"Colt, Colt, Colt."

Garnet puts her arms around her nephew who has given up trying to make sense of his feelings.

By the time he drives over to Rain's that afternoon, Colt has accepted the inevitable. He and Garnet have gone out to Tom's Nursery and purchased four large richly hued mums the color of amethyst, one for each member of his reconfigured family. He has put himself in charge of delivering them.

Eddie is out in the driveway washing Rain's car. Meg is helping, handling the hose, and rinsing off the soap as Eddie moves on with the big sponge. They do not notice Colt at first. It hurts his tiny, stony heart to see them laughing together as he unloads the mums onto the sidewalk.

"Daddy!" Meg says. "What did you bring us? Purple ones! My favorite."

Rain comes out of the house,

"From Garnet and me," he says, setting them two at a time onto the porch. "Congratulations."

"Colt, the announcement said no gifts."

"One for each of us," says Colt. "This little family we have here."

Unexpectedly, Rain's eyes fill with tears. "I didn't expect this reaction, frankly."

"It's not the reaction poor Garnet got, I'm afraid."

"Well, God bless her. I'm happy to see you let her unplug and reboot you. Sometimes that's all it takes. Why don't you get the spade from the garage and you and Meg can plant those on either side of the front steps."

Meanwhile, Franny has not forgotten about adopting a dog. "You sure that's a good idea?" Colt asks.

They are making toast and drinking coffee in Franny's minuscule kitchen, Colt in sweats, Franny wearing one of his shirts, when she mentions it to him on Saturday morning.

"It's a little apartment, Franny," he says. "Isn't there a 'no pets' policy? Maybe they'd let you have a small one, a dachshund? If you put down an extra security deposit?"

"I don't want a little dog. I want a big one, like Vera. Something I can wrap my arms around."

Colt thinks he fits that job description just fine. Why does she need something else to love when she has him?

"You're at the shelter as it is every Wednesday now," he says. "You don't get enough puppy love there?"

"Yes, I volunteer at the county shelter. One morning, once a week, until school starts."

"I worry about you winding up with eighteen rescues. A hoarder. Health department called in. Video on *The News at 6*."

He's only half-kidding.

Franny laughs. "And that is quite the leap, Colt."

"I know you, Franny."

"You do, do you? Okay, I confess. I have my eye on eleven or twelve right now that I wouldn't mind one bit bringing home this week."

"I know you're not serious."

"I'm not. About the twelve. But get used to the idea because it's going to happen."

It seems that they are gearing up for their first serious disagreement after four blissful months.

"And," continues Franny, "it just so happens I'm thinking about moving anyway. My lease is up September first."

For the second time, Colt is thrown for a loop.

"Moving? Where?"

"I'm looking."

Franny has begun to talk to Colt about her husband, his sudden death five years ago, the motorcycle accident in which neither one of them was wearing a helmet, how it affected her, still does, she, his passenger, thrown clear onto the wet, soft dirt of a freshly plowed field, the rain which contributed to the accident having ultimately saved her life. She admits to a survivor's guilt that has made her careful, cautious, responsible, as though by becoming the most grown-up of the grown-ups, misfortune might not ever again be able to find her, much less place her at ground zero. Though unrealistic, it makes her feel better. Safer. And she's told Colt that as the school year progressed, she'd observed his sense of responsibility, his parenting of Meg, noticed the way he treated his ex, Rain.

She's told him about the relationship preceding theirs in which things progressed too quickly; they'd moved in together after just a few months and everything rapidly fell apart. And, yes, Colt understands the subtext here. He knows it's too soon to bring up the subject of the two of them living in the same space. But he really likes not only making love to and waking up with this woman, but also reading the paper and drinking coffee with her. Taking the trash out. Drying dishes she's just washed. Or vice versa—no gender stereotyping here. He's a goner, he admits to himself. And he's pretty much decided the only way to deal with the situation is to make himself so indispensable that Franny will wake up one morning and realize she cannot bear to live without him.

At least that was the idea before she threw a monkey wrench, or rather, problematic canine, into his plans.

Later, after they're up for good and dressed, Franny shows him the places for rent she's highlighted in the paper, some already seen and crossed off. She's also searched online. Colt decides that if Franny is to be wooed and won, he'd better start getting involved too.

"I'll keep my eyes open," he says.

When he gets home, he tells Garnet about their conversation.

"Vera made her a dog lover? Amazing. Usually she helps

people decide a dog is way more work than they are interested in doing. Franny looking for something small? Tell her chihuahuas are the worst to housebreak."

"No chihuahuas. She wants a giant like Vera."

"Oh my. But her apartment is tiny."

"She's moving, looking for a bigger place."

"Really? With Remmy gone, I'd love to have someone else in that house with Bowie. Do you think she'd be interested?"

"Not in the attic. What about the carriage house apartment?"

"It needs work. Mostly cosmetic. Paint, cleaning, new carpeting. It is roomy. I'll talk to Tommie about giving her a deal. A big dog would be no problem there. We both know how much Bowie loves Vera."

Once Colt shares Garnet's idea with Franny, things move fast. Franny asks Colt and Meg to help her move. It's already the last week in August. She decides improvements can be made after she's moved in; the new sixth-grade teacher has already signed a lease for Franny's present apartment starting September first, less than a week away.

Franny also changes her final scheduled shelter day to the weekend, the last Saturday in August—school begins the day after Labor Day and the first Monday in September is fast approaching, plus she will be moving next week. Things are about to get very busy. She takes Colt and Meg with her for this last visit. She will help with feeding and cleaning kennels as usual, and she has asked in advance if it's okay for her two guests to take a pup at a time out to the fenced-in area for ten minutes apiece of playtime.

The facility is not fancy but Colt's first impressions are positive. They are greeted by a large, calm, and capable-looking woman, Maxine, in green surgical scrubs and blue Crocs, in charge at the front desk. The place is orderly and bright, its concrete block walls each painted a different soft pastel—blue, yellow, green, and peach. The linoleum floor with its black-and-white squares is clean.

"Max, this is Colt, and Meg, his daughter. Colt and Meggie, this is Maxine, or as I call her, Super Max."

"You are a funny girl," Maxine says.

She turns to Colt.

"We'd like your girlfriend here to quit her big bucks day job, apply for food stamps, and come work for us."

The noise that greets them when they enter the kennel area is deafening. It reminds Colt of a long-ago avant-garde concert of atonal compositions that Rain dragged him to. Here, there are howls and barks, yips and squeaks, there is keening, and one impressive basso profundo baying solo from the bloodhound in the first kennel.

"Do you ever get used to this?" Colt asks Max; he shouts the question.

He notices Max is wearing small flesh-colored earplugs.

"In a minute, they'll calm down." She smiles.

And when, as she promises, they do, Colt hears Mozart playing softly on the speakers overhead. She answers before he has a chance to ask.

"Not their favorite," Max says. "Believe it or not, Debussy wins every time. They also love Shania Twain. Brooks and Dunn is another fave. And they hate, hate, hate Ravel and Stravinsky and Aerosmith."

"How can you tell?"

"Lots of sarcastic howling. I guess if I were you, I'd start at the first kennel and just keep going. The names are posted for each dog as well as any special concerns."

"Surely they don't all have names when they come in," says Colt.

"No, but they all have names when they leave us," Max says. She adds, "There's a tub of toys right outside the door. And keep that big water bowl outside filled. Use the wall spigot."

Colt and Meg begin with Louie the bloodhound, who spends his ten minutes, nose to the ground, methodically vacuuming up all the smells in the play yard. It occurs to Colt that Louie would probably have enjoyed being last instead of first, after the ten other incarcerated canines had run around, rolled in the dirt, and in the case of some males, obsessively marked their territory, the females generally content to simply squat, pee without an agenda, and move on with their lives (no judgment). For Louie, Colt realizes after observing the dog, arriving before or after his peers is probably the difference between a *USA Today* and the Sunday *Times*.

By the end of the first hour, he and Meg have also entertained or been entertained by Pepper, Gunner, Ryley, Zoey, and Sam. Three are mutts, plus one rottweiler, a sad-eyed golden retriever, and Louie. Meg winds up refilling the large stainless water bowl three times.

By the end of the morning, Colt is exhausted. Franny and Max and Meg laugh at him, but he can tell Max's thanks come from the heart. And twelve dogs have had a bit of individual attention. Zoey, in alliterative allegiance to her name, spent her recess in crazed zoomies that made them dizzy, crossing and recrossing the yard, stopping only for one bowl-draining drink of water. Pepper preferred listening, head cocked, as Meg sat with her on the grass and talked to her. Colt tried throwing the ball but the dog ignored it, preferring instead ten minutes of belly rubs, ear scratches, and being told she was a good, good girl. And Sam broke his heart. He didn't want to play or retrieve the ball. There was no tail wagging. To Colt, the dog gave the appearance of someone on the verge of giving up on trying to figure out a really tough math problem, one involving subtraction with the subtrahend taken permanently away, and Colt himself unable to help. When asking the universe to mitigate a situation or, at the very least to explain much less justify it, more and more he hears only its implacable silence.

"Thirsty work for all of us," Colt says to Max, upending the last of the Dr. Pepper he's just purchased from the machine in the office. "Please tell me, what brings a beautiful golden to a shelter anyway?"

"You die leaving no plan for your pet, so your kid who lives in Seattle brings Sam here before he leaves for home after the funeral. Still, not the worst ending this story could have. He'll be getting picked up by a retriever rescue next week."

"Wow," says Colt.

When they leave, Max calls after them, "You're welcome any time."

"Don't be surprised if my daughter and I show up some Saturday morning," Colt says.

"I look forward to it."

In the car, Meg in the back seat, earbuds plugged in, listening to whatever it is that ten-year-olds are listening to this summer, Colt says quietly, "I was afraid to ask Max, Franny. The dogs we played with this morning, any chance of them being put down?"

"There's a reason I call her 'super,'" Franny says. "Max has through sheer force of will made the shelter no-kill, doing whatever it takes to find homes for every animal coming in. And that includes the cats you weren't interested in seeing. By the way, what is it with you and cats anyway?"

"Myself, I want to be loved not judged."

"I'll keep that in mind."

They drop Meg off at Rain's. She is missing Saturday night at Garnet's for a sleepover with three of her Girl Scout buddies, friends more and more assuming a greater role in her young life. Additional evidence to her glum father, though give him credit, he's trying not to show it, that time's winged chariot has no hand-brake option that might slow its ineluctable progress.

"How was your morning at the shelter?" Garnet asks.

Colt is making salsa, chopping up sweet onions, ripe peaches from the farmers' market, and the tomatoes he's harvested from the small garden Garnet cultivates in the one consistently sunny spot in her tree-shaded yard.

"You know, Garnet, I'm glad you asked because—"

"*Stop right there.*"

"What?"

"I know what's coming."

"How?"

"Because I've been on this earth forty years longer than you and have some experience with what happens when an animal lover spends time with the furred and homeless. Vera very much prefers being an only dog."

"Don't you want to know?"

"Actually, I don't."

"A golden. The owner died and his kid dumped his dog at the shelter. You have never seen a sadder—"

"Not one more word, do you hear me!"

They eat dinner in a silence unusual for the two. Garnet comments favorably on the salsa, Colt asks her to pass the artichoke focaccia she picked up on her way home this afternoon. She clears the table; he begins to wash the dishes. Garnet takes a clean dishtowel from the drawer.

"All right," she says. "What exactly is it you want from me?"

"Take Vera to meet Sam. Male, so no female rivalry. They might like each other."

"When pigs fly."

"This is not like you, Gigi."

"Okay, set it up. But if Vera doesn't take to this Lothario—"

"Lothario? Really? He's neutered, Garnet."

"If Vera doesn't take to this Lothario, then we will speak no more about another dog in her house. Agreed?"

"Agreed."

Vera, subject of conversation for the last hour, is sacked out nearby on her kitchen bed, as opposed to the four other beds scattered throughout the house for her not-always-serene highness's repose.

Colt calls Franny and asks for Max's home number. Then he tells her why.

"You're what?"

"I said I'm going to adopt Sam."

"I recall a recent conversation ostensibly about someone

else's lack of willpower. Who knew you were talking about yourself?"

"Don't hold back, tell me what you really think, Franny."

"And Garnet is okay with this?"

"Garnet is okay if Vera is okay."

"A big *if*. Call me tomorrow?"

"Will do. I love you."

Colt apologizes to Max for the late evening call. He asks if they can come by tomorrow with Vera. And if the two dogs get along, can he adopt Sam rather than have him go to the golden rescue in Syracuse.

"We always prefer local adoptions, so the answer is yes," Max says. "And I'll cross my fingers."

"Please do. We are bringing a diva. The household revolves around her."

"Interesting. We'll see if Sam is also a fan, won't we? Better to arrive early, before the shelter opens."

Sundays, the shelter opens at noon. Garnet and Colt are in the parking lot at eleven with Vera who is regarding them suspiciously.

"Oh no, sweetie, we are not dropping you off. You're not worrying about that, are you?" Garnet asks, scratching the dog's ears.

"I don't think Vera is even aware there are such creatures as homeless or abused pets."

Garnet covers Vera's ears with her hands and shoots Colt a dirty look.

"What? What did I say?"

Max pulls into the shelter's lot at 11:15, just as she promised.

"I haven't got a life, if you haven't already figured that out. What a magnificent Pyr. I do know that's redundant, by the way."

Together they decide it best to walk Vera around the building and enter the fenced-in play area from the outside gate, letting her investigate for a few minutes before bringing Sam out.

Vera does not deign to investigate anything. She sits and looks enquiringly at Garnet. Colt translates the look for Garnet as *WTF?*

"You know what it means, right, Gigi?"

Garnet sighs.

Max opens the kennel door and Sam steps out into the yard. He looks no happier than the day before. Vera gets up. Neither dog's tail wags. Both Garnet and Colt studiously ignore the retriever. Garnet has dropped the leash so the Pyr can move freely. Vera strolls over to the golden and sniffs him. He does not care.

"See," Colt says to Garnet. "He's depressed."

Vera begins herding the impassive Sam, moving him first to the bench where they're sitting, then back to the gate, then to the kennel door. Seeing that her imperial status is not being questioned, she has begun to wag her tail.

"Oh, all right," Garnet says. "But if it doesn't work out for any reason, you have to find him a home elsewhere."

Colt takes Vera and Garnet home and grabs one of Vera's bright pink leashes, Garnet refusing any semblance of gender neutrality where Vera is concerned. He returns for Sam, filling out the forms, taking out his Visa card, on which he adds an extra fifty bucks. Just because. They stop at the big box pet emporium next to the mall. Sam accompanies him inside. Max told him his age was given as four and that seems about right. He is a serious, well-behaved animal. They pick up a sober black nylon leash and collar, some toys, a bed, a water and food bowl nestled, like Vera's, into a plastic platform, and one large bag of premium kibble. Having pretty much ensured the bill for the month on this credit card will nudge its limit, they head to Garnet's.

Once there, the golden is completely non-confrontational. Vera finds she also has no rival for her crown here at home. She herds Sam at will, demands that he move off his very own new bed so she can plop down on it, even makes him give her the squeaky rubber frog, his only toy at the shelter, all without any demurral on his part. By the end of the day, it's clear that a peaceable kingdom has been established with Vera as self-appointed domestic monarch for life.

"I'm going to start calling your dog Ida Amin, Garnet. I had no idea Vera could be such a despot."

"They'll sort it out. It's working for now; isn't that what you wanted?"

"I feel like Neville Chamberlain."

"We are not appeasing anyone here. And you're lucky you're talking to me. No one your age would even recognize the allusions."

"So I watch the history channel. You think my generation is unserious, maybe a little stupid, don't you? Many my age would have caught those references."

"Let's ask your friend Booker, shall we?"

"That is not fair and you know it. Booker is still in the toddler phase of adulthood."

"You have a point."

"I'm going to have to speak to Vera if she keeps pushing my boy around."

"Knock yourself out."

That evening they feed Vera first and then Garnet takes her out for a walk. At which point, Colt feeds Sam. His depression seems to have no effect on his appetite.

He falls asleep next to Colt's bed that night.

❧

The last week of August arrives. Franny, Colt, and Meg spend Monday night helping to pack up the little apartment into cardboard boxes that Franny found piled next to the dumpster behind the liquor store. It does not take long, given Franny's penchant for plain and spare—except for a ridiculous number of books, their number unremarked upon by Colt who has after all been living for years with a self-described bibliophile.

Colt takes Tuesday afternoon off. He and Meg return to Franny's, helping her load everything into the medium-size

U-Haul Colt has rented. He's asked Booker to come over and lend a hand with the furniture after he finishes work.

"Sure, man. Yeah," Booker said. "I will finally get to meet the fox who kidnapped you back there in April!"

"Just behave yourself, okay?"

"Dude, no worries; you know me."

"Yeah, and that's exactly what worries me."

Booker shows up on time. Painted flames no longer lick the side of his vehicle, which has recently been repainted a metallic gold that glitters in the late afternoon sun. The muffler, however, still rumbles. In deference to the females in attendance, Colt figures, the radio blasts Springsteen rather than Eminem. It's the first time Colt has seen the 14-karat update; Booker drives a rusted wreck of a ten-year-old Ford truck to the jobsite. And, by Colt's side, his daughter—is it possible she's impressed?—watches, eyes wide.

Before Colt can yell, "Turn that thing down," both Bruce and the engine are silenced, and Booker has bopped up the front steps.

"Nice ride," Franny says, her arms filled with a large trash bag of bedding and pillows.

Booker blushes. "Thanks. Trying to class up my act. Not a teenager anymore, I guess."

Colt introduces Booker to Franny and to Meg. This time it is Meg who blushes.

He takes a closer look at Booker but sees nothing there to interest a ten-year-old girl, though he does seem to have shaved today and recently combed the hair that shows under his backward NY Yankees ball cap. He hopes this is not yet another sign that Meg is growing-goddam-up. He's not ready.

"Let's get this show on the road," Colt says.

By six the apartment is empty. Colt's truck and the U-Haul are full. Booker has gone out to lock up his car before they head over to Bowie's. Meg is carrying out the last of the boxes of books, setting them on the curb for Colt or Booker to stash in the U-Haul.

Colt puts his arm around Franny as they regard the empty space from their vantage point at the apartment's door.

"Thoughts?" Colt says.

"I'm not sorry to be moving, but I'm leaving a piece of my heart. Our first night together, here—"

"Our first night, period," Colt points out.

"Are you implying I'm easy?"

"I guess I'm just attesting to my lethal charm."

Franny laughs and takes his hand. "Time to get going."

When they arrive, Garnet is there ready to lend a hand. Bowie, always the interested spectator, has already dragged an aluminum lawn chair over in order to better keep tabs on what's going on, and to offer helpful suggestions, first telling Colt he could unpack the truck a lot quicker if he threw out every other box of books.

"Nobody needs that many books, son. You don't want a woman smarter than you."

Then he tells Booker to stop looking like an idiot and turn his hat around.

Only Meg receives unqualified support, *Good work, Meggie* ringing out frequently.

And Franny? Bowie pretty much ignores Franny until she pulls the other lawn chair over and sits down next to him. Vera is stretched out on the grass at his side, panting.

"Get my dog here some water."

No *please*, no *would you mind?*

Garnet, arms full of bedding, shoots Frannie a sympathetic glance. Franny gets up and goes over to the outdoor faucet under which Vera's bowl sits. She rinses and refills the bowl using the nozzle on the coiled hose, brings it back to Bowie, and sets it down. Vera rises and drinks noisily if not gratefully.

"I want to thank you," Franny says to Bowie.

"No thanks necessary. Rent is due on the first of the month. Security deposit due today. This is a business arrangement, you know."

"I left a check for both on your kitchen table, Bowie. Right next to your bag of Cheetos."

"I know you and Colt are friends, but I have to watch my bottom line if I don't want to wind up living under a bridge."

"I have something to ask you, Bowie."

"*Nope*. No, not going to happen."

"What?" says Franny. "I haven't said anything yet."

She wants to tack on *you old coot* but good manners prevail.

"No. Cats. Ever."

"How about dogs, Bowie? I'm thinking of getting one. Or two. Dogs."

"Dogs? Dogs! Why didn't you say so? Though you do look like a cat person to me. Single. Older. You know."

"Tommie's right. You really know how to sweet-talk a girl."

Bowie regards her suspiciously. "You're being sarcastic, aren't you? Very unattractive trait. You'll never catch a husband that way."

It's the end of a long day and everybody is hungry. The large tray of chips, veggies, and dip Garnet supplied has already been attacked and decimated. Colt has made a run to China Palace; Bowie provided the paper plates and red plastic cups for the beer and lemonade he's donated to the cause from his refrigerator, and Franny has thrown one of her pretty pastel sheets over the beat-up picnic table in Bowie's side yard and lit a row of votives down the center. There is a bouquet of Queen Anne's lace and purple phlox from the weedy perimeter of Bowie's yard picked by Meg. Tommie arrives with a bag of brownies and chocolate chip ice cream.

"*Yay!*" says Meg.

"Skip the work, come for dinner, cuz? Is that it?" Colt asks.

"We had orientation today. All day."

Franny looks at her with sympathy. "The bullshit always precedes the actual teaching, doesn't it."

"I don't mind. I'm excited I'm actually going to finally have my own classroom and kids."

Booker is regarding Tommie with great interest. She's wearing a pale yellow summer dress and her hair is pulled back away from her face. She doesn't look twenty, but in the golden light of the dying day she also does not look almost thirty either. She and Garnet are the only humans present, including Bowie, who are not some combination of hot and sweaty and dirty.

"Booker," Colt says, "meet my cousin, Ms. Tommie Delaney."

"Call me Tommie and please ignore my obnoxious cousin."

"Here, come sit next to me, Tommie," Booker says, patting the bench to his right.

Meg, who's sitting on his other side, looks put out though she loves Tommie. Colt shakes his head.

Bowie looks up from his moo shu pork; undiminished virtuoso wielder of chopsticks, he pauses eating to point them at Booker.

"She's also my daughter and she's entirely too old for you, young man. Pick on someone your own age."

"You could have maybe said 'too good' instead of 'too old,' Daddy. Or maybe 'out of your league'?"

"I say it like I see it," Bowie says.

"You know what," Tommie says, "I think I'm just going to sit right here on the end next to someone who I know appreciates me. Okay, Meggie? If you don't mind sliding down, Booker?"

Booker looks abashed and embarrassed. He slides down.

Later, driving Booker back to his car at the old apartment, Colt says, "Sorry about the old man; he's liable to say anything anymore. I really appreciated your help today. I owe you."

"It's okay. I have a granny losing it. Except sometimes I think she's faking it just so she can say whatever the hell she wants to anybody, anytime."

Then he looks sideways at Colt and asks, "How old is Tommie, anyway?"

"She is almost thirty, man. And a piece of work. I say that and I love her. My advice, don't go there."

"You owe me, remember? Give me her number?"

Colt sighs and says, "Don't ever say I didn't warn you."

Booker calls Tommie that evening and asks if she wants to hang out sometime. Tommie laughs, though not meanly.

"You're not a very good listener, are you, Book? You heard my father, right?"

"I listen just fine. My teachers did say I didn't follow directions too well."

"I stand corrected. You do know I am also a teacher, right?"

"But they all liked me. They still like me."

"You know this because…?"

"I shovel my third-grade teacher's driveway every winter. My high school history teacher hires me to clean out his gutters. Miss Potts, my kindergarten teacher, had me set up her smartphone last spring. I did that for free, by the way. I can go on."

Tommie admits to herself that she's flattered. The breakup with Ben has left her unhappy with the person she sees in the mirror every day. Booker is proof that everyone does not see her as she sees herself. Even so, they do not hang out.

School will begin next week but Ben will not be there; Tommie hears that the sabbatical Ben has been talking about taking forever has finally been granted. She learns this through the grapevine—in the person of the kindergarten teacher, Mrs. (never Ms.) Lee, who knows where all the bodies are buried and this year, to the relief of many, will take that knowledge with her into a long-deferred retirement. Ben already has a graduate degree in education, and Tommie wonders what in the world he is going to do besides put as much distance as fast as he can between him and her. On the other hand, perhaps she may not have figured into his decision-making at all? *Ha!*

In truth, Tommie will be happy not to have to see him every day, each sighting sure to bring up a tangle of emotions, none of them pleasant, all a reminder of who she was for so long, and in fact may still be, knowing yourself, seeing yourself through others' eyes, both tasks that have never been easy for her. She's trying for insight. Trying and, most of the time it seems to her, failing.

Colt, who's been lending Ben, as well as Franny, a hand with moving this week, tells Tommie Ben's sublet his apartment and will be putting the last of his belongings into storage tomorrow.

Friday morning, Tommie guilts her mom into making some brown sugar, cinnamon crumble banana bread for Ben. Then she swallows her pride and stops by his apartment to say goodbye. She carries the loaf as a peace offering. She presses the doorbell, and hearing its *bing-bong-bing*, grasps the recyclable plastic container with both hands, holding it in front of her like an offering—no, more like a shield.

Ben opens the door.

"Tommie."

He does not look surprised. He does look good, tanned, she knows, from a summer painting houses—the teacher's summer job from time immemorial—and from his daily swim at the public pool in the park. It seems Tommie has many eager informants available to her.

Then he laughs. She's forgotten what a great laugh he has. There was a time when "old" Tommie would have fixated on that little detail and figured out a way to wind up in bed with Ben, just for old time's sake, you understand. It also appears old Tommie has not been completely vanquished by her recent spate of good behavior. At least, she tells herself, she is now aware of it when O.T. makes an appearance. She is determined to resist.

"You look like the kid sent to the principal's office one time too many, the one about to be expelled," says Ben.

"I'd say that's a pretty good description of how I feel."

"Is that one of Garnet's treats?"

"Banana bread. She said to tell you bon voyage."

"I love your mom, Tommie. It really made me sad when I realized she was never going to be my mother-in-law."

"About that..."

She hears Moira's voice calling Ben from the apartment's interior. "I just want to say I'm sorry and wish you the best," Tommie says, speaking rapidly and shoving the container of banana bread into Ben's hands, her goal now changed to getting an apology out and herself back into her car before Moira appears.

Nevertheless, Moira appears. "Who is it, Ben?"

"Moira, this is Tommie."

Moira says nothing, standing now behind Ben, her arms folded tightly across her chest. She does, however, fix Tommie with a very unfriendly stare.

"I was just leaving," Tommie says, making eye contact with Moira as briefly as possible.

Moira makes a dismissive noise, turns, and walks back into the apartment's interior.

"Guess we can't blame her, can we?" Ben says.

"There was certainly enough bad behavior to go around."

Ben steps out of the apartment and closes the door behind him.

"I'll walk you to your car."

"What will you be doing?"

"Moira's taken a leave and we're going to travel, visiting good and bad elementary schools, hospitals too if she wants, as we go. Maybe wind up with a book. At the least a report for the school board when I get back."

Tommie thinks how much she would have enjoyed accompanying Ben on this adventure. She loves to travel. It could have been her packing things up back there in the apartment. Apparently some embers remain, aglow with regret for what might have been.

"No hard feelings?" Ben asks.

"Oh, lots of hard feelings, I think. On both our parts," Tommie says.

"I'm afraid you're right."

There are no tears in Ben's eyes. In fact he seems a little antsy, maybe even impatient for her to get going so he can do likewise? Ben does not kiss Tommie on the cheek. No embrace occurs. There are no tears. *Real life*, she thinks. *So often so very unsatisfying.*

Seeing Colt's truck in the drive, Tommie stops at Garnet's on the way home. Colt and Garnet are in the kitchen, Garnet paying bills, Colt texting reminders to subcontractors scheduled for the jobsite next week, both of them bent on demolishing a plate of snickerdoodles still warm from the oven.

"Cookie?" Colt says. "I made them."

"One of his better attempts," Garnet adds. "Crisp yet chewy, and lacking the usual charred notes."

"You're too kind," Colt says.

"Actually I am," Garnet assents.

Taking a cookie, Tommie says, "Ben and Moira? Together again? Who knew? Not me."

"On a need to know basis, there was just no reason to tell you," says Colt.

"She was *not* happy to see me today."

"You were there because…?"

"I delivered banana bread from Garnet."

"Sure you did," Colt says.

"You asked me to make it," Garnet adds sotto voce.

"I went to apologize and wish him well," Tommie protests.

Once again, Colt says, "Sure you did." Then he says, "Just can't leave it alone, can you, kiddo?"

Garnet stands up. "Okay, you two. That's enough."

And it is.

September

The dog cocks her head as we listen, together,
to the trees in the yard talking among themselves,
water from the night's rain moving, dropping,
susurrant, leaf to leaf, creating a murmur,
like childhood's sound of grown-up voices
downstairs after bedtime, the words here, too,
indecipherable to the eavesdroppers on the grass below.

Booker waits a week, until Labor Day in fact, before contacting Tommie again, trying not to seem obsessed, thinking to avoid any resemblance to a stalker. This time he texts Tommie, asking if she'd like to see a movie sometime. Tommie texts back that there's a new third-grade teacher, single, his age, at her school. She'd be happy to introduce them.

They do not see a movie.

The Saturday after school begins, Franny brings home not one but two adult greyhounds, recently of the dog track, a male and female. Besides the shelter, she's also been searching rescue sites since May, finalizing this adoption without telling anyone just before she moved. Their names are unknown. She tells Colt she's going to call them Heloise and Abelard.

"That's a terrible idea," he says. "Hell and Abe? You want literary, we can do better."

"Okay, let's hear it."

"Romeo and Juliet?" says Colt.

"No," says Franny.

"Wait! Bonnie and Clyde!"

"Really, Colt? What next? Simone and Garfunkel?"

The two graceful animals, having almost immediately discovered and claimed as their own Franny's well-loved, ancient (versus antique, she specifies if asked) damask sofa with its down-stuffed seat cushions, are intertwined thereon, deeply uninterested in human conversation, fast asleep.

Colt and Franny finally settle on Lucy and Desi.

"Not a very literary choice after all," Franny says.

"No," says Colt. "But what was left after we eliminated Leonard and Virginia, George and Martha, Scott and Zelda? Come on!"

"If you look closely, Lucy's coat does have a reddish tinge."

They are lovely dogs, and smart. They learn their names

quickly and respond to them. Bowie, hardly a surprise, falls in love, which tempers his initial decision to keep things businesslike, to regard Franny solely as *The Renter*. Instead, she becomes Lucy and Desi's significant other, someone he's required to remain on good terms with if he wants to spend time with her dogs which he very much does. It soon becomes apparent that while Franny is teaching, the dogs will spend their days in the house with him. No doggy daycare necessary.

Moreover, the advent of Franny and her two hounds works a minor miracle. It's not that Bowie is no longer forgetful or has regained all he's lost in the last few years. It's that he's happier, more engaged than he's been in a long, long time. He is, dare we say—not that anyone has bothered to do so maybe because of the fear of jinxing it—a pleasure to be around. Having practiced tough love on her inner brat with some success, Tommie tells Garnet she's even managed to tame her almost-jealousy of the way her father looks at and talks now to Franny, making her mother laugh and Tommie accuse her of being unsympathetic.

The only problem Franny encounters is how to convince Bowie it's better for the animals if they are not fed a constant diet of treats and scraps when he's in charge. But when Desi suffers an epic intestinal event after ingesting some (quite a lot, actually) leftover Hawaiian pizza, which Bowie has to clean up and then confess to Franny, himself miserable, feeling terrible for the suffering he's caused the dog, he begins to see the light. Not only does he see the light, but being Bowie he becomes the treat czar, parsimoniously rationing only the certified and the organic—whatever that means, Colt tells Franny—and scolding anyone he feels is not adhering to his new standards.

In turn the dogs adore Bowie, following him wherever he goes, leading him back home after long afternoon walks. No more getting lost; Desi and Lucy know the way. The exercise does him good too. His potbelly disappears and he tosses out his disgusting extra-large overalls and begins wearing reasonably clean jeans with a normal waist again.

Colt's boy, Sam (a.k.a. Sammy Boy, the Samster, also Samsam) and the greys, as Colt begins to call them, get along famously from the start. Vera, unsurprisingly, is another story. Garnet walks her down to meet the new dogs on an especially nice Saturday afternoon soon after they arrive, thinking it's better for their first encounter to have the dog off her own turf, free of the self-imposed obligation to rule and defend. Colt comes along just in case, leaving Sam at home. Once there, it becomes clear that Lucy and Desi are not submissive like Sam, or puppies that Vera can ignore, boss, or even, though highly unlikely, mother. The two greyhounds are at first respectful, and friendly, though not overly so. And Garnet is careful, basically ignoring their existence.

But Vera is not happy. She spends the brief visit with hackles raised, emitting an unhappy sound from somewhere deep in her throat that is not exactly a growl, but a sound whose volume nevertheless increases dramatically when Bowie comes out and the two interlopers rush over to him. This dog considers every person in attendance here—Garnet, Franny, Colt, Bowie—as hers, *her* people, *her* flock. Moreover, she does not like to… correction, she is one more family member who *hates* to share. Lucy and Desi, quickly taking the hint, keep a considerable distance from Vera in all her alpha glory, obviously classifying her in their canine brains, if push ever comes to shove, as "she who must be obeyed."

"I don't think we're going to be one big, happy family after all," says Colt.

"Why should they be any different than their humans?" says Garnet.

"We're going to give them plenty of time," says Franny.

"And hope for the best," adds Colt.

Garnet walks back home with Vera, the arthritis in her wrist kicking up from having held so tightly for so long onto the leash. For the next few days the dog sulks, the only thing causing the delightful Vera of old to make a brief appearance being a visit from Meg.

But should her owner decide mid-week to mosey on down, alone, to Bowie's on some errand, let us say to deliver a bag of apples from the farmers' market, Garnet is more than happily capable of making a fool of herself over Lucy and Desi. Even though she is aware that when she returns home Vera will read her, nose wrinkling at the scent, like some very bad novel, one she, Vera, intends to pan in a vicious *New Yorker* review. Her dog will then haughtily stalk away, snubbing Garnet for the rest of the day and feigning profound deafness when called, except, of course, for dinner.

Garnet wonders about the extent to which this really differs from Vera's everyday ignoring of commands she deems unnecessary. She finally decides it's the attitude that accompanies Vera's behavior here, an attitude Garnet regretfully sums up as, *the hell with you and the horse you rode in on*—though she fears instead of *the hell with you,* Vera is likely employing Garnet's least favorite two-word expletive. Given human form, her owner knows that Vera would be one tough old broad.

Garnet really does sympathize. She too has experienced betrayal. She knows exactly what a combination of disappointment and anger, the keen desire for revenge, feels like and how it leads to less than exemplary behavior.

Colt tries to reassure his aunt. "She'll get over it."

But Garnet herself has yet to get over it, to move on. Every time she sees Bowie, some variation of the feelings she experienced when she first found out he was cheating on her with Lily floods back. This, despite Jake, despite the ideal combination of payback and solace he represents to her. With such a bad example to emulate, she doubts her dog is going to fare any better.

And if that were not enough, now that Vera has turned nine, she has begun periodically to go lame. So far, each episode—there have been two—has lasted only a day. The next morning the dog is good as new, trotting down the stairs, through the kitchen, Garnet following close behind with the leash, the two of them out the back door, the dog demanding breakfast the instant she returns. The vet says Garnet has only to say the word and she will start Vera on medication, but Garnet can list every side effect, knows them all by heart, and is reluctant to begin the pills any sooner than absolutely necessary.

The two episodes do serve to bring Garnet face to face, once again, with the reality of her and Vera's situation. Time is short, and no longer on her side, if it ever really was to begin with, on either of their sides (and for that matter, not, she might also gently point out, on Mick's anymore either). She can feel it. She knows it. Each day, she must make a conscious decision to live that day, not as young people think, as if it were her last, but as though she, and Vera, (and Ruby, not so very long ago) will live forever, as though mortality does not exist, as though she has nothing but endless time before her. If she wishes to accomplish anything free of the dread of not being there to finish it, she must first perform this daily feat of magical thinking, her mind all the while stubbornly holding onto the realization that there is only one way any living creature ever manages to break free of time.

They say a sign of intelligence is this ability to hold two opposing ideas in one's mind at the same time without your head exploding. In that case, she thinks, she must be fucking Einstein—this thought, so prominently featuring her least favorite epithet, takes Garnet by surprise. Until it doesn't. Until she fucking embraces it, realizing there may be, after all, a space in present-day English usage for an ancient Anglo-Saxon obscenity. But this place is not, as the culture seems to believe, to be found in profligate ubiquity. Rather it is an expletive most effective when used subject-specific and sparingly. Garnet thinks of Ruby and all she will miss. Vera, at her feet, hiccups and begins quietly snoring. *Fucking death!*

❧

Colt's truck needs some work done. He's asked Tommie to pick him up at Ray's Auto, where he's leaving it for the day, dropping him off at the job on her way to school. When they arrive at the site Booker is offloading rolls of insulation from a van. It's been a few weeks since Tommie last heard from him. If she's honest, she's a little disappointed he hasn't tried again.

Colt disappears into the field office, a small trailer parked on site. Booker sees her, waves, and walks over. Tommie lowers her window.

He has a smudge of dirt on his cheek. When he leans in to talk, his forearms, muscled and tan, rest on her window frame, the left with its rather beautiful tattoo of a not particularly friendly looking wolf. Maybe younger might turn out better than age-appropriate, which has not been at all kind to her thus far.

"So, no how, no way," he says.

"How about you pick me up at eight on Friday night, Booker," Tommie says. "And we'll see about that."

Colt emerges from the trailer just as Tommie is pulling back onto the highway, having left Booker flatfooted, looking like a fastball had just whizzed past, barely grazing his forehead.

"You okay, buddy?" Colt asks.

"I don't know," he says.

Booker realizes he doesn't have a clue where Tommie lives. Somewhere in the city is all he knows. So he asks Colt. Colt says, *Oh man!* but gives him the address. Then Booker, no longer in love with the metallic sheen of a gold car, decides he needs a more serious color. He repaints it an iridescent deep blue that reminds him of a dark pool of water, but then cannot resist stenciling on the car roof, where they will not be too obvious, a sprinkling of stars. That way he does not feel he's completely sold out the free spirit he sees himself as.

He is a confident young man where women are concerned, a confidence built on repeated success. But when Friday night comes, he's nervous. Used to feeling in charge, to being the one who ultimately decides when a relationship—if you could even call it that most of the time—is over, he does not feel in charge here.

Booker checks the time on his phone and knocks on Tommie's door. She answers, ready to go. His first impression at the picnic was not wrong. Tommie wears jeans, boots, and a starched and pressed man's white shirt. Her hair, still damp from the shower, curls, loose, almost shoulder length. Her makeup, if she's wearing any—she must be wearing some, this *is* a date, right?—is minimal. As he feared, she looks terrific.

"Hey, Book," Tommie says.

No one else calls him Book. When he was a little kid, his dad had called him the Bookster. That was about the extent of nicknames (except for a short time in second grade when a nine-year-old tormentor dubbed him Booger until Booker, small but feisty, relieved the bully of a front tooth with a well-placed kick as they wrestled on the ground, and wound up himself with a two-week suspension and a hiding from his father).

"Hey. You look nice."

Tommie laughs. "You clean up pretty good yourself."

"What do you feel like doing?" Booker says.

"I decide?"

"You decide."

"How about a gallery opening? Rain and a few of her friends have a show at Big Art over on First Street. I told her we might stop by."

Feeling already out of his league, he opens the car door for Tommie, a nicety he hasn't observed in quite some time. It seems right in this case, however, and he likes the way it makes him feel. Respectful. Caring. Maybe he's more adult than he's been giving himself credit for. Before Tommie gets in, she places her hand on the car roof.

"Stars," Tommie says. "They're beautiful."

On the way Tommie tells him the gallery, which began as a pop-up in an empty storefront, has recently moved up in the world. Now an artist co-op, it comprises the main floor of a repurposed old warehouse. Once there Booker is impressed. The brick walls have been painted bright white; the refinished wood floors shine. Movable partitions on which work is hung, serve to organize the large space. Colt's ex spots them and comes over, giving Tommie an affectionate hug.

Booker has seen Rain before, dropping off Colt's daughter at the site at the end of the work week, saving him the ride over to her house to pick up Meg. Exes, yet they seem to get along just fine. He's also said hi a few times, running into her at the hardware store or at The Cup, but he's never been introduced. How does one family rate so many good-looking women? Even Garnet—he knows it's wrong to add the *even* but Christ, he's not saying it out loud for the PC police to hear, and, what? Garnet must be at least sixty (unimaginable to Booker that he might ever be that old)—*even* Garnet is easy on the eyes, and little Meg, same heart-shaped face as her mom, destined to be a looker too.

"Booker, this is Rain. Rain, Booker," says Tommie.

"Yes," says Rain. "I'm a big admirer of that shiny piece of art you drive. Still got the 14-karat-gold look?"

"Actually, as of this week, midnight blue," says Booker.

"With stars," adds Tommie.

"I'll have to have a look before you leave. Wine and cheese are over there. Help yourselves."

"Where's Eddie?" Tommie asks.

"He and Meg came earlier then left for a movie she's been wanting to see."

"Princesses involved?"

"Dog story. No princesses! No princes! No happily ever after. Franny, looking ahead I think, has requested no evil stepmothers either."

"Meggie is okay with that?"

"Meg is fine. She says she's outgrown all such juvenilia."

"It's going to be hard sending her off to Harvard when she turns thirteen, isn't it?"

"She scares me sometimes."

Booker thinks of himself as a kind of artist. When he lived at home, he'd set up a studio for himself in a bay of his parents' garage. No one except his family has seen his paintings. Here, there are paintings and collage and some small sculptures. This show, he judges, has both good and (surprisingly, to Booker) bad art. He likes Rain's work, finely detailed ink drawings that look to have taken hours, overlayed with splashy bright color, seemingly carelessly applied. He makes a mental promise to himself to retrieve his art stuff from his parents' and try this technique sometime.

Rain does come outside and approves the new paint job. Hungry despite the gallery's snacks, Tommie and Booker find a drive-through and order burgers and share an order of french fries, then find a small dark bar and listen to very bad jazz. At the end of the evening, he walks Tommie to her door. She does not kiss him good night. He is not asked in for a nightcap or a cup of coffee. *Nada.*

"I had a really nice time, Booker. Thank you," she says.

Tommie turns the key, opens the door, and smiles at him. Then she walks into her apartment and shuts the door.

October

Are you aware how strange the universe finds you,
with your unhealthy pallor, your yellow yoga pants,
celebrating arcane holidays involving orange gourds,
gathering family members around large avian carcasses
or dead trees dragged inside, lit up, and surrounded
by paper-wrapped consumer products? Having lost all
credibility, maybe it's time to consider yourself pot,
one unable to call the kettle anything but long-lost sister.

To both Booker's and Tommie's surprise, they continue to see each other. Booker, having now been at least introduced to most of Tommie's family members, is still getting to know them. Since they've begun dating, he's been the recipient of a volley of imprecations hurled by Bowie after accidentally spraying the interior of the windows-open Lexus one afternoon chasing the greyhounds with the garden hose (he was supposed to be helping Colt put together some Ikea for Franny). He's recently peeled spuds for Garnet as she prepared potato salad for another family picnic. Although Vera eyes him doubtfully, she appears not yet to have definitively made up her mind he's not to be trusted, so Booker makes sure he does not arrive in her presence without some special offering, a lump of cheese, a wax paper-wrapped slice of bacon, maybe a knuckle bone picked up at the village butcher shop on the way over, Vera, with great dignity, accepting all as her due. Meg's eyes follow him wherever he goes. Colt seems almost to view him as a younger brother now that he and Tommie are kind of a thing, although at the same picnic referred to above, he did take Booker aside and explained in some detail what he would do first to Booker and then to Booker's car if he broke Tommie's heart. Tommie had pitched a fit, having immediately been informed of the chat by an eavesdropping, gleeful Bowie. *Kicked his butt, he did. I don't expect that young man will be asking you out again, daughter. I'm afraid you just lost your last chance not to die an old maid.*

"I appreciate the thought, Colt, I really do," Tommie had said, "but first, I am completely capable of making sure my heart is not the broken one—"

"Yeah, right," Colt says.

Tommie ignores him. "And if you had to say something, why do it where Bowie can hear and hold it over my head?"

"Dementia has not slowed down that old man one bit," Colt says.

"Well, he almost has me convinced, thanks to you, that I need to give my Manolo Blahniks to Goodwill and buy some more appropriate, sensible lace-up oxfords for those fast-approaching declining years I'll be spending all alone."

"You exaggerate."

"Not much. Back off, cuz."

Booker, staying out of it, somehow knowing that nothing he might wish to add would be appreciated. By either one.

When Booker tells Tommie his mom wants her to come to Sunday dinner, Tommie is surprised. She's determined not to rush things; they've been going out for only a few weeks, and this seems way too soon. But not wanting to offend Booker's mother before she even meets her, she says yes. Book has not said much about his family so Tommie has formed her expectations based on little or nothing. In the (surprisingly elaborate) mental picture she has nevertheless constructed, she sees Booker's mom and his younger brother—she knows he has one but that's it—in a pre-fab, maybe a mobile home in a trailer park out in the whoop-whoops, his mother, a smoker, looking older than her years, works at a big box, struggling to make ends meet; his high-school-dropout brother, now come to Jesus, is working on his GED. Book's father is out of the picture—Booker has not mentioned him. Tommie is not nervous, having resolved she will not judge, she will be open and friendly, and they will love her. (She later admits to herself this scenario smacks of nothing if not a rabid case of rampant privilege on her part, noblesse oblige run amok. The only thing she'd left out, she figured, was making Book's mom a Pentecostal snake-handler speaking in tongues.)

Luckily, she shares none of this with Booker, and later, confronting in her very own mirror a person who once again must face the fact that she needs to do better, the harsh words that come up are "entitled" and "arrogant."

Booker picks her up at noon on Sunday and they head across

the city, driving to an enclave of lovely old bungalows, not mansions, but homes built by last century's merchants, doctors, attorneys, and other well-to-do denizens of the 1920s and 30s upper middle class. Nonplussed, she keeps her mouth shut. Booker is not talking either. He pulls up and parks in front of a large Craftsman, gets out, and opens the door for her.

"I'm not real happy about this, but my mom can generally get me to do what she wants. What she wants is to meet you."

The big oak front door is opened by a dark-haired woman with a gently lined face, along with a crazed, love-struck corgi who deliriously attacks as much of Booker as he can reach, which mostly means his legs, from the knees down. Booker scoops him up and holds the wriggling, actually quite hefty animal, like a baby. "As you can see, Charlie has missed you. We've missed you, Booker. I am so happy to meet you, Tommie. Please call me Arlene."

Once inside, the house reminds her of her mother's home. Books everywhere, no huge electronics in evidence. The Sunday paper has slid from the coffee table onto the floor. Tommie is introduced to Booker's father, Lowell, who emerges from his study where he's been grading papers for the Gaelic lit class he's teaching this semester, and to Booker's brother, Dylan, a junior at Cornell, home for the weekend. Lowell is older, maybe late fifties, even early sixties, his wife perhaps a few years younger, boomers who'd waited until the last minute to have their family, she thinks.

Booker, looking uncomfortable, says, "Guess which son is the black sheep?"

"Not so much sheep as renegade lamb who liked his gap year after high school so much, he's renewed it five times," says Booker's mother. "But we have not lost hope, have we, dear?"

"No, not hope. Not yet," says his father.

It turns out as they talk at the dinner table that Booker's mother is a CPA who has just sold her business and is looking for something new to do. Meanwhile, she's taking a cooking class.

"You, my darlings, are my guinea pigs today."

"Please pass the mashed potatoes," Booker says before he is corrected.

She has prepared a shepherd's pie, with Dylan acting as sous-chef. There is crusty bread and red wine picked up for the occasion by Lowell.

"I liked the truck on the label," he explains. "Though I almost brought home the angry housewife."

"Oenophiles we are not," says Arlene.

"Any new tats?" Dylan asks.

"Nope," says Booker unenthusiastically.

Tommie is aware of only the ink on his left arm. They have not slept together, something Tommie can hardly believe, so unlike herself it is—she's proud of her forbearance. However, it's becoming apparent that the better she gets to know Booker, the more attractive she finds him, instead of the reverse, her more usual reaction—always with the notable exception, of course, of the problematic Ben (though it has finally occurred to her that she may have been the problem all along rather than Ben). Discovering whether there are indeed more tattoos might just be the incentive (or excuse, she concedes) needed to push herself over the edge and Booker into her bed.

He's let Tommie set the pace thus far, though he's said it feels weird to be making out in a parked car in front of Tommie's apartment building instead of just heading on inside and doing it. "I think you need to know that referring to any eventual sex we may or may not have as 'doing it' is not a huge turn-on for me," Tommie had told him, adding, "neither the 'doing' part nor the 'it' part."

It would not be a stretch to conclude that Booker heard only, and took heart from, her reference to "eventual sex."

"Tell me about your boys' names," Tommie says.

"People hear Booker's name and are impressed that we named him for Booker T. Washington," says Arlene.

"Until they find out my namesake is Booker T of the MG's," says Booker.

"A terrific musician, son. We named you for the best," says his father.

"Let me guess," says Tommie. "Dylan for Bob?"

"That would be consistent, and a good guess, but no," says Lowell.

"Dylan Thomas?" asks Tommie.

"Dylan Thomas," says Lowell.

"I finally figured out that Lowell held out for the name Dylan," Arlene says, "just so every time the baby was colicky and kept us up with his screaming, he could intone...."

Arlene leaves the sentence incomplete.

"'Do not go gentle into that good night'?" Tommie finishes for her.

"Exactly," says Lowell.

"Please stop," says Dylan.

Tommie asks, "Is Lowell for Robert Lowell?"

"I'm afraid not. No, I was named for my dying, wealthy great-uncle Lowell, who himself was named for Lowell Thomas—don't ask—in hopes he would include baby-me in his will. He didn't. What about you, Tommie? Let me guess. You are named for the rock opera."

"To quote you—afraid not. My given name is Grace Anne, named for my grandmother. I ignored my dolls and played with boys; I had no girlfriends. I suppose today my parents would be signing me up for gender confirmation counseling. But I didn't want to be a boy. They were just way more fun to be around. I was full of the devil. My mom started calling me Tommie. Shorthand for tomboy."

On the ride home, Tommie asks, "Why didn't you tell me about your family?"

"Because I'm not like them. I love them, but I don't want their life."

"It doesn't look like a bad life, Booker."

"My goal is to be a self-made man. Colt works in the office now, ever since Nadine quit to go back to school. I'm taking his place as crew chief. I want to keep that job. And then I want my own outfit."

"Every time I think I have you figured out…" says Tommie, who is finding it increasingly harder to pigeon-hole someone so disinclined to show his cards.

"Grace Anne, huh? When were you going to tell me your real name?"

"No one has called me that in forever, not for years and years."

Yet, when they go to bed for the first time that night it is *Grace Anne* that Booker murmurs, Tommie surrendering to him the right to call her by that name. With it somehow goes not only the corporeal self that Booker has just made love to, but also whatever it means when we say we give our heart away, even though the mass of muscle and blood beating in our chest is not what we are talking about at all. Which is simply a convoluted way of saying that Tommie falls in love with Booker, though she does not say the words to him for a very long time, even though Booker after that night will tell her often that he loves her, will in fact get new ink the following Valentine's Day, a heart emblazoned with her name *Grace Anne*. He will feel no need to hear the words himself. He knows every time he calls her by her given name, she is telling him *I love you.*

Garnet is amused, or perhaps bemused, by the idea of Tommie and Booker as a couple—she cannot bring herself to take it seriously, this May, perhaps not December, but at the very least—say, August? romance. She feels sorry for Booker, surely on his way to becoming one more victim of her impetuous daughter—that is, until the first time she hears him call Tommie *Grace Anne.*

The two are helping Garnet and Jake rake up the drifts of leaves her trees, those profligate, gorgeous old giants who live in her yard, let go every fall. Garnet, as ever her own worst enemy, has forbidden the use of any and all gas-powered lawn equipment in consideration of beleaguered Mother Earth.

(When occasionally questioned about how that edict jibes with the Japanese SUV in her garage, she mutters ineffectually about consistency and hobgoblins, or perhaps some variation on "better than nothing," both of which are after all kind of true, she thinks. Or truish, anyway.)

"Really?" Tommie says, voice rising. "Really, Mother? We could have this job done in less than an hour using George's riding mower with the leaf bag, and his blower. You know that, right?"

"Grace Anne," Booker says quietly. "Grace Anne, take a breath."

Garnet would almost not believe her ears, but she has just heard Booker say the name out loud not once but twice. She'd been the one who'd chosen it for Tommie, a name she loved, her own mother's name, and she also the one who gave her daughter the nickname which superseded it. That the seven-year-old Tommie had then stamped her foot, and ever after would answer to no other, felt to Garnet back then like she'd lost her mother all over again. And, worst of all, no one to blame but herself.

Now, however, Tommie whirls around to face Booker. Garnet braces for the inevitable sharp and hurtful, possibly, probably, profane retort to the foolhardy peacemaker holding his bamboo rake. Instead, she watches Tommie stop, actually take that breath and lean into Booker, resting her head against his shoulder, his arms encircling her, despite the rake he holds, for that moment.

When she steps away, she says, "I'm sorry, Mom. Speed isn't everything, is it?"

And then she picks her own implement up off the ground where she'd thrown it and goes back to work.

Garnet knows that she, herself, will never be invited to call her daughter Grace Anne, but, besides Booker, neither will anyone else. Somehow that is enough.

At Jake's house later that day, the room darkening as autumn continues to steal a little more late afternoon light each day, Garnet sits on the edge of the bed buttoning up her sweater as Jake tells her what it was like to watch that moment as a bystander.

"I see those two and wonder if I was ever that young."

"Tommie is twenty-nine, Jake," Garnet reminds him.

But he continues as if she hasn't spoken. "And I wonder if I was ever in love like that. I love you, Garnet, with this old body and this old mind...but I think somehow I missed out on what they were feeling today."

Garnet replies with a quiet, "Come here."

The end of October already and the fourth graders are putting on a play for Halloween with Franny as director. For some reason no one in the community has yet thought to object to this Wiccan celebration of a pagan holiday involving ghosts and fairies, though Franny is holding her breath. She shares what she will say in her defense with Colt.

"If it's good enough for Charlie Brown, it's good enough for Rosa Parks Elementary."

"Will you be mentioning the Great Pumpkin?"

"Why?"

"Some say the whole rising-from-the-pumpkin-patch is blasphemy."

"What?"

"You know, that Easter thing?"

"Sweet Jesus," says Franny.

"Exactly," says Colt.

"You are pulling my leg."

"It could happen."

"You're right," Franny says.

Colt has been spending most nights at Franny's, returning to Garnet's on Saturday or Sunday to keep up with outside and inside chores for his aunt, but actually only staying there every other weekend with his daughter—no way he wants Garnet thinking he's deserted her. On this Saturday night, with Meg at her mom's, before Colt returns to Franny, they are having dinner. Garnet has prepared baked beans and Colt is grilling pork chops on the little hibachi on her patio. Another apple pie, Vera-proofed, is cooling on top of the fridge, and Vera, in protest, is lying on her side, effectively blocking traffic into and out of the kitchen. "I brought up moving in with Franny," he tells Garnet as they sit down at the table.

"And…?"

"She says no. I might as well be moved in, all the time I spend there. I don't understand."

"Did you ask Franny for a reason?"

"I guess I was too surprised."

"Ask her."

"Tell me what you're thinking."

"Franny has been single for a long time. She's two years older than you, right? Maybe she needs a better reason than you paying half her rent and drying her dishes to give up that independence."

"Maybe it's time for me to man up?"

"Could be."

Franny's class play is a great success The ten-year-old Great Pumpkin, having risen spectacularly out of the pumpkin patch, trips over a green garden hose vine and falls flat, gamely hauling herself back up to thunderous applause. Along with Charlie Brown's wardrobe malfunction, and Lucy forgetting her lines and uttering a less civil version of *drat!*, the production proves to be a big hit. Colt and Franny finish helping the custodian stack folding chairs, thank Mr. Mac, as the kids call him, for staying late, and send him on his way. They check the restrooms to make sure stragglers big and little have left, turn out the lights and, finally, set the alarm, before letting themselves out. Franny is exhausted and happy as she gets into the truck.

"And tomorrow morning you'll get up and do it all over again," Colt says. "Well, not the play, but school as usual."

"No. There is no such thing as usual," Franny replies. "That's why I love it. It may be a great day; it may be terrible, but it's never predictable, never the same."

Colt puts the key in the ignition, then pauses and turns to Franny. He's glad he was such a cheapskate when he bought his used pickup, choosing the plain bench seat, no buckets, no cupholder, no console. He can put his arm around his girl and pull her close and he does. He has no speech prepared, no ring.

"Franny," Colt says. "Would you consider marrying me?"

Her expression, what he can see of it in the darkened parking lot, its sole illumination the halfhearted light of a waxing autumnal moon—the only remotely romantic thing in this whole picture—is unsurprised and serious. She regards him for a full minute and then answers. "Maybe."

Colt is not unaware that the front seat of a working man's truck is probably not the setting of any woman's fantasy, but the timing of his question is as much of a surprise to him as it is to Franny. Once again, Franny has put him off balance. Even Rain, unpredictable as she was, did not upset his expectations this way. But he is beginning to understand this woman, and how he might manage to keep her around.

"I'll take a 'maybe,'" he says. "For now."

He drives Franny home. He pulls up in front of the carriage house apartment. Bowie's place is dark, Franny's two dogs probably asleep up there on the bed with him, something that now happens any time Franny is out for the evening. He hesitates, taking nothing for granted. Franny reaches over, turns off the ignition, hands him his keys, and gets out of the truck. Colt turns off the headlights.

Once inside, they walk back to her bedroom without turning on a single light. Once again, moonglow, filtered by the sheers that cover the windows, provides the only light. Clothes on the floor at their feet, they kiss and are about to tumble into bed, when Franny pauses, placing her hand on Colt's bare chest. She is tall, tall enough to look directly into his eyes.

"Probably," she whispers.

November

Effortless to be thankful for what's bright and beautiful,
uncomplicated; the benevolent, the temperate; but
what about hard, sharp-cornered things, the bruises

that result? What about the barbed, the rough-barked,
the shrill and songless, beaked and taloned,
the envenomed biters and stingers; what about them?

Who will be grateful for all that hurts and sickens
and kills? Who bless the poison ivy, sumac, oak?
The fire, the storm, the hurricane, tornado, tsunami?

Who among us willingly stands to embrace
the darkness, to heed its unreliable narrators,
the liar, the thief, the criminal, the saint?

Garnet announces early in November that she's hosting Thanksgiving this year. She will provide the turkey. Everything else is to arrive with the guests. In order to make things more interesting, she's added the proviso that no one is allowed to ask what others are bringing. She does not say how she plans to enforce this.

"That's crazy, Gigi," Colt says. "What if we get ten pumpkin pies and nothing else?"

"Turkey and pie. Sounds good to me. We'll spend so much time discussing it, there'll be no time for arguing about politics. Where is your adventurous spirit, Colt?"

Garnet's invitation includes everyone: ex-husbands, adultereresses, ex-girlfriends and boyfriends, current versions of same, brothers and their husbands, cousins, pets, and children, all welcome.

Colt says, "You sure about this, Gigi? Bowie and Jake have not been in the same room since your divorce."

"This is way, way too many people," he tells her.

"Are you losing it, Garnet?" he says. "Or planning to rent the convention center?"

"Oh, all right, Colt," Garnet finally tells him the week of Thanksgiving. "Just tell me who you wish to eliminate, and I'll let them know you've decided they aren't welcome."

Colt throws up his hands (a phrase that so reliably delights Garnet with its mental picture of its physically impossible alternative that she once wrote a poem about it).

"And you *will* help me anyway, won't you, dear."

"God help me, yes," says her nephew.

"The family that prays together…" Garnet intones.

"I do not understand, Gigi, with that mouth, why you haven't been struck by lightning."

"Because He, if He exists, or She for that matter, has a sense of humor. Just look around you."

On the Sunday night before Thanksgiving, Colt and Franny take Meg back home to her mother. "Thanks for helping me with my homework, Franny," she says.

It has taken Meg most of the fall to stop calling Franny Ms. Fisher when they are not at school.

"You're welcome," Franny says.

"Fifth grade is much harder than fourth. And I don't like having more than one teacher either, and I really, really hate changing classes," Meg says. "I just wish everything would stay the same."

"Growing up is hard," Franny says, turning sideways in her seat so she can better see Meg.

"If nothing ever changed," says Colt, "there would be no Franny to help you with your homework, to lose to you at Scrabble, or to go to the flea market with you to look for antique dolls."

"If Cabbage Patch dolls are antiques," Franny says, "then so am I."

Meg laughs, then pauses, thinking over what her father said. She leans forward. "I love you, Franny," she says.

After they've dropped Meg off, Colt says, "You're very quiet."

"I am," Franny says, breaking her silence. "And, Colt, yes. Yes, I believe I will."

The next day, Rain and Meg are walking home from school, where Rain has been subbing for the art teacher who's just had a baby, a girl. She has the job until after the holidays. Something else to be thankful for this coming Thursday.

"Mom, why don't you and Eddie have a baby. I could help take care of her," Meg says.

Rain smiles.

"Her? What if it's a him, Meg?"

"Well, there's a fifty-fifty chance it could be a her. Those are good odds, right?"

"You think so? And if it's a him, what? We put him up for adoption and try again until we get it right?"

"That's an awful thing to say, Mom."

"Yes, I guess it is. Sorry."

"You're not sorry, and you're not going to have a baby either, are you."

"No, sweetie, I am not."

"But why?"

"Because I do not want to tempt fate."

"That is a stupid aphorism."

"Okay, Miss Dictionary, I hit the jackpot once with you. Chances are I wouldn't do it twice."

"It's Ms. Dictionary, by the way."

"So what do you think of your father and Ms. Fisher? Are you okay with it?"

"I didn't like Daddy dating Franny at all. I felt like she belonged to me and he should stay out of it."

"Understandable."

"Now that I'm in fifth grade, I hardly ever get to see her at school, but thanks to Daddy, I see her all the time outside school. So, really, he saved her for me."

"If they got married or started living together, that would be okay with you?"

"Yes! Maybe then they could have a baby? I really, really want a little sister."

"Oh, Meg, you are like a pit bull with a bone."

Colt tells Garnet that Franny has said yes. She gives him his mother's diamond.

"She asked me to keep this for you, Colt," she says. "If Franny likes it, you two can take it over to Rodgers's Jewelers and have them put it in a new setting."

But Franny loves the ring just the way it is. The band only needs to be re-sized before she begins wearing it.

They decide the Thanksgiving feast will be held in Garnet's roomy, detached garage, like Bowie's, once a carriage house though never remodeled as his has been. Colt gives it a thorough cleaning and even throws a little paint on the inside trim here and there. Rain and Meg again volunteer to decorate. Instead of making Kleenex flowers, Meg cuts out colorful construction paper leaves and tapes them to windows Colt has washed inside and out. Rain and Eddie spend a day assembling a collection of straw bales, yellow mums, gourds, corn stalks, and pumpkins. They collect acorns and whatever else looks interesting and fall-ish on a Sunday walk in the woods that border Haven's cemetery. Colt borrows two quartz room heaters from work and long folding tables and stackable chairs from his boss who's connected, not with the mob, but with The Vineyard, new megachurch and furniture-source, off the Thruway exit on 96 where he's a trustee.

The day before Thanksgiving Colt picks up the two large, fresh turkeys Garnet ordered from the poultry farm outside town, figuring the giant birdzilla she would otherwise have required, if such a monster actually existed, would have taken two days to roast.

As it turns out, almost everyone has accepted their invitations. Lily, alone, sends her regrets. She will be in Paris with her husband.

"Wimped out," Colt says to Garnet.

"Wisely," Garnet says.

Remmy and Freddy fly in. Even Ben and Moira circle back for the holiday. Garnet is serene; Colt is a wreck. Franny tries to be supportive.

Garnet uses all her flatware, sterling and stainless, her crystal and plain old glass, her wedding plus her everyday china. Rain supplements as needed.

Colt says, "What is wrong with paper plates and plastic?"

Garnet says, "I will not dignify that with a reply, young man."

By Wednesday evening, the tables are set, the space ready. Rain has scattered votive candles and real autumn leaves on tables throughout.

Dinner is scheduled for four o'clock. Garnet gets up at five a.m. She prepares stuffing and readies the turkeys for roasting, putting one in her oven and one in George's oven, despite his desire to try out his new smoker. It turns out to be a lovely autumn day with a nip in the air. At quarter to three Rain borrows George's barbecue lighter, Garnet's incendiary pistol having mysteriously disappeared soon after her birthday. She touches its flame to each votive. Colt turns on the space heaters and opens the garage doors. The dogs have each been given a soup bone and are working on them in the grass of the side yard, the two greys and Sam, uninterested in wandering free, and Vera, securely leashed queen of her own dedicated space off to the side.

People begin to arrive. Remmy and Freddy bring champagne and Dr. Pepper for Meg.

There are five pies—three pumpkin baked by Franny, one apple courtesy of Meg, and a killer lemon meringue from Tommie (who knew?)—there is a carrot cake and two green bean casseroles. Someone comments that there are no brussels sprouts (Franny is the only one to hear Colt's *Thank you, Jesus*). There are sliced bananas and pineapple chunks preserved in Jell-O amber, a sweet potato casserole topped with an alarming number of mini marshmallows ("Let me guess," Rain says to her daughter, "your favorite?") and four dozen dinner rolls, plus the two beautiful birds that Colt and George have just finished carving, all arrayed on tables under the garage's side windows.

There is no assigned seating. After everyone has been encouraged to find a place and sit down, Garnet stands and asks each person to write down one thing for which they are thankful using the paper and pencil stub provided at each place. Meg collects them using one of Garnet's straw hats.

"What are you going to do with them, Garnet?" Bowie asks.

"I don't know," Garnet says. "I just knew if we went around the table and gave each person a turn it would be six o'clock before we ate."

"If I'd known that, I wouldn't have bothered," Bowie says, breaking his pencil in two.

But then just before everyone gets up and heads over to the buffet to load up their plates, instead of grace, Garnet asks for quiet and reads aloud W. S. Merwin's poem, "Thanks." It is a long poem, a heartbreaker, also one of Garnet's favorites, and it is her party. Somewhere in the middle, Bowie inquires loudly, "What's she saying? I don't get it." But Garnet soldiers on.

Reaction is mixed, from Rain looking stricken, to Booker jumping up from his chair with "*All right!* Let's eat."

Dinner is a success. Bowie does hurl a roll at Jake, who is seated across from him, but Jake makes a lucky catch, butters and eats it, leaving Bowie to grumble, "Show off!" Tommie and Moira studiously ignore each other while Ben and Booker talk cars. Meg sits between Colt and Franny until dessert when she piles a plate with samples of each offering and shares them with Rain and Eddie. Freddy and Remmy hold hands on and off during the meal. When Franny shows Remmy her engagement ring after dinner, Remmy, recognizing it, starts to cry.

Closing the garage doors after everyone has finally gone home and the mess has been at least organized if not completely eliminated, Colt says, "Gigi, you are going to have to go into party planning. Though I was sorry to see the pyrotechnic birthday option eliminated."

"It was lovely, Colt. Now please go. Franny is going to start wondering where you are."

Inside the house, Jake is starting a third dishwasher load, waiting for Garnet to come in. Vera has gone upstairs to Garnet's bedroom and is already sprawled, asleep in her preferred spot on the hardwood floor, next to, not on, the expensive, extra-large orthopedic dog bed Garnet bought her, large head resting comfortably on its bolster.

The next morning Garnet gets up at six, leaving Jake behind in her bed. Vera follows her downstairs. Garnet believes she may be as happy as she's ever been. Finally finished with the poem she began the day after her birthday, she's looking forward to copying the final draft in her small, neat script onto its own page in her journal. It is almost filled. But Garnet will not, tomorrow, begin the beautiful new lilac leather one that Colt and Meg gave her in May.

Of course, there is no way she could know (nor would she want to) but Garnet has finished her last poem. Though she will not die for another five months, just before her next birthday in matter of fact, the Garnet we see here will be gone by nightfall, felled by a stroke that will extinguish this sprightly intelligence with its slightly mordant sense of humor, erasing the totality of its memories, the sum of her loves, hates, and *don't-give-a-good-goddams.*

If Garnet were somehow, no matter how reluctantly, to intuit her future, she would say (and mean!) *Just kill me now!* But the universe is pitiless and entirely capable of, some would say prone to, unfairness. It does this to Garnet because it can, because, like the scorpion, it is its nature. Most unfair of all, her ex-husband, Bowie will not only outlive Garnet but die in his sleep in his own bed, back, as he wanted to be, in Garnet's house, after having lost a great deal but not everything, still able, if not as cogently as in his prime, to make his demands and opinions known to his family, still able to feed and dress himself no matter how badly, and with Vera, a pragmatic canine—who can blame her?—despite truly grieving the loss of her beloved, his dog once again.

After Reading the Obituaries on Your Birthday

Never mind. Go ahead,
pick up your birthday cake
at the bakery where once again
they will misspell your name.
Strike a match.

Light up that wildfire of candles
the universe has provided.
Set off all the smoke alarms.
Make your wish. Blow.

And in the charred aftermath of wet ash,
of singed streamers and melted ice cream,
rejoice, happy to be alive in such a world,
to have had the great good fortune
of an invitation to the party.

from *How the Universe Says Yes to Me*

Epilogue

The cosmos is not all-powerful. It cannot destroy what we leave behind, the good, bad, the indifferent. In Garnet's case, her legacy will provide solace to those who love and survive her. To Colt and Franny and their daughter, her small namesake, Gigi—at last the little sister Meg so ardently desired. To Tommie and Booker and their four wild boys, not one named after firearms. To the adult Meg, who will dedicate her own first book to her aunt and, in her thirties, edit a collection of Garnet's poems.

In the future, each time a dog is added to a household, Vera will be remembered fondly with stories and laughter, long after she has joined her mistress. This will happen many times. She will become a kind of creation story for all the dogs that follow.

And as for Bowie? Once he's gone, it will become harder and harder to remember what he looked like, he will be a phantasmagorical image crankily receding into the past until finally it resembles nothing so much as a faded, curling black-and-white photograph.

Acknowledgments

My heartfelt thanks to dear friends, Judy Johnson, editor, proofreader extraordinaire, and Kristina Onder, valued first readers who comprised our small writing group. They followed this book's journey, with encouragment and valuable critique, from its beginnings as a short story that refused to quit to completed novel. I am also grateful to poet, friend, and first reader, Cathryn Essinger, for her steadfast conviction that this story would find its way out into the world, and her suggestion that I submit it to Regal House Publishing. Love and thanks to gifted teacher and novelist, Katrina Kittle, another first reader, whose year-long class delivered on her promise that at its conclusion I would have a completed first draft. And I am indebted to my editor non pareil, Pam Van Dyk, for her dedication to making this the best book it can be.

I commend to you Jean Harris of Big Fluffy Dog Rescue in Nashville, Tennesee, whose witty, insightful, often heartbreaking posts on Facebook about her beloved Great Pyrenees breed (and dogs in need in general) were invaluable in forming the character of Vera. Her rescue, BFDR, is well worth your attention and support.

And to my husband, Jim, and our good girl, Zaza, my love and thanks for keeping those home fires burning.

All Garnet's poems (italicized) are my original work. The first and last poems in this book can be found in my poetry collection, *How the Universe Says Yes to Me.:*

"The Universe Speaks, #6," *How the Universe Says* Yes *to Me* by MJ Werthman White, Main Street Rag Publishing Company, 2017, p.48

"After Reading the Obituaries on Your Birthday," *How the Universe Says* Yes *to Me* by MJ Werthman White, Main Street Rag Publishing Company: 2017, p.72